THE MARKS BOY'S ROCK

HOMECOMING

LEE WIMMER

THE MARKS BOY'S ROCK By Lee Wimmer

Published by Hightower Publications
100 Minges Creek Place E-305
Battle Creek, MI 49015
www.hightowerpublications.com

www.leewimmer.net | lee@leewimmer.net

This is a fiction work. Any similarity to actual people, places, businesses, schools, events, or any other similarities is purely coincidental and should not be taken or interrupted otherwise. The Marks Boy's Rock novel is a work of fiction in the Life's Hard Places series.

ISBN Identifiers:
979-8-9883334-9-4 (EBook)
979-8-9916349-0-8 (Paperback)
979-8-9916349-1-5 (Hardcover)
979-8-9916349-2-2 (Deluxe Edition)

Library of Congress number - TXu 2-464-295

All addresses listed in this book are accurate at the time of publication. They are provided as a resource. Hightower Publications does not endorse or guarantee their performance after publication.

Cover and Interior Design by Emilie Haney, eahcreative.com

Creative and final editing by Deirdre Lockhart of Brilliant Cut Editing

Kathy, my wife and biggest supporter. Thank you for always being there for me and giving me the confidence to follow God's inspiration. Together, we did this .

PROLOGUE

TWO SUMMERS AGO, my life changed. Now, no matter how I look at it, everything is upside down. I had begun noticing small changes before then. But I shrugged it off, not realizing how *everything* was about to change. It's often said great things happen all of a sudden. Well, so do bad things.

Lily's words—"Do you wanna play?"—still rattle around my brain like BBs in a matchbox. I've heard and said those words thousands of times. I can't remember when that stopped exciting me. The fun we had and the closeness we forged, playing together almost every day for eleven years, once seemed an unbreakable bond. Why? Why did it end?

The memories linger. They start with blue skies and a young Lily —the all-smiles-and-giggles Lily—knocking on my door. We were always playing in our yards, up at the tree house, or on one of our porches. I especially remember her porch.

My thoughts progress to playing house, to missing-teeth smiles, and to the question "will you dance with me?" No, I'll never forget those days and the Lily I love remembering.

We played until our moms called us in for dinner. Oftentimes, we ate together. After dinner in the summer, we chased lightning bugs, laughing until dark. Chris, my twin, played too most days, though he claimed we teamed up on him. A girl our age, Emily, from down the street a couple of houses joined in sometimes. That's when Chris had the most fun. But that's a different story.

Now, today, there's the high school Lily, the no-more-games-of-tag, cocoon-busted Lily. The prettiest-girl-you-ever-did-see Lilly. And here I am—stuck. My life's become all about keeping on, keeping on, slogging on, fighting the whispers in my head. I don't know whether the whispers are friend or foe. Or if they're just part of the craziness getting in my way.

As a result of the whispers and what Mom calls "natural," my troubles have built a mountain I can't descend. I struggle, trying not to allow any outward signs, once hiding them well. Natural? It sure doesn't feel that way. I'm ashamed of it... all of it and myself. I haven't told Mom about the hiding-in-the-bathroom thing, not yet.

I've come to the point of desperation, beginning to admit most, if not all, of my struggles to Mom and Gramps. Some are fueled by what I want, what I need—I want and need to be a good man—not like my deadbeat, never-been-in-my-life dad.

Yes, I wanna play, but something keeps stopping me!

Sometimes, I call out loudly to myself when I'm alone. That's something else all this "natural" stuff has caused more of, me... alone.

Mom calls what I'm going through cocoon busting. She says every boy and girl goes through it to become an adult. It's the phenomenon called puberty. She says, "Sometimes, it takes years for the brain to catch up. Don't be ashamed." And, "Everyone experiences it differently, some having it easier than others."

I'm one of the others, something no one wants to be. Another reason I'm usually alone.

At least, I have a nosy mom. She hovers over us, Chris, Abbie, and me, making sure we're all right. She spends hours talking with each of us about what we're experiencing, how the natural process of growing up with other teens in high school can get messy. But she says not to worry, we'll all survive, soon figuring things out and forgetting all about it.

I hope so.

Chris mostly finished his cocoon busting over a year ago before he turned fifteen, no slogging for him. Abbie, my fun-loving little sister finished hers too as she turned fourteen this past summer. Her interest in boys and theirs in her drives Mom mad. So, as the oldest, why am I the late bloomer? That's what Mom affectionately calls my struggle. Experts call it delayed puberty. Apparently, it affects 2 to 3 percent of us.

With my delayed cocoon busting come a cracking voice, bad mood swings—really bad, the shaking kind of bad—swollen breasts, and uncontrollable acne. Oh, and not to forget, sweaty palms.

This wouldn't have been so bad had I gone through it at the same time as most of my classmates, like Chris. But doing it later, alone, and isolated is terrifying and embarrassing. I don't want anyone to notice, especially when my emotions melt down and erupt like a volcano—my feelings, moods, and anxiety going all over the place as my voice cracks. So I run and hide.

I'm an other. At fifteen, it's not a fun place to be. Everyone else has moved on, working on their brain part, girls liking boys, boys liking girls—and here I am. I wonder, does anyone else hide in the bathroom?

In school, I've had to run crazy fast five or six times, hiding so no one sees and makes fun. My anxiety becomes too much for me to function properly. Then emotions overflow the floodgate, melting down, and all I can do is blubber. I don't know why or what triggers it. So I run to the restroom, stand on the commode seat, and hide in a sometimes smelly stall, waiting for the eruption to stop, go away, or whatever it does. All while hoping no one sees me or my foot doesn't slip into the commode.

"Why me, God? Why me?" I often ask. Crickets.

Each time, I contemplate whether I should take the meds I've been prescribed. The meds have their fun side. They make me feel heavy, like I'm behind some sort of evil veil, seeing but only vaguely. I don't like that feeling, so I tolerate the mood swings. After all, Mom says they'll go away one day.

My friends add to the dilemma of late blooming. They're taller and bigger than me now, both the boys and girls and Lily. I used to be *that kid*, the one who seems so good at everything, at least in my own mind. Now those days are over. I'm not so much anymore. I was good at most sports, girls-be-watching-me good, especially when Chris and I played football in middle school. High school once looked like it could be fun.

Some days, I sneak over to the practice field and watch, hiding—again. Wondering what high school could've been, mine now a life full of could've beens. Thanks to this, there'll be no football or basketball tryouts for me, at least not for a couple of years, not until I grow more.

At five feet and a couple inches, I'm barely over a hundred pounds. There's only one thing I can do—wrestle. I can't stand wrestling. Who wants someone's smelly armpit in their face? No thank you. I'll pass. Chris has given up sports too, by choice, his pacifist side having gained control. "He's more of an academic," Mom says. Sure, but he'll fight me like a raging lion.

Maybe I'll try out when I'm a senior, if I grow, but not likely, especially after sitting out two years. Blooming late messes everything up.

Yes, I wanna play! A part of me cries out—desperately—deep within myself. Only, no one can hear me.

CHAPTER ONE

TODAY IS SUNDAY, a beautiful early October afternoon. The river down below the hillside must be glistening, sparkling, and cool as it roars over the flat moss-covered stones by the broken-down iron bridge. Gramps lives here, and they're the same stones he reminisces about in this story he's told Chris and me at least a dozen times. It borders on bizarre and quirky, the stones becoming part of a magical journey as he crosses the river on them.

Gramps leans back into the bench. "Feel that? The air is heavy, the weather changing. Soon, this old bench will be covered in snow." Reaching down, he rubs Butch's head. His old coon dog usually lies tight against our legs, the sunrays warming his tired old hide. He's almost a hundred in dog years.

"Yes, sir. Football is already on television." Sitting here with Gramps and Butch, I feel love, peace, and tranquility—things I need most. But tomorrow, that'll probably all change.

"I miss watching you and your brother play. I understand why you didn't. You must miss it, your friends and all, but there'll come other things—you wait and see. God has a plan just for you." Tussling my hair, Gramps curves his side to mine and adds an encouraging jostle.

"I'd love to play, but I'd have to be desperate." I sight of a chipmunk scurrying under the nearby shed.

"Extraordinary things can happen when belief is born out of desperation." Gramps braces his elbows on his knees, hunkering forward, smiling and dreamy-eyed. "There's a place where the elements around you appear to melt away, meshing colors so intense with sounds that not only provoke fear but also inspire excitement."

He stands and holds his hands and arms out wide, using them like balances helping him cross the river. Suddenly light of foot, he twists and turns like an acrobat, at times wobbling, and shaking on one leg, all while he shares the adventure of crossing those stones. Then he puts one hand on the back of the bench to steady himself. The gleam in his eyes ignites as his intensity overflows, so much so that in the past I've seen Chris moving his body like he was crossing the stones.

Gramps winks at me. "Are you desperate, Nickie? I've been desperate before. Everyone has a time or two."

Yes, I've been desperate. I am most days during his storytelling, just like now. But I won't ask him today why God let all this happen to me. After all, he's always telling me how much God loves me. Is this cocoon busting love?

I've always counted on Gramps for his wisdom and support. I need him now more than ever. When Chris and I were younger, he regaled us with stories of fantastical places, mystical beings, and harrowing adventures. Some, if not most, were from the Christian fantasies he likes to read.

The back screen door slams shut. Granny and Chris cross the thirty or so yards to our bench by the woodshed, our hangout. "Is he going off again, Nick?"

Gramps and I walk around the bench to meet them.

Chris snorts and moves to the side of the bench where Butch lay. "You'd think he was a circus ringleader."

Granny kisses Gramps's cheek. "Your grandpa's always been like that. He eats up attention like candy, and he loves make believe and fantasy. Don't you, dear?"

I fend off Chris over the bench, who starts picking on me right away. "He's the best storyteller. Sometimes I think he's reliving his tales while sharing them."

"Can't deny it, Gramps." Chris stops messing with me and grabs a handful of Butch's neck skin, causing Butch to stand up. "You sure make it real. A person wouldn't ordinarily feel anything in just any old story."

Granny hugs Gramps's waist and pushes him with her hip. "He should've been an actor."

I agree. "He kinda makes me believe his story about the stones." Okay, so I *completely* believe it, mostly because I need it, the Sea of Life that is.

"Leave us be, Helen." Gramps shoos her away, looking over his shoulder as Chris leaves too. Then he reaches over and pats my hand as we sit back on the bench. "This is one of my favorite spots. How many times do you reckon we've sat here just talking the hours away?"

"A lot. I like it here too." My chest warms. Most of them spent leaning against one another. My fingers stray to the woodgrain. The bench's wood has become dark brown and shiny from the years of wear.

Gramps takes a deep breath, eyes closed, and exhales soft and slow. It relaxes him more than anything, like singing his favorite gospel hymn. The bench overlooks his garden down the hillside, right beside the Roanoke River. That's where the stones are.

"O'Hanahans have gardened here for four generations. Bottom-land, where we plant, has the best soil for gardening. It's richer than the soil up here, less rocks too." He scrapes the ground with his boot. "It all starts with good soil."

What would it be like to feel as peaceful as he looks? It helps me understand that "peace that surpasses all understanding," the one the pastor always talks about. The one I need to find, the sooner the better.

The wind's gentle most times when we're sitting here. Occasionally, like today, it gusts all swift and chaotic. Seeming to carry an urgency that can't be explained away as if there's a secret to be found and understood, a secret we can't quite grasp any easier than those pieces of cattails flying by.

Gramps catches one of the twirling pods falling from nearby trees. They're blowing throughout the valley, searching for a resting place, somewhere to settle. "Fall will begin in two weeks." He hunches his shoulders in. "The wind's already becoming brisker, the heavier cold air roaring down off the nearby mountaintops, picking up speed as it reaches the valley floor."

I scoop his catch from his weathered palm. Gramps calls them helicopter seeds. Anyone who's ever swept a porch in the spring knows the ones. "I love watching the spinners come down off the maple trees in the spring."

Sitting on Gramps's bench, it's easy to tell when the seasons are changing. In the fall, pumpkins get cut loose or rolled off their vines. Once they're ripe, ready to become pies or jack-o'-lanterns, that's how I know fall is here. Spring has its signs too.

"People have seasons too. You boys are in the spring of your lives." Gramps sinks back against the bench, arms crossed over his wide chest. I hear him breathe in the fresh air.

"I hope this season I'm in hurries up and ends." Thinking that explains some of my dilemma. When spring comes out here in the country, there's the smell of manure being turned into the ground, yuck. Maybe cocoon busting is like spring. It sure stinks.

"Shh, listen," Gramps whispers. "Hear that? That's a momma deer calling for her babies."

"I don't hear her. I can sure hear the river today, though."

"Yep, she's going strong today." He kicks his long legs out, crossing his ankles. "All depends on how much water the dam keepers at the reservoir release upstream. Most days, the river barely has enough water to meander through the valley. Mind you, remember it can become deadly."

Several times it washed away the lower part of Gramps's vegetable garden after too much water was released.

"I hear you and your neighbors talk, saying all your gardens will end up over in Roanoke someday if dam keepers aren't extra careful." I slide my foot over a clump of grass that somehow managed to survive us sitting on the bench.

Roanoke. That's where we live, Mom and us kids. We also live near the river. Roanoke was first called the "Big Lick." I know, it's a funny name. Now, it's called the Star City, because of a big star high on one of the mountains facing the city.

Gramps's feet rock side to side, digging his boot heels in. "The dam's destroyed the natural flow of things."

His feet keep rocking. He lives in the moment, having told me at his age he's learned to appreciate the little things in life. He is my rock, my role model.

Simple things can be calming, even comforting. It's nice to have unchanging things in your life, things you can count on, people who are dependable. Kind of like the old oak tree beside their driveway where we sometimes swing. It's been here for hundreds of years. Gramps swung there too as a child.

"Doesn't take much to alter the flow." Gramps's voice flows around us. "Our surroundings, people, and things, sometimes lead us to make decisions that alter everything." His shoulder bumps mine. "Believing is the most important thing, especially when cocoon busting. Not making rash, impulsive decisions or doing things that alter the normal course of one's life."

Now's when Gramps starts talking to me about girls like he's been doing lately, how to respect them and enjoy their presence, but not get carried away. Sometimes he talks about how he met Granny, how she swept him off his feet at hello.

He leans over, a gleam in his eyes. His smile says it all. "Good people in your life are a blessing. I got the best in mine. You, your brother, and your sister. Your mom and her sister and..." He slaps my knee, then tugs Granny's picture from his chest pocket. "She'd just turned nineteen."

The age my mom married my deadbeat dad. "Granny was so pretty."

"That she was." The fire still burns hot in Gramps's eyes for her.

"I'd have done anything to have her hand in marriage."

I believe he would've too. They're always holding hands, and he's always opening doors for her. It's the way I want to be.

"We grew up in a time when girls and boys didn't do the things they do now." He pats Granny's picture face, then tucks it back in its secure place over his heart. "We respected our partners and ourselves. There wasn't anything but holding hands, and as far as I'm concerned, that was enough. Our wedding night was magical, and it couldn't have been any other way. Your grandmother is a special woman, so are your mother and sister. Lily is too. You should always look over them, protect them, and love them—no matter what."

"I will Gramps. I promise." We sure need each other, though sometimes I wish Mom wasn't quite so overbearing. Nothing misses her scrutiny. Most times, that's good, but I'm at the point now of liking some privacy, especially with all these changes happening to me.

"Keep God first." Gramps rubs his hands and wrists. "And everything else will work its way out. You've got a lot of living to do and no need to do it all in one day." His smile flashes wide, the leathery wrinkles on his face full of years and confidence. "Experience is an excellent teacher."

He grips his knees, and gnarled fingers dig into denim. "So…"

CHAPTER TWO

"SO?" I mimic, ready for his special story—again. I know he hopes it'll help me believe, something he says I need. He never misses an opportunity to share that faith of his, and neither does Granny, no matter who's around.

Now, the pulse at his neck quickens as if his heart begins to race faster than the clouds can trace their shadows on the fields below. My shoulder nudges his. "You know, Gramps, as I've grown older, the adventure has grown more daring, bolder." Maybe out of necessity to keep my attention.

His shoulder bumps mine back. "Maybe the more I tell it, the more I remember."

"Remember, huh?" I dare not confess it aloud, not to him. But I've begun to think he's making the stories up, something to keep me, us, wide-eyed and entertained. "It works for me. Too bad, Chris has grown bored now that his life is so focused on academics and girls." Like now, he goes inside some days before the stories even get going.

Gramps shrugs it off. "You're like two identical trees planted in a garden at the same time, eventually growing and branching out, each in their own way."

He nods toward the river. The worn-out path leading down to the stones appears to jump to life. Blowing past cattails and through the field brush, a gust of wind shares a secret, surprising element. Something's calling out to me, beckoning in my spirit—*"Come to the river."*

"Now where were we?" He flexes his grip on his knees. Then his voice dips into a low rumble, more like a motor than words. "Ah, yes, the Sea of Life's a magical place where you can fix things, kind of like playing God. If things have gone wrong in your life…"

How entranced he keeps me!

"There you can fix them," he promises.

I want and need it to be true—badly. I know more than most teens my age what is meant by "necessity being the mother of invention."

The breeze tugs on Gramps's hat. He reaches up and grabs it before it can blow away. "The wind's as stiff as the sun-dried towels slung over your granny's clothesline." He resettles the hat. "You know the way they get when the night air turns cool."

The air smells different, even tasting funny, probably from the honeysuckle, lilacs, and lilies growing in the fields. Moments earlier, butterflies and bees frolicked in the sunshiny fields nearby. Now, they've abandoned the fight and headed for cover, disappearing as the stiff breeze overpowers them. Only the sweet fragrances remain, flushed by gusts of wind trying to shake the foundation of the shed behind us.

Here, the old buildings and benches, combined with the garden and uncut fields, make you think you're years behind people living in the city just a mile away. Kind of like you stepped back in time. The pace is slower, you're loved deeper, and your troubles never appear as big.

Today, though, it feels like something wants to reveal itself to me, something my senses can't explain, even while all of them are wide-eyed and on high alert. Gramps has a way of doing that, getting me all worked up. But he also has a way of bringing me down, gently, back to reality, back to where he can talk man stuff with me.

I jitter on the bench, more curious than ever—out of necessity. Is the story true? Something feels different today. Back then, the river down below flowed swiftly through Gramps's land. That's where he first discovered the Sea of Life. Or it discovered him.

"Gramps, do you think I could find it?" My breathless question rushes free. I've been edgy, even cruel. I don't like how I've felt inside. Mom better be right, and I'm just going through my cocoon-busting stage. But the Sea of Life could erase all of my troubles if it's real. I struggle with far too many almost impossible things. I need his story to be true. If so, maybe I could get a few redos and change things for the better, including some of my decisions.

He rubs his beard. Like an actor on this stage, he purses his lips, looks high into the heavens, and chooses his words. He waits *forever*, and my heart becomes as tight as a balled-up fist, squeezing, constricting, tightening ever more with each passing second. Now, it seems unable to beat.

"Nickie, relax. It's going to be okay." He grips my knee. "I don't know why you get so wound up. Have you ever searched for it, deep in here?" Patting my heart, he raises his chin and squinches his eyes.

Maybe it's from the cattails and seeds in the wind. Or maybe he's being dramatic again. I know what he's getting at. He knows I'm at that age, and I know it too—the age of accountability. At least, that's what the pastor calls it.

"No, that's not it. I want... Well, Mom needs a husband." Best to disguise my needs by sharing Mom's. My teachers say you can deflect from yourself by pointing at others, and I'm not ready for the in-depth conversation that ensues somedays.

Pastor says the time of accountability is when pathways begin to form and help determine how easily I will become a good man—or not—answerable for my transgressions, whatever those are.

Why? Why is everything on me?

Gramps knows my needs. He was there when someone triggered most of my bad thoughts—about myself. He also knows what I've wanted more than anything since I was two years old, a dad. Before long, it won't matter anymore for me. But what about Abbie? I'd give anything to keep her happy and safe. Her heart is pure and full of love, like Mom's.

Most of my bad thoughts began on a Father's Day Sunday, nearly two years ago, before my cocoon busting began. Pastor taught that for a boy to become a *good* man he especially needed a dad at home, a good dad. Mom said he was only sharing that with the fathers in attendance to explain the importance of their role in the family, encouraging and appreciating them. She said he wasn't talking about us.

But some whispered and pointed at Chris and me. Some of those whispering people were supposed to be Mom's and Granny's friends. That's what hurt the most. I heard them, so did Gramps, as they talked behind our backs, and the thing is you never know what they might be saying.

Gramps waved it off as busybodies doing what they do, even in the church. Propping themselves up at the expense of someone else. Although he straightened a few out, the damage was done. I want to be a good man, not like my deadbeat dad. But what if the pastor is right? What chance do I have without a dad? Do grandfathers count? It's the biggest, toughest, and longest battle I've fought during my cocoon busting. *Thanks, Pastor!*

Whispers, cold stares, and rumors return and call out the loudest during the long and lonely nights in the quiet darkness, sometimes mocking, even becoming a taunting voice, especially when I'm alone —in bed—during the wee hours. Even Chris said so, and that's something for Mr. Placid, who never *ever* shows emotion.

Gramps's feet rock side to side, the hole under his heels deepening. A playful smile flashes. "Let's see. I was down by the river, crossing those large flat stones right there under the old iron bridge. See... they're right there."

He points down the slope, toward the fallen-down trestle. "Back in those days, the railroad trestle was still in use. That's the only place you can find the big flat stones to cross over on, and you can only find them when the river goes *really* low. Then you can see the minnows swimming around and the sun glistening off the fool's gold on the river bottom. But you'll never find them when the water is deep, swift, and muddied."

His expression changes. He mustn't want to miss anything. He takes his Norfolk Western Railroad hat off his silver-covered head, wipes his brow, then puts it back on. "I'd always walked across those stones to get to my friend's house, even when water covered them some."

I stretch my legs out to mirror him. "Now, it's the only way to cross unless you go down to the bridge where the Sheetz is, and that's a good little hike."

"That day, crossing the stones didn't seem any different."

A crow circling high above our heads lets out a caw, probably tracking a field mouse.

Gramps shades his eyes to look up. "That's funny. In this breeze, you wouldn't expect that. He must be hungry. I was hungry then— not the food kind of hungry. Something had been gnawing my insides for months after I turned twenty-four, just eating at me. I became weak in my faith, almost lost, going out with a few of my service buddies, doing the unthinkable."

Unthinkable. That's how Gramps thinks of it.

"I came to my senses though. The day I found the Sea of Life, I never touched the water crossing to the other side. My shoes didn't have a drop on them. I remember pulling up on a small sapling, one I'd never noticed there before. I held tight to it and climbed up the slippery riverbank. When I reached the top, I was somewhere else, and I regretted my past indulgences right away."

Indulgences isn't a pretty word to him either.

The crow dives, touches ground, and swoops back up.

"Do you remember what I've told you? How, minutes earlier, I'd wished I were God and wanted more than anything to go back and change some things." His happy eyes and a big grin return. He must be there now, at least in his memories, hopefully not his imagination.

"Can you show me?" I spring to my feet, my shadow covering his boots. "I have something important to change. Do you think the Sea of Life can help me?" My hands fist, and my pulse beats out of control again. I lean in over him, and my shadow inches up his legs. He's become so serious. Normally, he's goofy, but when it comes to the Sea of Life, he loses forty years somewhere, like how he becomes light of foot. He says the magical place changes things, the past, especially people.

"I haven't been the same since." The story ends the same every time.

CHAPTER THREE

I HAVE TO FIND IT. Knowing Gramps wasn't always perfect helps me believe it could happen for me too. I'd never thought of him any other way except how he is with me. I guess we all have our things to deal with.

The tall field grass almost bends down now, touching the ground as the wind races by on its journey and scuds the clouds along.

"It can help anyone who believes." He waves me back into my seat. "Remember, you have to believe. Then you just might find it."

"Even if I'm not perfect?" I slump to the bench.

He pats my leg.

The sun fades behind the same fast-moving clouds as if on cue, as if a curtain closes-in the heavens. Is it hiding something? A chill runs up my spine as the wind whistles off the shed door, slamming it open, then closed again, startling Butch. I rub his head, and he leans back against my legs, calming me as much as easing his fears.

"No one is perfect, especially your mom or me." Gramps picks up a stone. "We just believe really good. Believing is the power behind the Sea of Life, even life itself. Without it... I don't know if it even exists. Believing is the greatest power on earth, next to love."

He tosses the stone. It sails over the path, strikes a sunflower, and shakes its head. "Not bad for an old-timer. What do you say?"

"That was sweet, Gramps." I admire his smile. It's easy and real. Nothing's fake about my gramps.

Even forty years later, his story gives him a new youthful energy, a deep joy, hiding the stain of his years on the railroad yard and life's hard knocks, at least temporarily. Maybe it's true. I'll continue to hope, desperate for answers, desperate for help.

"What's it like, Gramps? How did you know where to go, what to do?" Once, I never would've considered it could be the answer to my problems, thinking it was only a fairy tale. Now, I'm ready for a fairy tale. It could be my salvation. Especially since school began again, and for the first time ever, I've come face-to-face with my stepsiblings.

I'm desperate. Seeing my dad drive them home in a fancy vehicle, while he never even waves at Chris or me, cuts to my core. I cringe, remembering Chris saying maybe Dad didn't recognize us.

But Peg and Craig recognize us, and we never attended the same school with them. So someone must've pointed us out.

Gramps grips my shoulder, turning himself toward me. He looks deep into my eyes, almost like he's looking into my soul. Mom must've told him about the encounter after school, how Peg laughed at Chris and me, taunting us.

"Remember, I said there was a river bum, a hobo, only I don't think he really was. Looking back, I think he was on an assignment." Gramps half whispers and looks around all dramatic-like to ensure no one's listening, making it feel and sound supernatural. "He took me inside and explained how everything worked. He was an expert. Angelo was his name, only Angelo, no last name."

His hand slides from my shoulder, landing in his lap. "Once Angelo explained everything, he left me to do what I had to do. I was so excited... at first. I knew I could bring my folks back, if only for a little while, to say goodbye. They passed away while I was away in the service. But soon, the crystal-clear Sea of Life filled full of people, time, and life, scaring me. I didn't know which lever to pull or button to push, and I realized it wouldn't be so easy to fix my world, at least not mine alone."

His smile disappears. His hands take to rubbing the soreness from each other, their worn joints screaming out from years of hard work, arthritic fingers and knuckles showing their toil. He stops and sighs.

"It was confusing. I don't know how, but the Sea of Life became a place of trillions and trillions of light streams, four different colors, each leading from someone's life, then connecting to others. I realized, if I changed one thing—just one—everything would change. That scared me. I didn't want to cause a spiritual collapse of my church or, worse, my parents' beliefs."

Something shivers over my shoulders. "That would've been a huge burden."

Gramps snorts. "I didn't know what to do. When I had time to complete my changes, Angelo came back and talked to me. He said the changes I made or didn't make would take effect as soon as I left or pulled the lever. If I needed to change anything back, I had to do it in forty-eight hours, or it would be changed forever, regardless of the consequences."

"Right." I'd heard that part so many times. "He said that was the price of playing God." I could handle that, couldn't I?

Butch whines.

Gramps bends to fondle his floppy ears. "I'd already met a pretty young woman, your grandmother. Such a beautiful Irish lass, sort of a spitfire back then. I was smitten by her passion for God and life the first moment I laid my eyes on her with the pastor. It was so easy to see the way she carried herself, her modesty. Her hair was a beautiful deep auburn and long, like your sister, Abbie's, and she wore it under a white scarf. Abbie and Helen look so much alike at Abbie's age. I don't know if you could even tell them apart."

I nod. "Must be the special genes in our family."

I'd rather think my genes carried on Mom and Gramps's, than Dad's side.

"I didn't want to chance never seeing Helen again. It made making my changes even harder. I couldn't risk losing her."

Gramps grew up in a time when everyone had a sense of community. Our country was booming. His generation built factories, homes, roads, and railroads. They fought wars supposedly to defend it all. He still proudly wears his N&W hat even though he's retired, the same type of hat he wore at work for forty-odd years. Sometimes he joins his coworkers at a café near the Yard where they ate lunch together every day.

Butch stands, stretches his front legs forward with a deep groan, then pads off.

"So... What happened?" Automatically, my hands reach out, pleading. "Did you do it, you know, fix your world?"

He must have, and I need to know how. His life is so good, full, and rich. He's wise, and I love him, but most of all, he loves me.

That's the way the world is supposed to work. At least, how I believe it should, how I was told it was intended at first.

That's how the pastor describes it. But he grew up in a home with a father, not left out like yesterday's trash, so what does he really know?

"The Sea of Life makes you look at yourself and others differently. Standing on the Sea of Glass before that great throne, I saw how everyone was connected to each other in some way." He loops his arm over my shoulders and bends toward me. "That's why I asked, do you believe—do you really believe? It's the not-so-secret secret to the secret of life."

I wonder if I believe. What am I supposed to believe for? Why do my emotions bounce around so much? Could it be that hard?

"Do you think we could go together? If I go by myself, I'll mess things up. I could use your help, Gramps." He always supports me. He'll, for sure, say yes.

But he takes his arm away and straightens up. "Nickie, I'd love nothing more. Boy, that sure would be a great adventure for us! But it's not allowed. It's yours alone to do, to choose your way like you do every day. No one can walk in your shoes, not even your twin. If you change something—it's on you."

With my hands behind my head, I close my eyes and raise my face to the sky, exhaling loudly. I didn't know what to say.

Gramps squeezes my leg as if to reassure me. "I think that's why Angelo left me alone, so I could make the decisions I needed to make about what to change or not. Since I would be accountable for all my changes, I alone had to decide what's most important to me, like you have to decide now."

He stands and stretches, reaching toward the sky. Right on cue, the sun comes out of hiding. He must be right. He has that look he only gets when he's convinced of something.

"But, Gramps—"

He holds up his hand.

The breeze has stopped. The sweet familiar scent is gone. Only Gramps and I remain. Butch has left, and the magic has left too—just like that. How quickly things can change.

"This is your fight, son, your one life. I can't fight your battles for you. No one can. I'll be here for you, and I'll always love and support you, but if you believe—if you really believe—you'll have the best Helper. You know that secret friend you used to talk to? Well, the Helper's your real friend, and he shouldn't be a secret. Let him show you the way."

I don't go looking for the Sea of Life or a new secret friend, the Helper, whoever that is. Though I always try to put on a good show for those around me, I'm too scared. Gramps is my hero. This Helper better be my hero too. And soon.

CHAPTER FOUR

MONDAY, after classes, I press my hand to the cold locker. The chatter in the school hall around me isn't loud enough to drown out my thoughts. My fingers inch up to touch the photo of Abbie, Chris, Lily, and me, all goofy smiles from three years ago. Mom took it, of course. Who else? Not like Dad was around. He and Mom split up while she was pregnant with Abbie. He never touched our lives again, not in the smallest of ways. He never looked into Abbie's eyes. She never knew his touch. Why I still bother to call him Dad, I don't know. Probably some deep-seated need to have one. I don't remember him, and neither does Chris.

The hallway ruckus increases. Lockers slam. Sneakers scuffle. Giggles rise.

At least, they all ignore me. No one can know how Chris, Abbie, and I felt not having a dad, especially on birthdays and holidays. Mom is great, the best. But knowing Dad's living across town with two other kids our age, loving them and not saying one word to us, his real kids, hurts. Weren't we good enough? Mom says he was the loser, but it doesn't change how I feel about me.

I tap the photo. Then my finger traces a circle that loops me and my siblings together. Mom often put the three of us on the sofa to watch reruns. She propped Abbie between Chris and me to keep her from wandering or falling off. Abbie would look up as she wobblily leaned on me. She called me "Bubba." I felt more peace and love in those times than any other, toward Abbie and life in general.

My finger moves to Lily. We all played together on Lily's front porch. Covered with clusters of wisteria blossoms and hidden behind snowball bushes, it felt like a magical place, and now, I know it was.

Lily was always in control of herself—and in control of the games we played. Her imagination and flare captivated me. I liked that, but Chris didn't, at least back then. I think, now, he'd like to go back and change a few of his words here or there. He butted heads with her a lot, often going home in a huff.

Easy to hear him now. "You always must have your way. Well, you can have it, Miss Blue Skies! I'm going home." He'd shake his head, then stomp off. The pain in her eyes bothered me then. After all, she was my best friend, and he was my twin. I didn't want either of them hurt.

As we got older, natural attractions took over. She paid more attention to me than to Chris. He became frustrated, wanting his way, so he stayed in our house, not coming out to play. He'd like to change that now, but it's too late. Lily and I became closer than two kids have a right.

The games we played began to change. I never realized we were play pretending like we were a couple. I thought it was something kids do, but Lily was changing around the time we were eleven. We had played together for over eight years, and with that comes an emotional attachment that's hard to replace or explain.

After eighth grade, she began busting out of her cocoon. Stunning how things have changed in two years. High school Lily is amazing.

I close my locker and schlep out front of our school. Great. The bright-blue Hummer's waiting by the street for Peg and Craig Holland. I try not to look inside at their stepdad—*my* dad—behind the wheel. Footsteps jostle past me. The duo races to the vehicle and jumps in, saying hi to their driver. Their dad, their real dad, died in the Marines serving our country—giving everything. But he was there for them while he was alive.

"I wish my dad died in the Marines." Did I say *that* aloud? I've thought about it maybe once or twice. Mean that it is, at least I'd have a hero for a dad, someone to look up to. Just one more thing making me feel bad about myself. I jolt, jerking around to see if anyone heard me.

Chris swings his book-loaded backpack over one shoulder and lopes up beside me. He's smiling, so he didn't hear me. "Hey, what's got you scowling?"

I shrug. Maybe, since I'm thinking this way, I'm gonna be a bad man. *Where are You, Helper?*

Then I jab my thumb toward the Hummer, numb watching it play out. Numb and numb, unwanted. Like most of the teens streaming out of the school, Peg and Craig are laughing, poking, and punching fun at each other.

Chris has nothing to say. He and I shuffle down the school steps. All this being new, it mesmerizes us.

Peg, the youngest, sits on the side closest to us. She puts her hands to her face and makes a mimicking pose, showing her distaste for us. We're her stepbrothers, the driver's flesh and blood. Why so much hate?

"Stuff it, Red!" I shout at her.

Chris slaps his hand over my mouth. We are total opposites at behaving nicely.

I shove his palm away and spread my hands out wide. "Why? Why'd ya do that? They are rats, no better words for them. Their driver is worse. He is... he's—well, Mom won't let me say that word, but he is!" Even though I'm nearly sixteen, I mostly minded Mom's teaching and wishes. Mostly.

"Mom says God will make things right one day." Chris swipes his palm over his jean-clad thigh, wiping off my spittle. "We only have to live good. That's all."

"Sure, *little brother*." He's a minute younger than me, one minute I never let him forget. "When donkeys fly. Dad is living proof. Only a good knuckle sandwich will stop those two! I wish I was God. I'd fix them all." Our pastor, whose preaching I am beginning to dislike, says carrying a grudge only hurts the grudge holder. I gotta agree 'cause I'm hurting.

Other kids push by us to get home, almost knocking us down. I stand firm. Chris steps to the side. Yeah, opposites.

The Hummer pulls away. Peg waves, mocking us. They'll drive to the other side of the school district and a big fancy home made possible by their mother's inheritance before she married Dale Marks, our dad.

"C'mon. I'm hungry." Chris sprints down the steps, making me jog to catch up for our mile-long walk in the opposite direction to our old brick home. We could ride the bus, but our house is the last stop on an hour-long route. "You gonna keep up or what? A rain's coming."

He's right. The air has that prerain smell and feel. We hustle it. Even after avoiding the house with the big dogs out front by crossing over the street and then back again, we almost reach our porch before the downpour begins—almost.

The wetness reminds me I haven't always been lost in myself, just mainly since that Father's Day. Around then, I also first noticed my body trying to leave boyhood behind, to become a young man. I sure wasn't ready for that. I'd had a great childhood.

"Smells good in here." Chris swings the door wide. "Like the syrup we had breakfast. Bet Abbie's already looking forward to dinner."

I drop my backpack by his. "I wish Mom could have someone to love, to love her, beside us kids, a good husband." I slump onto the hall bench. "She deserves someone special."

He toes off his sneakers, not bothering to sit. "Granny says she isn't interested, at least while she has three teenagers to look out for."

To protect is what Granny actually says. Protect? Kinda weird wording. "Why's she feel she's gotta watch over us so closely anyhow?"

"Come on. Aren't you hungry?" He grabs my arm, hauls me to my feet, and shoves me toward the kitchen.

"Let me get my shoes off, why don't ya?" I dig my heels in. Ridiculous to get hustled around by your *little* brother.

"So get at it, why don't ya?"

The pacifist, it appears, only wants to fight with me. We're starting to become polar opposites, but we still share a few of our special twin bonds, at times. Impulsive and growing more combative with each passing year, I sometimes think I have a thorn like that guy in the Bible. Most times, it feels like something's pushing me.

That is why I want—need—desperately, to find the Sea of Life. If not, maybe I'll become a bad man.

I sit back down and unlace my sneakers, taking my sweet time just to irritate him.

Chris stands there tapping one socked foot.

Sometimes, I know I'm doing something wrong, but I still do it. I don't know why. Is everyone fighting these same battles? I hope so. I don't want to be weirder than everyone else.

Why me, God? Why do You dislike me so much? I don't understand why I think that way, but I can't help it.

CHAPTER FIVE

THE WEEK WAS off to a rough start. Tuesday wasn't looking like a fun day either, at least in homeroom. First thing coming in the door, Peg struts up to me. I don't know what's pushing her buttons. I try to stay on the other side of the room from her, but even then, she manages to get a jab in.

"Hey, loser, did you get wet yesterday?" She laughs until her sleeves ride up her arms. She reaches to slide them back down, turns, and huffs off.

I shiver at the sight of bruises on both her arms.

What could have caused those? Even the mean in me feels some compassion for her. I keep seeing them all day. Now, walking home with Abbie, Chris, and Lily, I tell them about the bruises.

Chris shrugs. "She was probably fighting with her brother. You know how we get."

"Maybe." He might be right. "Or maybe because of her light complexion, she bruises easily." I let it go. Anyhow, it's not any of my business. If she wanted to share or get help, she wouldn't have worn the long-sleeve shirt.

Oddly, Lily doesn't say anything. She's acting strange. Even though she's been standoffish for a while, she's never been like this, even purposely walking on Abbie's other side, almost mean to the point of ignoring I exist.

The days blur—crammed with homework and cocoon busting—I almost cannot recall the day before. Thursday evening, I smell Mom's kitchen magic at work. She's the world's best cook—ask the whole neighborhood of taste testers. The aroma wafting up the stairs tells me dinner is almost ready.

Abbie pokes her head through our bedroom door, her long brown ponytail swings side to side as she bounces. "It's pizza night."

I grin back. Our favorite weekly meal.

Abbie struggles with dad issues like me, partly my fault. Once, without thinking, I blurted out: "He left because you were born. He couldn't handle another kid." She's never forgotten it, and neither have I. Why did I say such cruel words? What could they change?

Sometimes, especially now, I'm too impulsive, even hurtful. I hope I never say ugly spiteful words like those again. It wasn't her fault, but I can't take my words back. I love Abbie, even though she is nosy like Mom.

Maybe the pastor's right. Maybe I won't be a good man.

But now, my senses overpowered, I jostle her downstairs, drawn to the kitchen as if on a hook and line. Mom has her ways of making our home special, like pizza night. She has every meal scripted to be fun for us, and most importantly, we can count on it.

Cara Worley, Mom's best friend and the big sister Mom doesn't have, helps her get everything cleaned up before the pies come out. A little compulsive, Mom likes to have her kitchen prep put away before eating. Even in our chaos, she's calm and organized.

Every night after dinner, we kids take turns washing the dirty dishes while she relaxes from a long day at the factory. Tonight, that'll be with Cara. In the winter, they often take refuge in front of our living room fireplace. I don't know how they have that much to say.

"I wondered if you were coming down. I had to send Abbie. Thought maybe you were taking a nap since it took you so long." Mom hugs me and looks me over with a sharp eye before kissing my cheek and turning to check on the pies.

I can still smell remnants of the chemicals they use to make parts at the plant where she works. She runs a machine molding parts for electronic ignitions or something for cars. It's a very distinctive smell. Must be something they use to clean.

"Nah. I was daydreaming and doing homework. Thinking about visiting Gramps again. Soon, I hope. I need to talk to him. Do you think we can go over tomorrow after school?" Gramps is the only man in my life.

"We'll see. Don't be rude, Nick. Say hi to Cara."

"Sorry. Cara, how are things?" I hug her. She's still dressed in the black pants suit she must've worn to work at the local newspaper. The nicest sort of soul one can be, she's fun to be around too. I guess that's another reason they've been best friends since first grade. Theirs is a friendship stronger than blood, cut and bound together by endless heartache and joyous love, Mom says. Their spirits are kindred, like mine to Lily's once.

"Nickie. Wow. You are getting more handsome by the minute." She lets out a whistle. "If only you were ten years older. No wonder Lily is mad about you."

She winks at Mom. "Ruth, you're going to need a big stick. With two handsome boys in it, this house'll be crawling with lovesick girls."

When she grabs my face with both hands and kisses my cheeks, I wrestle against her and reach for the counter to pull away. But it's too late. Her grip's too good. "Yeah, yeah." I laugh, getting a banter going. "I bet you tell that to all the boys for a kiss."

"Got me one too, didn't I?" She pushes her golden locks, this month's color, over her shoulder and winks as she sits beside Abbie and hugs her, then helps fix her ponytail.

She works Abbie's long, thick hair through the band, glancing my way once in a while. Mom must've told her about my recent struggles, the whole coming-of-age thing. Cara, also our godmother, knows everything about us.

Mom slides on her oven mitts. "Nick, would you get the plates and glasses down? The pies will be out in a few minutes. Abbie, get the lemonade out of the refrigerator and pour everyone a glass, please? Oh, pour one for Lily too."

We spring into action, anything for Mom's pizza pie and lemonade. There were never any squabbles on pizza night.

"Where's Chris, Mom?" I clatter the stack of plates. He never misses pizza night. He may be late for some things, like our birth, but he's always at the table first on pizza night.

"He is going to miss a lot of pizza nights. His new debate team meets every Thursday afternoon." She sets her cooling racks on the counter to put the pies on them. She always bakes three large pies, one cheese, one pepperoni and mushroom, my favorite, and one with everything but the kitchen sink, Cara's. "We may have to shift pizza night to Mondays, so he can be here too."

"Not Mondays!" Abbie slams her hands on her face, shakes her head side to side, and rolls her eyes. "No. Please, not leftovers night."

That sounds strange. But Mondays are cool. We can eat anything in the refrigerator, mainly things from our special weekend meals, doggie bags from our two meals out—Saturday supper and Sunday lunch at a restaurant after church. Our extravagances were so good that we often argued over who ate what on Mondays. Unlike pizza night when there's plenty to go around.

"Why can't he just eat cold pizza?" I reach for the glasses. "He's the one changing things."

After our brief uprising, Mom waves us back to our tasks. "Abbie, honey, it'll work out. Would you go see if Lily wants to have pizza with us? Her mom's working late. She was out on her front porch reading earlier. Hurry back. Only two more minutes on the pizza."

Mom helps Kayleigh, Lily's mom, and vice versa. The entire neighborhood is made up of single-parent homes, with the exception of two. Mom once told Cara there must be something in the water here, whatever that means.

Abbie bounds out the door, her ponytail now bouncing wildly. She returns, Lily in tow. Lily loves pizza night. When she and her mom used to come over, she always sat beside me. How I cherish those memories. If only we could go back.

I guess I outgrew playing together. She didn't. I know she likes me, but I'm not ready for any girl stuff yet. Besides, she lives right next door, so there'll be plenty of time for that later. But her stares have been growing colder, even angry. Why?

"Lily, how is school coming for you? Anything exciting or new? Your mom said you were enrolled in Home Economics." Mom slides the everything pizza over so Cara could fill her plate before we say a blessing over our food. A requirement.

"It's kind of fun. We're learning how to organize the cabinets and stove this week. But it's all backward from home." She giggled, getting ready to bow her head.

"Maybe you can show me a thing or two. Okay, bow your heads." Mom says grace, thanking God for our food and gathering. Then everybody gets busy.

"Mmm. Mrs. M, I hope I learn to cook like this." Lily closes her eyes, tasting the pizza. She loves Mom's homemade sauce. Who wouldn't?

"You're welcome here anytime you like. We can cook together." Mom winks at Lily. She'd already helped Lily learn to make sausage gravy, another Lily favorite.

After everyone finishes and wanders off, I take my turn to clean the kitchen. Then Chris stomps up the back steps. He sniffs and opens the refrigerator.

"How was debate club?"

"Fine. Can't believe I missed pizza night." He plops three cold slices onto his plate and slumps into a chair at the kitchen table.

"Sorry, bud." I dry Mom's favorite mixing bowl. "Lily came too."

His shoulders slouch. Yep, he's more disappointed he missed Lily than the hot pizza. He likes her.

I pat his shoulder in passing, then head off to our bedroom. He must've scarfed down his pizza because he's only a few minutes behind me.

With a full belly, sleep comes fast....

Then I'm on the river. Word comes down from someone called

the Helper. "Angelo's been assigned to help you get your joy back, helping your belief."

Huh? I hoped he'd make Dad set things right.

"Gramps O'Hanahan?" Angelo asks.

"Yes, Gramps O'Hanahan," a second man responds. "He knows the way. We will tell him in his sleep."

"Do you think the boy can handle it? He's not too impulsive, you don't suppose?" Holding onto the Helper's sent word like a key, Angelo and the second man, whose name I don't catch, do everything as directed.

The wind begins to howl like when I was at Gramps's house. I shade my eyes from the dust and leaves slapping by while I struggle down a path. I pass by the fields of lilies and honeysuckle, the strange fragrance stronger than I remember. I push on down toward the old iron trestle. With each step, it's getting darker, the sun now hiding behind roiled clouds. The closer the river gets, and the more urgent the surroundings scream out—like a horror movie.

Murders of crows fly up, their caws loud as if something were chasing them. They dart back to the trees, then even higher into the sky.

At the river, I can barely see the stones. The river's deep, no minnows or fool's gold in sight.

The birds flock at me, then shift course, skimming me as I topple to the ground. I dare not cross the fast-moving current. Moss on the stones would make them slippery. I can't see the river bottom or all the stones anyway. The brownish water hides everything, just the opposite of how Gramps described it should look. I knew it was useless!

Angelo speaks to the second man. "He can't make it. He doesn't believe. What should we do?" Wind whips his long gray hair, and his garments flap as he leans in, fighting to withstand its strength, beard waving back and forth. His legs bracing him, he points to the railroad trestle. "Maybe he should cross up there?" he half shouts against the river's roar and the wind's violent gusts.

As he speaks, part of the trestle collapses. I charge ahead, jump, and dive into the river, barely escaping the falling iron. Hunks of it splash mere inches from my feet. But the stones weren't so lucky. Now, they're buried under iron. I can't see even one of them.

"Where is this Helper? How will I ever find the Sea of Life?"

Angelo turns and stands, and everything falls quiet, as if a stage curtain opened. "He is where He always is. With you, for now."

He? Must mean the Helper. Must've read my mind.

"Find your belief, son."

Then Angelo disappears.

I toss onto my side, pulling the covers tighter.

Wait. Covers?

I'm in my bed. I'm not wet.

Great. It was just a dream, a glimpse, a horrifying warning maybe. But it begs the question: Who is this, Helper?

I sit up against the headboard, prop my head up with my hands, and plant my elbows on bent knees. I began to think finding it may only be in my dreams. But that was no better than some cheap B movie. How can that do me any good?

Oh how I'd hoped there was more to Gramps's story, that it is not simply a fantasy. If not, I'm in big trouble.

But somehow, something I can't explain, I knew the power of the Sea of Life must be real, greater than anything anyone had ever seen. Maybe even more powerful than Gramps said. I felt it in my spirit. If only I could reach it, now, before it's too late.

But, how?

CHAPTER SIX

COME FRIDAY MORNING, I sure wasn't ready for the first person I saw in homeroom—Peggy Holland. Talk about a way to make my nightmare even darker.

Why am I being punished, God? What have I done?

What a fun year this would be, every day getting trashed—first thing. My anxiety level ratchets up, approaching the extreme. Maybe it's time to go hide... just for a moment.

"Well, well, if it isn't the Marks boys." She saunters over. Her designer sneakers squeak into my view. "Did you know my mom sells junk—just like you—every day?"

My head snaps up, and my mouth hangs open.

She laughs, shaking her head side to side like a twisted victory dance. A fiery redhead, she's pinned and braided her long hair perfectly, matching her spotless clothing. She's everything except good. Obnoxious and mean-spirited, she holds her nose high in the air.

Why so mean? We never even met before this year. Wasn't it enough that our father didn't pay any attention to us, but hung on to her every word? Maybe mean people run together.

I shove my hands into my hoodie pouch to keep from pushing her down. After all, like almost everyone else, she's three inches or more taller than I am. So, I hold my tongue. No matter, she's above what I can say. At least, I think so.

Chris goggles at me, waiting for the explosion, his eyes big, his face expectant.

I shrug to let him off the hook. One won't come, not in class. Thankfully, neither of us has her or her brother in any of our other classes. One is too many, but it alone reinforces my desire—no, urgent need—to find the Sea of Life.

Gramps's story better not be something he made up to keep me occupied and entertained.

Shoulders hunched, I excuse myself with the teacher, then pivot, and run to the bathroom. A good ten minutes allows my frustrations and anxiety to ease. The doctor told me to picture a favorite time, focusing on pleasant memories. Lily, of course. Lily and me playing on her porch.

Then the doubts sneak in. One of the boys sometimes says he thinks he was supposed to be a girl. A teacher even heavy-handedly offered that suggestion to him. It almost seemed like I was being recruited too.

I squash that.

What was it Mom said? Right: it is our mortal enemy trying to steal lives and souls by sowing seeds of doubt. She got mad talking about it.

Pastor taught about it one Sunday. I whisper his words now, "'We're each wonderfully and fearfully made in our mother's womb by God.'"

Yep. So that is that.

All these strange thoughts make it hard standing in the bathroom stall. But I do it, and my foot doesn't slip. Finally, I trudge back to class. Not daring to tell anyone the real purpose of my trip and never wanting to share my thoughts either. They are weird. It is a very dark place.

Unlike the first days of the trimester, we now sit at our desks the entire class. At least, I am safe for now. Still, I feel Peg's hard, cold stare at my back. Spending the whole time worrying about it takes a toll on the rest of my day.

Maybe Chris has it right. Maybe I should let it go, going with the flow. Like a log bouncing in the river with no set course of action to guide it. But that would be like the sun hiding behind the clouds at Gramps's, as if something were missing. I can't do things that way, not yet. Like Mom, I have my own form of OCD.

I survive classes, and Friday passes. After what seems like an eternity, one of those days everyone must endure occasionally, the final bell rings. Then I race out, first dropping off my books at my locker, no homework this weekend.

Let the fun begin. Time to go to Gramps's.

I hustle to the school's front doors, step out onto the sidewalk, and dash out into the sunshine. Its rays warm and energize me. But I forgot the Hummer would be waiting, probably because I didn't see Peg or Craig. Whew.

I hunch into my hoodie on the front sidewalk, waiting for Chris. Then a push from behind slams me to the ground, and the Holland siblings run by to the Hummer.

"Loser," Peg shouts, laughing as she goes, using her thumb and forefinger to make an *L*.

I scoot to my butt and can only sit and watch. *Helper!* "If You are real, why do they have to be so mean?"

Nothing, not a word responds to my whisper.

I scramble to my feet.

"What happened to you?" Chris frowns as I dust my pants off.

All I can do is point. What's worse? This rage over being bullied or the pain of their ugliness? "Why do people have to be so mean?"

Chris picks up my backpack and holds it out. "Seems to me, at times, you've been one of the worst meaners."

I shrug it over one shoulder. But I can't deny it. "Guess I'm going to have to work on that. I don't want to be *anything* like the Hollands." I want others to like me.

We fall into step, the girls not with us today. He kicks a pebble, and it skids into a crack in the sidewalk. "School was good this week."

"Sure."

He toes the pebble out and sends it skittering further along. "Lily's not interested in me."

Deep down, he probably always knew she likes me, and—in an unseen way—I like her. But I'd taken the back seat on her, allowing Chris to pursue her affections, only not on purpose at first.

"You better decide fast, bro. Several boys in her anthropology class have been hanging around her a lot, and who can blame them? If you keep waiting, it will be too late one day soon." He tries to smile through his disappointment. You'd think he thought I had something to lose.

I hug him as we walk. I guess it is a twin thing. I'm as confused about that as anything. At times, he's my worst enemy. No matter how different we become, though, something always wants to bring us back together. I hate that he's disappointed. I need to figure out how all this works. Today, he's looking out for me, but tonight, he might be my mortal enemy—again.

I sling my backpack to my other shoulder as we turn onto our street. The homes here were all built in the 1940s or so. Most are similar brick two-story buildings. Almost all have wraparound, columned porches with a separate porch out back. All are huge with three to four bedrooms, large kitchens, and family rooms. All the important stuff for the big families during that era.

A leaf flutters past, and I catch it. I twirl the stem between my fingers. "I do kinda, um, *like* Lily."

The confession clogs my throat and sounds silly—after all, she's my best friend, so of course, I like her.

But Chris slaps my back and smirks. Yeah, he gets it. "Maybe go say goodbye to her before the weekend?"

This weekend, our moms are going away with Cara to attend a women's retreat our church is sponsoring. So Lily's gonna visit her dad.

At our house, I hand off my backpack to Chris and trudge the extra steps to Lily's. My hand shakes as I ring the doorbell. What's up with that, anyway? I've rung this bell a million times probably.

The door swings in, and she leans against the doorjamb, looking real pretty, big-girl pretty, I suppose. Even though she is only fifteen, almost sixteen, she's so mature. It's like I've missed something. Like Chris, she's shot up five inches. Now, she's taller than me.

Uncomfortable standing there with her taller than me and all, I edge to the porch swing. She gets the hint and sits with me. Our small talk grates my throat. Fisting my hands inside my hoodie pouch, I jitter the swing to set it rocking. *Just do it, buddy!*

I clear my throat. "Want to see a movie next weekend? I hear the new Spider-Man movie's coming out."

Her favorite. She'll say yes.

"Nick... I'd like that, but I already promised Eric I'd go with him. Maybe some other time, okay?" She gives me this half-hearted smile, and a disdaining where-have-you-been? look sets her face.

The screen door squeaks, and her mom carries out a travel bag. "You all packed, Lily?"

"Yes, ma'am." Lily's on her feet already. The swing careens as she leaves me without looking back.

"Hi, Nick." Kayleigh locks the door. "Say hi to your mom and tell her I'll see them in a bit."

Then they're gone. Lily's gone, my secret hopes and ambitions leaving with them. All I can do is watch.

Chris was right! But what did the look on her face mean? Where have I been?

I schlep back to our room, dump the backpack Chris left by the door, and stuff clothes into it for my weekend. Then Mom drives us across town to Gramps's. My forehead rests against the back passenger door, and my teeth worry the insides of my cheeks. If the Sea of Life isn't real, like Chris says—lately, he's more right than wrong—what will I do? The preacher's words rattle around in my head, louder than the other thoughts swirling there. I begin to sweat, a sure sign of cocoon busting, Mom says. Hopefully, it won't mean more acne.

Mom was talking to Gramps on the phone in a hushed voice before we left. Probably about me. When Lily turned me down, I felt like someone had punched me in the gut, my world slipping another notch further down the slope of ugly.

I had thought the Sea of Life was so important, that getting a dad to love me was the most important thing. Now, I ache. I hadn't even known my own heart.

The Sea of Life becomes more important, more than anything, almost. I clench my fists, wadding up the hoodie's fleecy pockets. *I have to believe. I have to believe.*

I have to talk to Gramps.

After talking to Granny and Gramps for a moment, Mom drives away with Cara, waving as she leaves us behind for their girl time. Mom doesn't know about my conversation with Lily, so Gramps doesn't know either.

Then Granny hooks her arms around Abbie and Chris. "Did your mom tell you how delighted we are to have all three of you here at the same time?"

Abbie snuggles in. "We still going to the mall tomorrow?"

"And making popcorn tonight?" Chris pipes up.

I zip my hoodie all the way up. Gramps winks at me and starts for the backyard. While my siblings head inside, chattering with Granny, Gramps and I relax in our favorite spot. His right arm slung over my shoulder feels good. Light spills from the family room. Chris and Abbie must've already set up camp there, playing on their phones, texting their friends, and watching television with Granny. Her favorite program, *Star Trek*, replaying for the thousandth time.

Butch flops at our feet, his old body warm over my sneakers.

"Gramps, why are girls so fickle?" A dramatic sigh escapes. "I thought Lily liked me, so I asked her to go to the movies. We've always hung out, but she said she was going with *Eric*." Oops. I didn't have to be so emotive, did I? Maybe I did. Putting special body language and emphasis on his name releases my disappointed frustration.

Just as petting Butch restores my peace, somewhat. A smile comes. "Gramps, whoever said your teenage years are your best must be living in a different world—or on a different planet, like Granny's shows. Life gets really bad. What with cocoon busting, stepsiblings, and girl confusion, who can know how to think? Maybe this is why some boys become bad... or switch."

"Oh, so that is what's eating you." Gramps's warm, heavy arm jostles me in tighter. He smells like medicated lotion. "Your mom said you were upset, almost crying. What happened?"

Even though I'm getting older, I need his caring hug more than he can know. Sitting so close, side by side, me staring straight ahead, I don't even notice the deer in the field beside us, a mother and her fawns foraging, until Gramps pointed to them. Butch never wavers or thinks about going after them. I guess he's too laid-back—or old.

"I waited too long." I push the fleece harder against the hollows of my palms. "Chris warned me other boys were swarming around her, talking to her."

The pain's so real, my heart so heavy. Is this my first heartbreak? I've heard Mom talk about her heartaches with Cara. She had lots of her own, especially with Dad and then Jim, a man who used to attend our church.

"Swarming? Okay. Well, I hope that's an exaggeration. But she is a sweet and pretty girl." Gramps kinda smiles. He loves Lily too. Maybe swarming wasn't the right word, but what does it matter? She's still going with Eric to see Spider-Man.

CHAPTER SEVEN

STILL CLENCHING the fleece hoodie pockets, I squeeze harder, then let go. One of the fawns tries to approach us. The mother noses it around, and they retreat into the high grass and brush, out of harm's way. My thoughts cease the essence of the momma deer's guidance. Turning sideways, I face Gramps, his arm still on my shoulder. I need him as much as those fawns need their mother.

"Tell me more about the Sea of Life and believing." I don't need the whole story, only the important stuff.

"Nick, did I ever tell you I've written in a journal every day since I was younger than you?" Gramps pulls a toothpick from his chest pocket. "Your great-granddad, my father, was a writer for a small newspaper here in town. He taught all his children the value of writing their thoughts down, our visions and dreams, even our innermost secrets—the ones we don't dare share with anyone."

He sets the toothpick between his teeth. For a bit, he's quiet, his lips and tongue working that slip of wood around. Then he points at me with its gooey end. "If we write our thoughts and things down, we can read them later and, looking back, realize the problems we saw were always smaller than they first appeared, at least in hindsight.

And that, most of the time, they're only temporary. But the important things in life remain."

He gnaws the toothpick again and regrips his hold on me. He's smiling as we resume watching the deer amble out of sight.

"I don't know why I never discussed it with you before. It could help—more than you know." He winks, takes his arm off me, and locks hands together behind him, stretching and supporting his head as he leans back. A sigh escapes his thick chest, the relaxing kind.

"Yeah, but—"

Gramps places a finger on my lips. "You need to be careful. You can 'yeah but' all your life and miss the good things if you're not careful. I know it. See, you're looking at the best yeah-but man ever."

He sets hands on knees, hunching over them, the lines creasing his face falling into deep shadows. "When I returned home from Vietnam and found my parents had already gone to heaven, I was torn. I became so angry with God, with the world. I screamed inside myself, 'I've given six years of my life to fight for what I love most. Then I came home to find they were gone!'"

Whoa! Gramps mad at God? There's so much about him I want to know—*need* to know. I straighten up, all ears.

"Nickie, we all have hard times. But hard times aren't meant to hurt us. We have a finishing point, a point to go home. Once I began reading the journals I'd written, I realized, over time, believing was the crutch that always supported me—no matter what. Then I found the Sea of Life. Angelo made sure of it."

Gramps slides over to the end of the bench. Leaning down, he pulls the head off a dandelion, the fuzzy kind that scatters seed every-where. He blows on it while turning it so the seeds won't fall on himself. "Not every seed will end up growing, and not every dream's going to come true. But God takes care of the seeds that can. He makes sure of it, especially when you believe."

I grind my teeth, tired of hearing about believing. Why won't the Helper just give me what I want? Why is believing so important? My body begins to shake, and my voice cracks again. I thought the anxiety was over. Am I imploding? No dad... and now, no Lily. Why believe? What good will it do?

It would be so much easier to believe if I ever saw good come out of it.

If he notices my uneasiness, Gramps doesn't let on. "Why don't you try journaling? I have an extra journal. You can start writing your thoughts and dreams every day, every time something comes to your mind. Then in a week or month, read your past thoughts, put a check beside them as you look back to keep track, and write notes beside them if it helps. I'll bet you'll see how everything is working for your good, in time, and it may show you what's important. And tomorrow does come, regardless of what we write on paper."

Gramps is speaking from experience. If I were honest, I'd realize losing Lily—if I had lost her—is my fault. I always assumed she'd be there. After all, she lived next door, and she liked me, right? I didn't give thought to her finding someone who returns her affection because they liked her. How had I gotten so caught up in becoming a good man and this cocoon busting that I couldn't see the good things right in front of me?

I chuff out a breath. "I'm afraid if I start writing my feelings down, I'll..." Have to face some hard truths about myself, as well as others. But am I ready to admit that, even to Gramps? I shrug, then confess, "Self-sabotage is so easy, and I may be the best at it, Gramps."

Do I really want to know the truth? The question almost eclipses my obsession about my dad and becoming a good man. Gramps is a wise man. Maybe too wise.

So he lets me stew on that one.

The world drifts by, unconcerned over my problems. Birds dart from tree to tree. Bees buzz the honeysuckle. The deer family moved on to new feeding grounds. With such calm all around, I'm battling a new chaos about Lily and Eric, plus myself on the inside, afraid of what I might learn.

The pastor always said, "Wait a while, for these problems too shall pass."

What does he know that I don't?

Leaning sideways toward me, Gramps bumps my shoulder with his. "Did I ever tell you what makes the Sea of Life so special?"

He raises a brow like he's recalled something, things he called *nuggets*, meant to build up the Sea of Life in my imagination. Real or not, I want to find it, desperately. So I hang on to his every word.

"Is it like becoming God?"

"No, no." He softly shakes his head several times. "It's what the Sea of Life teaches you about being you. Only God can be God, and only you can be you. Every decision, mistake, or accomplishment you make is a part of being you. If you change one thing, just one—your whole world might change too."

A horn blares out in the driveway. Aunt Rachael, Mom's baby sister, parks off to the side. Butch rises, stretches, and pads toward her, tail wagging. If he were younger, he'd have run.

"Let's go welcome your aunt." Gramps gets up, waving. Gramps and Granny have two girls. Their third child, the last—the boy Gramps so desperately wanted—they lost at birth. Granny nearly died during delivery. The baby suffocated. Gramps doesn't like to speak about it. Only skill, quick-thinking, plus what he said was the hand of God, saved Granny.

Shorter and rounded, Rachael's the opposite of Mom. What I would imagine Mrs. Santa Claus to be, she's quick with a smile and a plate of cookies, which may explain the round part.

"Hi, Nickie. Where's your brother and sister?" Rachael gives me a big hug and kiss, then hugs Gramps. She always smells like fresh-baked bread. Granny has taught her girls well, raising them to be sweet, loving, faithful to God, and devoted to their families, like her. Now, they work to instill that in us.

"They're inside with Granny." I jerk a thumb toward the boxes and grocery bags in the back of her car that might be for Granny. "Need any help?"

"No thanks. They're for your mom's retreat. I'm going there next." She scoops a letter from her dash. "Just gotta run this inside from the mailbox."

With the driveway so long, Granny and Gramps seldom walk to their mailbox anymore.

Gramps follows her.

I head back to the bench, still stuck on what he said about believing. The seats have chilled since we left them. I wiggle back into place and rub a finger against a groove in the wood. Lily's a believer. She even sings on stage, quite talented that girl. She loved to hum while we played those games she made up. Could that be why she's losing interest in me? If I never believe, will she like someone who does?

I shiver. Probably because nightfall's coming. Since the sun's evening shift came to an end, it's gone down behind the hillside. Shadows became longer, crickets chirp louder, and lightning bugs dot the hillside. The moon will soon be out, the other half of the world coming alive. Nighttime. A time when young minds like mine run wild.

The pastor talks about that a lot, saying, "Godly people walk in the light, while darkness shrouds the ungodly."

Makes sense. Most bad things happen in the late-night hours in our neighborhood. Timmy Moran, a boy two streets over, had his bike stolen at night. But that's not what Pastor meant, is it? It's kind of like what I think about in the bathroom stall, my darkest thoughts. I don't want to be ungodly.

Was that because they don't believe? Could it be that simple? I simply need to stay away from the darkness and believe? Were the bad people only those who didn't? That couldn't be right. I've seen lots of "believers" do stuff. Is Eric a believer?

And what about writing in a journal?

I scuffle my feet, uneasy.

Gramps is right. Lots of times, I've felt one way about something, only to find out I was wrong. Maybe if I talk to Chris, I can find out how come he believes so easily.

The cool night air begins to feel damp. I can't see the river below anymore. Still, the sound of water rushing over the low rapids resonates through the valley. My senses take everything in, magnifying my uneasiness. Unknown demons and characters lurk behind the long shadows in my imagination, causing more thoughts about light versus darkness.

I push to my feet and shuffle to the house, but my shoulders stay slumped. Do I want to know the truth? The truth about me, about my fears—my flaws?

CHAPTER EIGHT

"WHERE NO MAN HAS GONE" now scrolls down the TV screen from Granny's *Star Trek* episode. My siblings sit mesmerized by their phones. Gramps must be in the basement tinkering with his ERECTOR set. He loves to create things, some useful, some not so much.

I snuggle in beside Granny, and she leans in to accept my love. The familiar smell of her light perfume, sort of a flowery sweet smell, relaxes me.

Comforted, I fall asleep. Then I'm waking up, the bacon frying and biscuits baking. Gramps must have helped me up to bed. Breakfast smells amazing, and my stomach rumbles.

Chris, now also awake, races down the steps with me after washing up, a requirement in our world. Abbie's already at the table, waiting for us and the food. With her hair down this morning, she looks just like Granny in the picture. If I hadn't known better, I'd say she could pass for eighteen—easily. Somehow, like Lily, a certain glow came upon her after her cocoon busting, and she was already pretty and adorable.

My baby sister isn't a baby any longer. I nearly trip on that one. Where's our wonderful life going? This may explain why some of the boys and girls from her school have been hanging around our front porch. Abbie's popular. I slump into my usual chair as if I woke up ten years later, and everyone matured overnight.

Gramps pulls up his chair. Granny places the bacon on the table and sits between Abbie and him at the large oak table. We all join hands as he asks for God's blessing over our food and lives. "Heavenly Father, thank You for this treat of having our three grandchildren with us today. We ask that You bless this family and our gathering, along with the food, in Jesus's name. Amen." He releases my hand. "Everyone, dig in."

Then our forks and spoons get busy.

"Man..." Chris sighs out contentment. "Granny's bacon gravy is the best."

"Her biscuits as well," Abbie mumbles around a full mouthful.

"For sure." Aunt Rachael has *nothing* on Granny. Hers is country cooking in its finest, truest form.

After breakfast, we clean the kitchen for her. Then she takes us to the Roanoke mall. With its two levels of stores, the place has become a hangout for kids from our school on Saturday mornings. Entering beside the food court, I recognized several popular girls from school. They don't give me or Chris a second look, spellbound by a store window, pointing and giggling before scuttling in to find their favorite shoes. Mom says it's a girl thing.

Strangely, like Lily, they no longer look like the young girls I went to school with most of my life. They look more like pretty young women. I guess their cocoon busting's over too, or has my perception of them changed? Has the whole world changed, moved ahead, while here I am—stuck in my lousy cocoon?

The boys usually hang out around the food court fountain. It offers the best view of this end of the mall. Most of the boys I never considered as competition before, but after the Lily-and-Eric thing, my views have blurred. At least I don't see Eric. Will she tell him I asked her to the movies? Eric and I were never friends, but not enemies either.

Is this what grown-ups go through? Was I becoming a grown-up? Mom said cocoon busting would change my body and my outlook.

Maybe that's why Chris and I don't get along like before. Is *he* a grown-up? But I'm older! How does that work? My journal will be full in a couple of weeks if I don't slow down. I have to stop all this, or my anxiety will come back.

"Nick... Nickie!" Granny calls. "Are you okay?"

I must've mumbled something. She turns to the boys laughing and cutting up, watching the girls going into the shoe store, making rude comments and gestures just loud enough for us to hear.

"That's what happens to boys who don't go to church. It's like the pastor said." Crimson washes her face, sharing the horror that we could—*would*—become like them if we didn't go to church. "Their mothers ought to be ashamed."

Does everything have to be right or wrong, light or dark? Why does everything have to contrast its opposite? Where's the fun in that?

Normally, Granny leaves Chris and me in the food pavilion. Not today. She mustn't want us mixing with the other teens.

Fine by me. But Chris may have wanted to join them. He turns and watches them as we walk toward the center of the mall. He talks to several of those guys at school.

"Here, boys." Granny gives us ten dollars for tokens. "You two can play video games while Abbie and I have our fun girl time."

Shopping. Abbie will love it. She comes back with a skip in her step and a box with the Nike swoosh. "Check these out." She whisks off the lid, and we crowd in.

"Seems the company couldn't make up their mind," I blurt out. The front of one's red, the same as the back of the other. The rest of both shoes is gold.

"Cool, huh?" She wiggles them like they're dancing. Her radiant smile and gleaming eyes warm my heart.

"Supercool." Chris flashes a thumbs-up.

Super *ugly*, but I keep that to myself even without Chris elbowing me. We love our little sister. Sure, we have our moments, but most of all, we want good for each other.

But now, Granny's drooping. She's been wearing down quicker. Mom says it's because she's getting older. Gramps says she watches too much television and won't go walking with him anymore, not getting exercise like they used to. She's afraid of falling and getting hurt. I scooch around Chris to walk at her side. "Can I carry your bags?"

She loads me up, no resistance. Her hands free, she ruffles my hair. "Shall we get our usual stromboli and soda at the pizza place?"

"Man, what a real treat." Christ starts ahead. "I'll get in line."

Soon, I slide into a chair at the food court and stack the packages at my feet. Abbie scoots in beside me, takes off her shoes, and steps into those weird two-tone things. While Granny goes to pay, I watch the rude teens. I guess they think they're cool, but the girls don't think so. Neither do I.

"These are sooo cute!" Abbie gushes, wiggling her toes and turning her ankles this way and that.

A flash of heat sears my chest. Imagine if they said such things about Abbie!

Chris carries over a tray. I pop up to pull out a chair for Granny. Abbie tucks her feet back into her beat-up sneakers, and we wait for Chris to say grace.

Taking a page out of Gramps's repertoire, he finishes with, "And bless our family, in Jesus's name, amen."

Granny nods her approval. "Since your gramps is an elder, he sees and hears much more than most at church. He said Lily is going to be in an upcoming play. Won't that be exciting?" She tests a bite of her stromboli, then wipes her mouth.

My hunger quelled somewhat, I set my stromboli down and wash the last bite down with soda. "Does Gramps like praying in church?" My feet kick back and forth. "I mean, it seems hard to stand up before the whole church and ask God's blessing on the collection of the offering."

"You simply say what's in here." She leans over and pats my chest over my heart. "You always thank me for cooking breakfast or buying lunch. How do you feel when someone does something kind for you?

That's what you express. His prayers are much of the same thing—all prayers are. Sometimes, we go in need. Other times, we give thanks for our needs being met. God gives you the words if you take the moment to understand those feelings inside."

Granny takes another nibble, then peers over her sandwich at our still-glowing Abbie. "How is school, Abbie? Your mom said you've made quite a few friends this year."

"A few?" Chris chirps. "You can't even get on our porch so many of them come over." He ducks his head and returns to stuffing his mouth.

"School is good." Abbie pushes his shoulder, her glance rolling around the ceiling somewhere in obvious dispute. "I've taken more preparatory classes than some kids, but I like them. It helps me know school is serious business, unlike some of us."

At Abbie's too obvious dig, Granny turns my way. "And how about you, Mr. Marks? Is school going well?"

"It's okay." I chomp a big bite to finish my stromboli, accomplishing that and ending the questioning.

"Your mom was an excellent student—both my girls were. It runs in your genes to do and want more. You'll see. God has great lives in store for you."

It's always nice hearing about Mom's childhood. It helps me gain more perspective about my amazing mom. She rarely disappoints us. We have rules—rules help us know what to expect, what to trust.

I need to write this in my journal. I want to remember it. I don't want to be cool at the expense of hurting others, especially girls, and definitely not Lily.

Back at Granny and Gramps's, they all go inside. I plop myself onto Gramps's favorite spot by myself to ponder life's hardest decisions again. What did the pastor mean, saying believing is the most important question in the history of mankind?

I'd felt the darkness in the boys' conversation at the mall, their cold attitude toward goodness. Was Granny right? Should their mothers be ashamed?

I'd never thought about it that way, that my actions and words could shame my mom. But I'd felt the same coldness Granny felt. Does that mean I'll still be good?

Something strikes my back. Ha! It's only Butch's tail hitting me. I don't know whether he planned on his tail hitting me or not, but I call him around the bench. We sit there, Butch and me, his presence soothing me, stilling my doubts. Even if only temporary, it feels good, not being alone—with myself.

After going to bed, I lay awake replaying the scene at the mall. I don't want my mom to be ashamed of me. She works too hard and loves me too much for me to let her down. "I have to believe."

Helper, I need You. Where are You?

I must be going bonkers. I'm wound tighter than a ball of rubber bands.

I fall asleep whispering to myself.

"Aren't you up yet?" Chris bangs our door inward.

I push up on one elbow. Sun's already up.

He fits his hands on his hips and stands over me. "You wanna miss the world's-best breakfast?"

"Don't let Mom hear you call it that."

Chris rolls his eyes. "I'd never say that to Mom. But, man oh man, bro. Today, Granny made *sausage* gravy."

I smack my lips together and find my pants. Country sausage gravy. "Yum. Abbie's favorite."

"So hurry it up, why don't ya?" Then he's gone, clomping downstairs and probably drooling the whole way.

I only take minutes to wash before joining my sister smiling, waiting for the gravy and breakfast. I tug her braid as I pass, and she gives me a shove. Kitten-sweet Abbie can be a tiger when riled up. So, it's best to keep on her good side. Still, I can't resist another tug at that braid.

She'd give the shirt off her back to help someone. That's the way Mom wants all three of us to be, but it seems easier for Abbie. Maybe because she didn't have to share kindness and elbow room with a twin—even before birth.

"So Abbie"—I slide into my chair—"how do your new shoes feel this morning? I'll bet you'll be the talk of your school. A lot of kids at the high school wear those." Sometimes I forget I'm so lucky to have these two. Mom, with no help, except Gramps and Granny, has raised at least two great kids. Now, I'm trying hard to make it a third.

"They feel great. I can't wait for my friends to see them. I didn't think you liked them by your expression."

"Well, they look great on you, but they aren't for me." I scooch over as Gramps sits down and begins giving thanks over our food.

I think back to the dream with the fallen trestle, hoping it's not a harbinger.

"Nick, pass the rolls please," Gramps asks.

I guess grace is over. I slip my hand from Gramps's grip and stifle a groan. I'm doing it again, daydreaming. I'd best stay alert or the rolls will be gone, along with all the sausage gravy.

"You children need to come over more." He pats Abbie's shoulder. "Your granny fixes the best breakfast when you're here. No Slim Fast this morning."

Granny smacks at the air with her left hand as if to wave off his comment, rolling her gaze in the way she does. Huh, maybe that's where Abbie gets the eye-roll thing.

"By looking at your stomach, big fella"—Granny bats her eyes— "I'd say you haven't missed too many meals." She dips her head and tilts it. Going all squint-eyed at him, she purses her lips and displays her playfulness. Even after all these years, their love's so plainly visible.

"I don't want you to think I don't like your cooking," he chuckles.

The love at the breakfast table overwhelms my senses. It could've been a Norman Rockwell morning, Mom's favorite illustrator. Too bad Mom's not here.

"That's okay. Chris and Abbie will finish it up if you don't. Won't you, children?"

I'm too busy wolfing down to respond. So are my siblings, so all she receives back are grins and chewing gestures.

This is what I like more than anything in the world. That feeling of warmth that overflows every pore and fiber of your body, and you can only sit and marvel at it. I didn't realize it until now, but at home, I feel it all the time with Mom, Abbie, Chris, and Lily. Especially when Lily was with us before my cocoon busting began numbing my senses with questions I haven't any answers for.

Abbie's watching Granny's clock again, the one that looks like a black-and-white cat. Its eyes rock back and forth as its tail swishes the seconds away. It's mesmerized her ever since she was a baby.

"Eat up, children." Granny waves at our plates. "We've not much time. We don't want to be late and have everybody watching us."

She grew up in an Irish Catholic family in Boston. She loves greeting and praying for people in the sanctuary—before praise and worship begins.

That's partly what upset Gramps the most on *that* Father's Day. Several of those whisperers knew her well. She has the kind of spirit I imagine an angel would have, always looking to serve. Mom and Rachael learned well from Granny. Maybe I see myself in a bad way because everyone else is so good, so at peace with themselves and others.

"Hurry up now," Granny urges us again. She gets so excited going to church—I'm talking crazy excited. Mom says she likes to see souls saved. Supposedly, they all do in the church. Only when some leave church, they act as if they never went, like Dale Marks, my dad.

I don't understand. I hope to find out one day, but for now, I must learn to believe.

Didn't Gramps say that once you believe it's like when the sun comes out of the clouds? Then, supposedly, everything appears different, hope overpowers all your doubts, and you're seeing things afresh for the first time. Sounds good, but unlikely. Like the Bible story about Saul. The light hit him so bright and harsh, he heard a voice and couldn't see. He even fell on the ground.

"That's what the Sea of Life does too," Gramps promised, "like believing."

Gramps gets up early every morning to read and study "the Word," as he calls it. He says it helps his belief. I don't understand, but I don't get up early either.

CHAPTER NINE

FED AND DRESSED, I trek after the rest of them into the church.

Chris falls back in step with me. "Eat too much? Or why so glum?"

I shrug. "Guess we won't see Lily today." She's usually here on Sundays.

"She's still at her dad's, right?"

I nod. They go to a different church. My shoes scuff along in my vision, my head ducked. "I figured out why her saying she was going to the movie with Eric was such a gut-punch." Since I'm speaking to my shoes, maybe he won't hear me. "I've gotten so used to being with her."

Subconsciously thinking she'd always track me down, I stopped looking for her, not realizing how important she was to me. Not sure I want to explain that to my twin though. Probably because I was never the one doing the pursuing, I'm now finding out how that changes everything.

My lips curl. My shoulders hunch. My shoes stop scuffling along. "Remember how she ran down the church hallway ever since we were preschoolers, looking for me, calling out my name?"

Somehow, it stopped being special. What I wouldn't give to see her beautiful smiling face today, eyes sparkling—as blue and deep as the ocean—her long shiny black hair bouncing as she ran, giggling, reaching for me. Then she'd hug me, and I hug her.

Why was I so blind to my feelings for her? When did I lose sight? How did I become overwhelmed by imaginary loses when I had everything I'd ever needed—right in front of me?

Chris bumps his shoulder to mine. "It'll be okay."

A favorite memory is how she began hugging me ever so tight as we've gotten older, closing her eyes, taking all of me in. Sometimes, she seemed to shudder, taking hold of the front of my shirt in her balled-up hands, pulling tight to me. Lately, though, she hasn't run down the hall. Sometimes, she doesn't even come down it, instead going outside and sitting on the picnic bench in the warm months with the other teens.

Chris lopes on ahead up the stairs and into that hall. That's when he started hanging out with her. I didn't pay much attention after a while. It began shortly before my cocoon busting became evident to me and hers was over. It was right when I slipped into my meaner stage, and I have been mean—even to her. My most precious friend in the whole world.

As Lily has gotten older, she's taken on more responsibility in the church. She joined the young adult choir over a year ago and is active in all their dramas. All this happened after her cocoon fell off and her life changes became more dramatic. How much longer can I hope she'll be interested in me, my boyish ways still not letting go of me?

I snap out of my daydream as the pastor comes down the hallway. Bracing myself, I won't let self-doubt eat my soul again today. Still, my first thought after seeing him is boys need a dad to become a good man. Mom said that's not how he meant it to sound, but it's like dirty water in a well. It's still in there, getting deeper and deeper, ever harder to get out.

I guess I shouldn't be so uptight. Chris tells me that all the time.

"Good morning, Nick. Ready for a great service?" Pastor pats my shoulder and reaches for my hand, stopping for my reply.

"Yes, sir." Shaking his hand feels strange. The service passes while I'm still figuring on things, missing most of the message, except the salvation part.

Mom won't be home from the retreat until five, so we head back to Granny's for lunch. There won't be any leftovers from this weekend. I can see Abbie calculating what tomorrow will bring for dinner. Chris and I don't mind, but Abbie always looks forward to Mondays, no matter what the leftovers.

Granny's fried chicken is fabulous, and the smashed potatoes and chicken gravy wow us. "Granny, do you have enough leftovers we can take some home for tomorrow night's dinner?" I wink at Abbie whose eyes light up, the fire deep inside stoked. "We have leftovers every Monday from our weekend meals out."

"Yes, Granny... please?" she begs, a smile bursting out where a blank expression resided seconds earlier. Mom's dinner schedule and rules give Abbie something she can rely on and comforts our little planner.

"I'm a step ahead of you. I packed up some for you to take home before we ever sat down. You know your mom grew up on Monday leftovers."

"Ha ha." Chris points at me with the world's largest drumstick. "I thought Mom came up with that. I thought she was the clever, fun mom."

I ogle that drumstick. That must have been one big bird. I like white meat the best myself. Opposites!

"She *is* the clever, fun mom!" Abbie snaps.

This is what I need to write about in my journal—my family. *Oh, Helper, please don't ever let me forget this again!*

Now, why did I think that? I don't know any Helper. Is this what Gramps meant about talking to my secret friend?

"Now simmer down. Just because you didn't think of something doesn't mean you're not clever. Quite the contrary, the best quality in a person isn't necessarily coming up with things that make life easier or better, it's using them. No matter." Granny pinches Chris's cheeks gently. "Your mom is the most wonderful mom in the world. You children are lucky. Most women would have withered away, but not your mom. She's devoted herself and loved you even more, being her best. But you all know that, don't you?"

The same fire that brought joy to Abbie's eyes moments earlier now brings determination to Granny's. Must be an O'Hanahan thing. Gramps sits back, watching, not saying a word. Obviously admiring his family the same way I did.

"God has blessed our family." He reaches for the chicken platter. "When I look at you all, I know there is a creator and He loves me. No man has ever had more than I. Your mom and granny will do whatever they can to make sure you and I are getting what we need and we're loved more than a body has a right."

He passes the chicken to Chris, who goes digging for another leg.

Before Chris hands me the platter, I refill my lemonade glass and reach to top up Abbie's and Chris's.

After I take some crispy wings, Gramps accepts the platter back. "It was my dream long ago, when I was a young man, to have and love someone who loved God and would hold their family up to shine brightly, letting her children become the fine jewelry of her life. I found that in your grandmother, and I thank God for her every day. Your mom and Rachael are the same. Theirs is a special kind of love."

I pick up one wing with my fingers, glad Granny never frowns on letting chicken be finger food. Even gladder Gramps always finds a way to appreciate God's goodness to—and in—our family. Maybe one day I'll find my way to it also.

"Don't ever forget, you children have O'Hanahan blood in your veins, not just any old blood. That makes you special, and God has an important purpose for each of you." Gramps pats Granny's hand. The look they share shows a love still growing stronger through the years.

He doesn't mean to demean other families, only sharing our special heritage, what he says is a calling.

Later, when I'm so stuffed it's hard to move, Abbie and Chris take off.

"Lunch was good." Gramps pushes back his chair and rubs his belly.

"Granny's cooking beats all. Glad she taught Mom how to cook." I stack plates, it being my turn to clear. Flatware rattles against china as I add it to the tower. "You know, Gramps, every time we eat at your dinner table, Granny fills us up with good food, and you fill us up with good beliefs. Must be why Mom believes so strongly."

"Your mom's faith began to become real when she was young, like Abbie. She had some things come up, and she needed help. I can't tell you what that was—it's personal, she'll have to—but it was a hard time for her. The Helper revealed Himself to her, and through His love and mercy, she made it through, as we all do. That worked out for her good." His thick fingers hook around several lemonade glasses as he starts toward the kitchen with his load. "When you need the Helper the most is also where you encounter your hardest decisions. But if you'll believe, the Helper will never let you down."

Dishes loaded in the sink, I follow him outside to climb into his car, my siblings already buckled in.

Smiling, he comes around to my side.

"Nick, believing comes with a special gift. As you grow in your knowledge and love of Him, He reveals Himself to you, in your spirit, and that makes you want to know more. The Sea of Life is all about believing. I hope you get to see that soon. We'll talk more next week, okay?" He hugs me tight, then bends, and whispers in my ear the very thing I need. "I believe in you, Nickie."

"I love you, Gramps." A tear tries to find a way out of its home. I wipe it on my sleeve, getting into the car. My internal struggles ramp up once again. Now I'm shaking on the inside as night comes.

Mom comes out to the car when we arrive, kisses Gramps and Granny, and thanks them for looking after us. Taking the large box of leftovers from Granny, I admire their bond, so loving, special, and sweet. I hope I always love Mom like I do now. She's the best.

Inside, Mom hugs each of us, kissing us on the cheek, looking us over real good. Though our home isn't fancy and doesn't have the latest gadgets, love always overflows. Oddly, now I feel more at peace. Why my emotions change so drastically in mere seconds, I don't know.

I can't wait until Lily comes home. Maybe we can talk. Gramps says I need to believe. First, I need to learn how to believe. Maybe she'll help me.

Well into the night, I wait for her by my window in our bedroom, but she doesn't come home. Each passing hour leaves me more jittery. Is everything all right? Is there something I don't know?

CHAPTER TEN

THE ALARM RINGS, welcoming me to a pounding headache after unsettling dreams. Sure, they're only dreams, but they're all so real. I run to the window and scowl at the dreary gray morning, perfect weather for a Monday. Fog lays low to the ground, blurring the tree shadows stretched underneath it.

My thoughts feel gray too, my soul hurt. Is Mom ashamed of me or of herself because of what I've become? My imagination is often unsettling like fog, hiding or distorting truth, becoming hard to control at times, about who I am, what I'll become. Reality blurred.

How can two people share the same womb for nine months and feel so differently about themselves? Chris has it all together, me—not so much. How can you know what someone else is thinking or feeling? Does Chris *really* have it all together?

I can't speak at breakfast. Of course, only Mom notices. She rests a hand on my shoulder as she passes by bringing Abbie more milk. "The fog got ya down, Nickie?"

I shrug. I've never been able to hide anything from her. Sometimes, being under her scrutiny is a pain, but she always takes the time to talk things out, to lift our spirits, our hopes. She says she can only be as happy as her saddest child. I guess I've made her plenty sad these days.

Abbie and Chris scoop up their cereal, spoons clanking and milk dribbling. And I shift. And wait. *Finally*, they clomp upstairs to get dressed.

"So..." Mom turns from the sink and braces herself back against it. "What's bothering you?"

I just figured that out myself. "The gloom bothers me more today than most." The window by my bed faces Lily's bedroom window. I used to wave good morning to my best friend. It was the first thing I did every morning. Soon, we'd be out front talking, laughing, enjoying being together. But now, there's no waving, no getting together. "When did it stop?"

"When did what stop?" Mom unties her red apron and hangs it on the back of the glass pantry doorknob, antique, like the rest of the house. She looks great in her khaki slacks and blue button-up shirt, her work uniform. The heels on her work shoes sound like clackers hitting the tiled floor. They usually make me smile. Not today.

I drop my spoon into my empty cereal bowl and begin to get up to put it in the dishwasher, but Mom grips my shoulder and motions for me to stay. "I was wondering out loud, Mom. That's all."

She cups her hand alongside my face.

For some reason, I burst into tears. "Mom, am I a bad person? I feel so empty inside, and I've lost my best friend. What's wrong with me?"

When I duck my head, ashamed of my outburst, she holds me firm and adds her other hand to my face. "Nick, you are the sweetest boy I know, maybe impulsive, but your heart is good. Why do you doubt yourself so much?"

She slides closer and snugs her arms around me. Man, it feels so good.

When did I become so emotional? Lately, my eyes are rivers, feeding tears down my face. My head pounds, and my sinuses clog from crying. I wanted to run, to hide—from myself, from everyone.

Instead, I fidget my hands, picking at a cuticle. "Are you ashamed of me? Of something I've done?"

She smiles. Her face so full of love and compassion, her eyes go moist. "Nick, don't you know? I could never be ashamed of you. You're always going to be my son. Will you make some mistakes? Sure, we all do. But you are good." She pats my heart. "There's nothing in there to be ashamed of. This is nothing but a stage you have to go through. It'll be over soon, and you'll see."

Her loving pep talk helps. But my pain lingers deep inside, the self-inflicted, self-accusing kind. I want so much to have good friends and Lily. But I've become my own worst enemy.

We head out. The fog's finally lifted, and the day doesn't feel quite as bad, except for my pounding headache.

"What's going on with you?" Chris nudges me after we drop Abbie by her school and start up the sidewalk to ours. "You're a basket case."

He knows me better than anyone, even if we're growing in different directions.

"Don't you get it yet? Life is about choices—you get to choose!" He pushes me, hard, sideways.

I almost stumble. "I get it!" I'm so not ready for him to start busting my chops, so I push him back, hard. "I've just made some bad ones."

"No." He scoots around to plant himself in front of me, legs spread wide to straddle the sidewalk. "You don't make *any* decisions."

Huh? My backpack starts to slip, so I grip the straps at my chest. "What's that supposed to mean?"

"Think, buddy. Like with Lily. You stopped showing up. She asked me why you were mad at her. She thought she'd done something wrong. That's when she started coming to the picnic table with the other kids." His voice starts getting loud—like attention-attracting loud. "You've checked out of life for a year! What did you think, everyone would just keep waiting for you? You don't get it, do you? She was crazy about you. I thought you were crazy about her. Then one day, you checked out, nowhere to be found."

He's shaking his head, his hurt eyes questioning.

Where had I gone?

Dumbfounded, I can't say anything.

So he frowns, shakes his head, and keeps walking to school.

Entering homeroom, I hunch into myself. It's been a bad morning. I don't need Peg pounding on me too. During roll call, Mrs. Manning calls Peg's name, then mentions she's on a field trip with her anthropology class. I sit up in my seat and look at Chris, hands out as if to ask. Lily's in anthropology too. That's where she was this morning. My headache fades. My hopes rise. It's a two-night trip. She won't be home until Tuesday evening, late.

On our walk home, I loop alongside Chris. "Why didn't you say something?"

He feigns a laugh and stops walking. Red blotches his face again. "You pushed everyone away, including Abbie—and me—your twin. I didn't think that would ever happen! Say something? You fought with me every day, never giving me any slack, always right. Yeah, say something? Well, I'm saying it now—you're a jerk."

I flinch. He's angrier than I'd ever seen him, fighting angry. But is he right? Maybe the preacher was only half right. Maybe I was the only one who'd become a bad man.

"I wish I were dead!" I shout. I gasp, cover my mouth, and run home, leaving Chris behind, his jaw hanging. He can't know my battles, but then, I don't know his either.

After dropping my books off on my bed, I run out to our spot, the same spot Lily and I used to spend hours together almost every day, laughing, playing... and falling in love.

I finally know I love her. I don't know whether it's a big-boy love or not. But I know I hurt inside.

"Helper, where are You?" I cry out, unashamed who hears—now.

Our spot is an old tree house. Mom gave it to Chris and me for Christmas when we were seven. The. Best. Gift. *Ever.*

We've spent tons of time here, with and without Lily. I get why Chris likes her. He's been here most of the times with her too. She sort of sides with me, though. I'd never thought about it that way before. Is that why he's so angry? Did he want her to be his BFF, and she chose me? Did I push her away from me—and him?

I stay in the tree house until suppertime when Abbie climbs up and hugs me. "Mom said for me to bring you in for supper." She reaches down, takes my hand, and winks. "It's leftover night, ya know?"

I follow, the cocoon weighing on my soul.

CHAPTER ELEVEN

BEFORE LILY COMES HOME, the following day's an emotional roller coaster, all downhill. I'd never said I wished I were dead before. Have I fallen that deep into misery? Before school, Mom talks to me about it, but I can't answer her questions, save one. Did I want help? Yes, I do. Where is He? This Helper Gramps talks about. He said I only had to talk to my secret friend. But I can't find Him, so what do I do?

I couldn't say it aloud. I could only stare blankly.

Mom's eyes tear up, and her lips quiver when she sees my tears.

I hurt, but I didn't want her to hurt too. I can't speak. I don't know where or how to start.

Why do I feel like this? My mood swings are so wild. At times, I can't concentrate, and all this acne keeps popping up. I've never had acne before. Neither has Chris. But more than anything is this feeling I'm falling, spiraling, into a black hole of oblivion. With my anxiety skyrocketing during those times—the times I hide in the bathroom, not wanting to be seen—it hurts to be in my own skin.

Mom takes me in her arms and holds me, rocking me back and forth. It always helps—tonight, not so much. She finally holds me back and looks deep into my eyes, our hearts sharing a hard pain.

"When you want to talk, I'll be here, even if you have to wake me up. Okay?"

I head upstairs alone and flop onto my bed. Did I really want to die? Am I that bad? Do I hate myself that much? "Why did I say that?"

Do I really want to die and why? It becomes a loop, playing over and over and over, my anxiety almost unbearable as I prep for school. After school, I wait, watching for Lily. She makes it home around seven thirty, too late for me to go over. My heart's too weak to be tested again so soon anyway. Instead, I head to the tree house.

Abbie's there, talking on her cell phone. She hushes when I scramble up, saying goodbye.

I slide in and sit on the other side. "Who were you talking to?"

"Oh... just a boy from school. Nothing important." She shrugs, then eyes me. She's got this... questioning smile. "Chris told me what happened. Are you okay?"

"I don't know anything anymore. It's like I've been asleep for two years and I'm waking up to find out I've missed so much. I've lost Lily. I never knew I was in love with her. I hurt so bad. I'm sorry for being mean to you. I love you. Please forgive me!"

It's a shame hurt doesn't go away when you hit a tear limit, sort of like an earned reprieve from heartache. If only it worked that way. I had busted through my tear ceiling, not knowing why I was so emotional. I never was before—before the cocoon busting.

Abbie crawls over and hugs me. We sit nice and quiet. No more words, just love. I don't know how, but not having a dad has caused us to rely on each other more and maybe love each other deeper. That's better than having someone around who'd rather be some-where else.

Come morning, I rush to my window first thing. Lily isn't at hers. So I take a plastic ball, throw it, and hit her window like old times.

A few minutes later, she comes to the window, her hands apart asking why?

I wave and smile, admiring her.

She doesn't stay there long, just waves half-heartedly and leaves.

It's a start, but Eric can drive. I'm still too young. Besides, I'll have to wait to get a car until I can work for it, and Mom doesn't want us working on school nights.

I rush through breakfast, then get ready for school as quickly as I can. Chris still isn't speaking to me. He makes it clear he's angry with the way he cocks his head sideways during breakfast. I've apologized a hundred times, but he won't let it go. Like he said, I was a jerk, and that carries a certain punishment, I suppose. Unless I find the Sea of Life.

Kissing Mom goodbye, I'm ready to rush out the door, sit on Lily's steps, and wait on her. When Mom catches my arm, I try to swing loose, but she won't let go. "Mom... I'm in a hurry. I want to catch Lily before school."

Though every fiber in my body tells me not to, I have to tell her how sorry I am and how much I like her. It must be done.

"Are you sure? Before school?" Her eyes search mine. I get it more now. She wants to understand me so she can help. I didn't know she'd been through something like this herself. I guess we rarely see our parents as young and in love once.

"I want to apologize to her." I hold my chin up, even though it's probably going to be taking one very soon. Tension rises up in me as I prep to race out the door. Every second's an eternity.

"Okay, Nickie, good luck." Mom raises a hand for a high five. "Remember, I love you. It's not the end of the world if she's upset with you. Things like this have a way of working out."

"Thanks. I love you too." I sprint out the back screen door and rush over to Lily's as fast as I can go. I'll soon have everything patched up, and we'll be back together.

I plunk down on her front steps and wait. Twenty minutes later, our screen door slams shut. Chris must be heading out to school. I didn't know whether Lily left or not, but if I don't leave now, I'll be late. So I hustle to catch up with Chris and Abbie.

Chris doesn't talk all the way. Thankfully, Abbie keeps up a good conversation. But his silence drowns her out. Why wasn't I aware of the distance I put between us? If I was the bad guy—if I'd *decided* to be bad—I should know, shouldn't I?

Gramps better be able to help me understand. That's all I can hope for.

At school, Lily's talking with one of her girlfriends. I run over and wait for her to say goodbye to her friend. Then she stands there, shifting from foot to foot. Long black hair wisps past her blue-blue eyes. She tucks it behind her ears.

Other kids rush by to class, chaotic evidence of a bell ready to ring. A lump climbs from my gut into my throat, and I struggle to speak.

"Well..."

Man, she looks *so* good. I can't believe how grown-up she is. How'd I miss it?

"I'm sorry if I hurt you," I blurt. "I don't know what happened to me, what came over me? I miss you so much, Lily."

I swallowed down tears. No way will I cry now.

She doesn't say anything, simply stands still, watching me. Did I take her by surprise? Every second drags by and yet flies too.

I feel so small, so alone.

She has all the power, the right to speak mean, but she doesn't. The bell rings, giving us five minutes to get to homeroom.

"I've got to go. See you," she says. Then she's gone.

And I'm standing there stung, numb, no more knowing how she felt than before. My soul naked, exposed.

Do I still have any chance to be her boyfriend forever?

I pivot and head home, skipping school.

CHAPTER TWELVE

I KICK CANS, weeds, and most of all myself—all the way home—not wanting to consider the consequences of my actions. I don't want to be her best friend forever anymore. I want to be her boyfriend, I think. Maybe.

Maybe I'm getting over the cocoon-busting stage. Have I entered the accountability stage, the one the pastor spoke of? If so, I might be failing that one pretty quickly.

Mom will be so ashamed of me!

Why? When did everything become so life or death? Black or white? Urgent? I'm not even sixteen, why do the worries of the world have to fall on me? I don't remember being worried.

What was I thinking or doing during the time everyone else went their separate ways, even Chris? I didn't make a conscious decision to fight with him or not hang out with him or Lily. Did I?

Reaching home takes an hour longer than usual. Hungry, I trek into the house and grab a sandwich, then head out to the tree house. A quietness, a stillness, settles the air. The leaves and insects appear to stand still, everything in super-slow motion, except my thoughts.

I climb into the tree house, and Toby, Lily's great big yellow cat, rises. He stretches his legs and yawns a big cat yawn, then saunters over to where I'm sitting. His purr motor rumbles, and he rubs against me.

He always came up with Lily back when she'd come over. Back then, we laughed at him because he followed her around like a dog. Good thing he's here before the storm hits.

I'd done it now, skipped school for the first time ever.

Kinda eerie being in the tree house while everyone else is in school, almost unreal. Anxiety begins crushing my thoughts. I curl up in the corner under a picture of all of us kids, including Lily. All I can do is stare. I can see the feelings we shared, Lily and I, even in the old photograph.

I fall asleep, Toby cuddled beside me.

Who knows how much time passes before I hear the whispering, the slam of hands and feet slapping up the ladder. I can't tell who it is, but a reckoning's coming for sure.

Ready or not, here goes.

Chris and Abbie scramble up. I stare, waiting to get my chops busted.

It doesn't happen. Chris and Abbie sit on opposite sides of me like when Abbie was a toddler. Only now, I'm in the middle. No words are spoken, just love shared, even from Chris.

Then Chris's shoulder bumps me. "Gramps called, said he had a present for you. He's coming over tonight, him and Granny. They're going to bring over Mexican so Mom doesn't have to cook."

Chris gets up.

Abbie hops to her feet. "Are you going to be okay?"

"Yeah, sooner or later. Thanks."

They climb down the ladder. Toby's now nowhere to be found, but I have an amazing brother and sister, even though I question Chris's intentions lately.

I slide onto my knees. The tree house has a good view of our backyards and houses and our white wooden carport where Mom parks to keep her car sheltered from our old oak and maple trees. I frown at her car now. She must've taken off early.

I don't understand why I keep thinking I'm in trouble. Mom has never treated us like that. She's our biggest supporter and wouldn't come down hard on me. It's not her style. She must've gotten that from Gramps and Granny.

Still, I can't force myself to leave the tree house.

Trouble is, I still didn't know where I stand with Lily. How'd it all take place anyway? Did I stop showing up like Chris said? I didn't even know how I did that.

Once my anxiety rises again, I can't control my thoughts. They just scatter, popping up randomly. Mostly when I'm alone. Maybe I should take the medication the doctor prescribed for me.

What about that thing from Sunday school? It went something like "He who rules his own spirit is better than he who captures a city."

If only I could rule my thoughts.

Mom doesn't come out to the tree house, so I wait. An hour or so later, Gramps comes to the bottom of the tree house ladder. "Nickie... Nick, are you still up there? I have a surprise for you. Can you come down?"

Now I've dragged Gramps and Granny deeper into my troubles. Great.

"I'm coming down." I back down the ladder, my chest so tight I'm not sure I can breathe, my head pounding so hard it can't think, my heart ready to explode. Why am I so uptight? This is *Gramps*. He has nothing but love for me.

He's holding something under a cover. He plants it on the ground, then hugs me. I must've grown lately. Now, I'm not much shorter than Gramps. Had I grown or had he shrunk? Soon would I be too big to hug?

"Nickie, I have something your mom and I think will help you. Whenever you need to talk, I'm here, and so is she. Day or night, whenever you need us. You know that, don't you?" His tight hug feels so good. "We didn't realize you were struggling with this cocoon busting as bad lately, but you're going to be okay, I promise."

I've got to believe. I've got to believe. More than anything, I want to be a good man like Gramps. *I've got to believe.*

I'm so desperate. The hollowness in my spirit lifts while I hug him, but it's only temporary. Something inside keeps accusing me, pushing me deeper and deeper into hopelessness.

"Thanks, Gramps." Saying it seems enough for him, but not so much for me. If only I could blurt out all my problems to the world, demand to know where they came from. I have to let it go. I ease away and pat his back. "So what's under the cover?"

"Well, we thought you could use a new friend." He raises the cover to reveal the world's most awesome puppy. A red-and-white King Charles spaniel with big floppy ears and big shiny eyes blinking inside big patches of red. "He's weaned from his mom and eight weeks old." Gramps puts his arm around me, and we admire the pup together.

Great, my joy overflows in a torrent of *more* tears.

"What are you going to name him, Nick?"

"Really, he's ours? Mom's going to let us have a pet?"

Mom wouldn't ever agree to let us have a pet. What changed?

"Yes." He hands me the puppy. "Your mother, Granny, and I talked about it. You know how I love Butch. He's my best friend. He listens to everything I tell him, and he never ever judges me. That's what best friends do!"

I hold him, looking into his eyes, and my heart melts. It feels so good.

"So, what do you want to name him?" Gramps's thick arm jostles me.

What a huge decision. Something the puppy will forever go by. It has to fit just right.

"Can Chris, Abbie, and Mom help?" I half shriek, the excitement and my cocoon busting merging. "They're going to love him too."

Everything seems better—now. I hadn't noticed they were all watching from our back deck. Now, they head inside while I admire the pup.

"That's a great idea, and there's no need to rush. Let's go inside and see what they think. Besides, dinner is getting cold."

Another thing I didn't notice until we neared the house. Lily was watching too. She half raises her hand and waves at me. I wave back. But a chill rises up. Does she know I skipped school and why? The chills try to take over, but I hug my new best friend. Loving on him makes the cold sweats leave almost as quickly as they came.

Everyone's sitting in the living room, waiting, talking in hushed voices, probably talking about me. I feel so small, even though they love me and want the best for me.

Chris eyes me. I can see the pain in his eyes, and he must feel my pain. I've felt his.

Gramps slaps his hands together, breaking our silence. "Nickie wants you all to help name his new puppy. Now, there's no need to rush into it. It took me two days to name Butch, and I don't think another name could fit him better."

I plop onto the sofa between Chris and Abbie, so they can pet and hold him. We've been wanting a dog for so long. Mom said we couldn't have one. Until now. Getting him is great, but it reaffirms my suspicions. Something must be wrong with me! Maybe I should've taken the medication.

We eat dinner, and everyone gets a chance to pet and hold the new addition to our family. Then Gramps and Granny head out. Gramps whispers in my ear before leaving. "Time for you to believe, Nickie." He tousles my hair, which is getting long. "I'll see you this weekend. We'll talk. Okay?"

"Sure, Gramps. Thank you for my puppy. I love him." I snuggle him up to my face. He's so soft and warm. "I love his floppy ears, his large eyes, his, well, *everything*."

Then the door closes behind them. Soon, their car rumbles away. Then Mom takes me by my hand. I leave the pup with Abbie and Chris and let Mom lead me to her room. She shuts the door behind us, so she's going to set me straight.

"Nickie... Nick, I'm so sorry." She pats the bed beside her, rumpling up her blue and gray striped bedcovers.

So I sit myself down.

"I knew you were having a hard time busting out of your cocoon, but I never knew it was affecting you like this. When Chris had his turn, he was younger than you, and it wasn't all that bad. I spoke to someone today after Chris called to tell me about your walking home alone, not going to school."

I kick my sock-covered feet back and forth, scuffling up the grain on her bedside rug, then smoothing it out.

She takes my hand. "You're going to be okay. But the doctor said you're having anxiety issues, maybe because you're older during all this. He said lots of boys and girls can have anxiety. He thought a pet might help, giving you someone to talk to when you feel bad about yourself or lonely."

I touch a picture of all of us on her nightstand—Abbie's thirteenth birthday, one of my favorite memories. Mom always keeps reminders of our fun times close by. She claims it helps her remember how blessed she is.

She rubs my shoulder, then fits her right hand to my cheek. Her love for me radiates through the warmth of her palm.

"I'm sorry, Mom. I don't mean to be this much trouble. I'm so ashamed everybody has to make all these changes for me." My stomach clenches. The Sea of Life is my only way back to normal. If I can get to it and change this dad situation, everything will be better.

"Honey, we all love you. We're here for you. That's what families do—look after each other. Wasn't it nice for Gramps to find you such a beautiful puppy? He's special like you. Now, we need a name for him." She kisses my forehead, then holds me at arm's length. Her shoulders sag with her exhale. This must've been a long day for her too. After all, she's my protector in her eyes, and she's only as happy as her saddest child.

CHAPTER THIRTEEN

THURSDAY COMES and goes without a hitch at school. Craig and Peg aren't much of a problem. After Mom gets home from work, we pick up a dog bed, food, and supplies. Toys to keep him occupied when we're away at school and lots of papers and blankets for his makeshift playpen, for potty training.

King Charles spaniels like constant companionship, so his barking kept us awake a little last night. He's still small, so it wasn't too loud. Our bedrooms being upstairs helped too. Abbie, Chris, and I spent several hours in the tree house playing with him, racking our brains for a name. But none came, and it's gotta be perfect.

Friday, Peg gets up to her old tricks, trying to pick at me, but Chris takes care of her. I knew being a twin would come in handy one day. I guess this was another one of those days. I feel more peace today than I have in weeks. I don't know what came over me. Since talking to Lily about the movies, I've been sort of lost, reality never close by. Finally, I know how much she means to me.

Now, I lean back against the tree house's wood wall. Toby comes up to inspect and approve of the intruder. The puppy runs toward him, and Toby bounces backward. Then they replay it.

Abbie giggles. "Look at him trying to play with Toby. He looks so funny all riled up."

Chris and I laugh too and eye each other. I tried to avoid the name Riley because it was the name of a dog in a movie we liked. She was a King Charles spaniel too. But it did fit him now when Toby's got him all riled up. The puppy was already fulfilling his intended purpose. We loved him.

I let out a deep breath.

Chris laughs even more.

And Abbie points. "We've got to name him Riley. We just *have* to! Let's ask Mom what she thinks when she gets home."

Already, it's a foregone conclusion. Not that we'll call him it without Mom's consent.

I flop onto my stomach, elbows propping me up while Toby and our puppy nose around sniffing each other. "Looks like they're gonna hit it off."

"Yeah." Abbie mirrors me on her belly, except she kicks her feet up behind her. "Good thing Toby's so laid-back."

Chris snorts. "And the puppy is too young to know any better."

Hands slap the tree house ladder rungs. Then Lily's head pops through the open treehouse door. "I heard a commotion up here."

"Hi, Lily." I gulp, all awkward, and hurry to sit up. "I thought you were going to your dad's for the weekend."

"I am, but with Abbie shrieking and laughing and the puppy yipping, I didn't want to miss the fun." She plops down next to Toby and scoops him into her lap.

"Hi, Lily." Chris gives her a wave, happy to see her. We all are.

"See Nick's new puppy." Abbie pushes up to her hands and knees and crawls over to us. "Isn't he cute? We're going to ask Mom if we can call him Riley. What do you think? We wanted to name him something else, but it does fit him. Don't you think?" Her face shines, reflecting her joy like a full moon.

Nice to see her and Chris happy to have the puppy too. He's great for all of us, and I don't mind sharing him. A puppy's gotta have enough love for everyone.

Did Lily know I got a puppy? Of course, she did. Abbie would've run over and told her about the puppy first thing. Not much happens that we don't share with Lily and her mom. That's one of the best things about having friends.

"Hi, guys. Wow. Abbie, you were right. He's adorbs. Can I hold him?" She nudges Toby from her lap. He's generous enough to leave cat hair on her black hoodie and snazzy jeans. She's all dressed and ready for her dad's.

Man, she looks great. How'd she go so fast from being the adorable girl I've played with all my life, to, well, *this*? Even the blue of her eyes is bluer. Is that a word? I don't know, but they are. And I feel different having them looking back at me.

Picking the puppy up, I hand him to her, belly first, looking into her eyes. She stares into mine while taking him. The warmness in them wasn't there the last few months or longer. It feels good. This puppy's working better than I'd hoped. In the movies, dogs help people connect. There must be a special kind of magic God puts in them.

"Riley's a wonderful name." She strokes his head, and lying in her arms, the puppy tips his adorable, loving face up at her, soaking up her love.

I snort. "This is going to be one spoiled puppy." How great is that?

Adding one small puppy to the tree house sure changes things. It's like my troubles aren't worthy of a mention, much less the driving force of my recent decisions. Toby doesn't mind either. He's made a new friend too, and if the puppy gets rambunctious, Toby can hop up on one of the window ledges encircling the tree house. Problem solved.

Soon, Mom comes home and heads straight to the tree house and climbs up. She slips through the open door and sits on the threshold, one foot and leg on the ladder and her other inside, and laughs at us engrossed with the puppy. "I can see now I should've let you have a dog years ago. How's he doing?" She reaches toward the puppy, and he edges over to her, first allowing her to pet his head. Mom's going to enjoy him as much as we are.

"You're such a cutie-pie. Yes, you are. Yes, you are." Yep, she's already talking baby talk to him. She rolls him side to side, shaking her head back and forth.

Love's such an amazing thing. On one Wednesday night Bible meeting, Pastor taught us love was patient, forgiving, and kind—it's not rude or resentful. He probably could've gone on to a couple more. I was glad he didn't at the time, and I don't understand why all these things keep popping into my head. It's like every sermon I ever heard is somewhere inside, bouncing around, waiting to come out.

Mom slides her other foot back to a ladder rung. "You'd better come out to the car and help me with the groceries. Cara, Kayleigh, and Lily are having dinner with us."

Lily lifts her head and blinks. "We are?"

"Yep." Mom's already climbing down. Her words float up after her. "Hot dogs and french fries—Cara's favorite."

Abbie's eyes get large. "What about my tacos?" Her lips purse. It's easy to see her calculating the situation.

We all troop after her. The fun's probably only beginning.

"I grabbed two for you at Taco Bell. I'll make it up to you next Friday. I promise." Mom carries the puppy. We carry the groceries, Mom still whispering baby talk. Her smile's so pretty and playful. Nice to see her get a break from my troubles. Believing became a lot easier after seeing the puppy's love bring on the changes.

Mom nestles the puppy into his crate under the hallway table near the front door. "Nick, start the gas grill. Abbie, can you cover the table with a cloth? Chris, get the twigs and leaves swept from the porch."

We hop to, knowing the drill. We spend lots of afternoons on the porch—more like a deck—grill blazing, sending heavenly scents throughout the neighborhood.

Our neighborhood's mainly single parents, but we sure know how to have fun. Almost every afternoon someone on our street is cooking out, kids screaming and running around, moms or dads laughing in the background. This afternoon has the flavor of fall. A breeze stirs the treetops, the heavier fall air rustling the limbs and leaves. The sounds and squeals of us playing with the puppy must carry through the neighborhood, along with the smell of the charred hot dogs.

Emily, the pretty blonde who lives five houses down, pops her head around the corner. "I heard quite the ruckus and wanted to see what's up." She plops to her knees and ruffles the pup's ears. Then she's on her feet again and gone just like that. Her dad's super strict. Maybe that's why she is the top student in our class. She never seems to get to have very much fun, though. I don't know, but I saw Chris watching her closely. He might be moving on from Lily. I hope so.

Soon, Lily comes back over with her mom, who brings an apple pie for dessert. Having Cara and our neighbors with us makes naming the puppy even more fun. We dub him Riley after all. A perfect fit, everyone agrees.

I don't know how Lily feels about me, but I'm going to try to find out.

Bellies full, we head back out to the tree house. Soon, Lily's dad arrives to pick her up. She starts toward the ladder, then pauses, and touches my shoulder, sharing a soft smile. "I think he's perfect. I'll see you soon."

"Bye, Lily," I say as she turns to go to her dad's car. Maybe she'll begin coming out to the tree house again now that we have the puppy. Maybe it won't only be for the puppy. Maybe he'll just be her excuse.

"Bye, Lily!" Abbie chirps behind me. "Have fun at your dad's."

Chris says his goodbye too, watching her walk across the yard. His heart's probably heavy like mine.

What an evening. One of those you hate to see end. Everyone's worn out, even Riley. We put away our things before going in for the night.

Still, I write a few lines in my journal.

Dear Journal,

I couldn't have imagined all the fun having a puppy would be. We named him Riley. We're going to have so much fun. My problems don't seem as big anymore. I'm sure like, Gramps says, I need to face them still, and I will. One at a time. Good night, Journal.

CHAPTER FOURTEEN

AFTER BREAKFAST SATURDAY MORNING, we pack a bag for Riley and head over to introduce him to Butch. As I hold him looking into his eyes, I feel our bond growing. Mom sees it too. Chris and Abbie also cuddle with him on the way, but soon, their phones beckon. I've never been one who stayed on the phone much. I prefer to interact face-to-face.

Maybe I don't have as many friends—acquaintances Mom calls them. She says you're lucky to have one true friend at any given time in your life. She's extra lucky. Cara's a good friend, almost family—nah, no almost about it. She is family. I love Cara as much as my brother or sister. She's the best. I love tussling with her, giving her some good-humored grief. She likes to give it right back, and I wouldn't have it any other way.

Turning onto Gramps drive, I spot him and Butch at the bench on the hillside overlooking his mailbox. He must be waiting for the mailman. As soon as Mom lets me out, I tromp up the hillside, tall grasses tangling around my sneakers while Riley romps through it. The calming easterly breeze lifts my hair, fall fully in the air. "What a beautiful day, all sunny," I call as we near.

I drop onto the bench beside him. Their home and property has evolved into "comfortably convenient," as Gramps describes it. Their benches and outdoor furniture aren't fancy. The worn wood has survived the generations through heat, snow, and insects, giving them an old-country look and feel. But these benches await them so they can enjoy the peace and talk to the Helper. I think Gramps talks to the Helper a lot.

"Have you decided what to name him yet?" Gramps teases Riley with his finger, then rubs Riley's head, and bounces him back and forth, the way one does when adoring a baby or, in this case, a baby dog.

"Yes, sir. We named him last night." Will he approve? "We're going to call him Riley."

A passing car on the nearby road causes Riley to stir in Gramps's arms.

Butch sniffs around on him.

"We tried to think of something else, but it fits him."

Gramps hands him back to me, so I hold him up away from Butch by putting my hands under his front legs and wrapping them under his belly. He blinks at me, then yawns of all things. Tired or riled, imp or angel, he so stinking adorable.

Chris and Abbie had gotten out of the car too and hiked to join us while Mom drove to the house to help Granny with lunch. After hugs all around, the four of us laugh and play with Butch and Riley.

Gramps sits back down, us by his side, and we wait on the mail. Riley climbs all over Butch as he tries to soak in the sun. Butch has finished his sniffing and ignores the newcomer—until Riley steps on the wrong thing or nips at his nose.

I laugh, our conversation different today. If a puppy can help me this much, how much more could the Helper?

Soon, the mailman leaves his flyers, and we begin our journey up the long gravel driveway.

Chris toes a rainwater rut. "No wonder Granny's afraid of falling. If you're not watching, your foot could slip into one of these."

Gramps hunches his shoulders. "If I'm ever going to get your grandmother walking down here with me again, I'm going to have to get my tractor and put some gravel down. I've been a little lazy, I guess."

I can't imagine him lazy. He's always helping me and my siblings or Mom.

"I suppose that won't matter till spring." I hand Riley to Abbie so she can play with him during the walk. "With fall gearing up, these types of walks will have to be put on hold."

Butch slumps along, falling behind, no longer running ahead like he did only a couple of years earlier.

"He's getting old like me." Gramps beckons by slapping a hand against his leg. "Come on, boy. C'mon, kids. Let's see how your grandmother's coming with lunch. I'm starved." He picks up his pace.

Butch doesn't or can't.

We pass by the old white oak, probably a hundred feet tall. The tire swing still hangs on a rope under its shady canopy, now lonely, neglected. Memories of the warm afternoons spent here, swinging, playing, and picnicking, flood back. Many include Kayleigh and Lily, times taken for granted, then. Now, I long for them.

I close my eyes. I'd forgotten all the times, outings and such, spent with Lily. My whole life's wrapped around being with her. Chris's and Abbie's too. No wonder I'm going insane, and Chris found himself liking her—a big piece of our lives is missing. What have I done?

I fling open the storm door, though silent hinges give no testimony. Gramps keeps them oiled. Instead, Granny's garlic bread baking tempts me. "Hmm." I give an exaggerated sniff.

"Homemade buss-ghetti too." Abbie scrunches her nose and brushes past me. That's how Abbie pronounces spaghetti. Mom says it's cute and lets her alone with it, even though she knows how to pronounce it now.

"Buss-ghetti's good, but ya can't beat Granny's garlic bread—her own recipe."

Chris toes off his sneakers. "Mom uses it all the time."

I sit on the hall bench to unlace mine and take them off proper. "It's still Granny's recipe even if Mom uses it—right, Gramps?"

"Leave the puppy outside," Granny calls. "I don't want any dogs at my dinner table."

Abbie, still holding Riley, stops in her tracks, turns like a robot, and hands him to me. "He's your dog." She grins, rolling her gaze in a circle.

Chris laughs.

"Oh, I see how it is!" I cackle. Abbie's such a ham. Good thing they didn't mind Gramps gave him to me. Yes, I'll share Riley—his heart's big enough for us all, and I want them to love him too—but he's mine.

"Put him in Butch's doghouse... and put that two-by-six across the opening so he can't wander off. Last thing I want to do is go looking for him after lunch on a full stomach." Gramps shoots back from the washroom off the kitchen. He washes his hands for the longest time. I'm surprised he still has skin. He must get a special kind of heavy-duty dirt on his hands. I never have to wash mine that long unless I get ink on them.

"Yes, sir. Thanks, Gramps." That's a heartache I don't want either. There might be red foxes in the area, and Riley, almost all fur and ears right now, is barely more than several bites.

By Butch's doghouse, not far away from our special bench, I sense something different in the air, some kind of presence. I don't see anyone, so I push it off as overactive nerves. Placing Riley in the doghouse, I prop the board up like Gramps said, good and solid. Hopefully, he can't knock it down or scramble over the top of it.

CHAPTER FIFTEEN

AFTER FILLING up on Granny's spaghetti, Gramps and I return to sit in our spot. Looking down at the river, I'm more at peace than I can remember.

"I think Riley and you are going to make a great team." Gramps grips my knee and gives it a shake. "You look calmer today. How do you feel on the inside?"

"Better. How did you know Riley could help me?" I sink against the wooden backrest, the world passing. Riley's still in Butch's doghouse, but Butch takes up his usual spot with us, basking in the sun. I pet his side, and he raises his head enough to acknowledge me. Then he's down again, ready for a nap.

Now I understand how much Gramps loves Butch. He truly was his best friend. I love Butch too. He's always here with us. Impossible to imagine these times with Gramps without him.

"Just an educated guess. My first dog, Rover, helped me through some tough times when I was no older than you. The great thing about a dog, and maybe even a cat, is they give unconditional love. They don't care if you're short, fat, or can't sing. They only want your love and care. Rover and I were a team. I'd do anything for him, and him for me."

I cross my arms. "Did you always have a dog? Even when Mom and Aunt Rachael were little?"

"Yep. She forgot how much love they give everyone. She didn't want to get a pet for you, said they're like having a baby around and three at a time was her limit." He ruffles my hair. "She probably regrets that now."

I bat my mussed-up hair back into place. It is getting long. Usually, when Gramps does that, it doesn't bother me, but now, it's hanging in my eyes.

"Nick, sometimes your mom can't be there for you, and you'll have to work things out for yourself, things like finding the Sea of Life and the Helper. But, Riley... he's always going to be there for you, on your best days and worst, and unfortunately, you'll still have plenty of bad days."

I tilt my head back against the worn wood, close my eyes, and pick my words. "Do you think I still need the Sea of Life and the Helper?" I know I will. I still need—*want*—to be a good man and to be Lily's boyfriend. Yep, I want that more than anything in the world. There, I admitted it to myself again. I want to be Lily's boyfriend forever, not just her friend.

"Yes, you need Him more than ever. You'll always need the Helper. He'll guide you through your cocoon busting and get you back on track. He'll help you be that good man. More importantly, He'll give you a new spirit inside you—His." He drapes his arm around my shoulders. With his other hand, he points to the moon. It's just hanging there low on the horizon in the daylight.

"See the moon there? It might not be shining brightly now, but on days like today, you can still see it there. It's always there. You just can't always see it. It's the same way with the things bothering you. They might not be so big right now since you have Riley, but they're still there. One day, again, maybe soon, you'll be dealing with those same thoughts. The Helper can teach you how to solve it for the last time." He squeezes my shoulder, leaning until his hair tickles my forehead. "Who knows, maybe Lily will start coming out here with you to see us again. Just like old times."

They love Lily and she loves them. She hasn't seen her grandparents much lately, but mine see her most Sundays at church because she makes sure of it. They always fuss over her. I love watching them and her soaking in all the love. I'm beginning to understand and appreciate how our ability to love can be endless.

"Look, look. Go get Riley," Gramps whispers and points to two adult red foxes beneath the trees, less than fifty yards from where Riley's sleeping. "They're searching for food, probably to feed their pups."

I'm on my feet already. Riley isn't going to be their dinner, not on our watch. "Will they hurt Riley?"

"No, most likely not, but no use leaving it to chance." Gramps winks. "They're probably more scared of us and not looking for a puppy for a meal."

Riley whimpers, waking up.

The foxes' ears perk up when they hear my pup. I cuddle him even tighter, then hustle back to the bench with Gramps.

"You know, Nick, that's the way the Helper looks over us. He reveals Himself little by little and not the same to everyone. Most times, He leaves us be until things get rough, staying quiet, sometimes even until we call to Him out of desperation. But when a fox pokes around our lives, He's right there with us. That's why it's so important for you to believe."

Riley's little tail slaps my stomach. His paws knead my thighs. His ears slip through my fingers.

Gramps reaches over to scratch the pup's back. "Having Riley makes you feel better, but there comes a time in life where only having a dog won't cut it. We need divine intervention. That's when not just believing, but expecting, knowing He's going to show up, is so important."

The foxes have left. The time for us to leave comes quickly too. Mom comes out with a dish of Granny's spaghetti and a plate of garlic bread for our Monday night dinner. Abbie's got her head cocked to one side. Yep, she's already calculating it. She's always looking ahead, never back.

CHAPTER SIXTEEN

SUNDAY MORNING CAME in raining one of those steady, hard, cold rains. Since it's supposed to rain all day, it was a good day to laze around the house binge-watching sitcoms after church. Now, Riley barks at the window, and I crane to it as Lily gets out of her dad's car and rushes into her house to stay dry.

Man, it's still pouring down. It better stop by morning, or we'll have to ride the school bus.

I much prefer the long walk to the bus, even in winter. Abbie would have to ride a different bus, but that's only ten minutes, not an hour. She doesn't like it much though. The boys are always flirting or messing with her. There's one boy she likes a lot, but Mom says she's still too young for any boy talk, and that's that.

Minutes later, a knock brushes our front door. Abbie hops to her feet and runs to answer it, Riley snuggled tightly to her shoulder. From the muffled voices, it must be Lily. She's asking to speak to Mom. Soon, she slumps around the corner, shoulders down, head ducked. She rushes closer when she sees Mom and hugs her, shooting a teary-eyed glance at Chris and me. "My granddad passed."

"Oh, honey!" Mom holds her as she sobs.

I go over and hug her too. We all do, our hearts breaking.

Lily drops onto one of the long, fluffy, red floor pillows we kids watch television on. "Mom's going to the hospital to be with everyone, but I just don't want to go, even though my grandmother's there." She wiggles onto her belly, elbows on the floor, chin in her hands, glum as the weather. "We sure hadn't seen Granddad much lately. It must've been Christmas—or maybe it was Grandma's birthday we saw them last."

The dark gloom penetrates our home, making the rainy day more dismal. Our sitcom binge over, I turn off the TV.

Abbie hands Lily Riley, his role as comforter once again being put to the test. He doesn't disappoint, licking Lily on her nose, causing her to giggle. It's the sweetest giggle I ever heard. It seems he knew exactly what she needed.

I sit beside her, watching her with Riley. She's so pretty. Even with a tearstained face, she shines as brightly as any star ever could—in my eyes. I touch her shoulder.

She leans against me, and we play with Riley together.

"It seems like bad things happen more often when it rains cold," Mom says.

Maybe so. I've got nothing to say or offer. Though Lily's granddad had been sick for quite a while, it still hurt her and her mom. Lily appears to be in a fog. I imagine she hurt so badly inside, as much from the confusion of love's complexities as anything.

The next morning, I go to my window first thing to see if she might be looking back. Surprisingly, she is. My heart aches for her pain, but still jumps for joy seeing her looking for me again. The next days are good that way, sad, but good. Then the day before the funeral, she comes over to talk. I grab up Riley against my shoulder and take Lily to the tree house. Just the three of us. Since I don't know what to expect, my heart pounds as I follow her up the ladder.

Toby's already there, basking in a ray of sunshine with not a care in the world—until Riley pounces on him. We laugh as Toby raises his head and gives us this funny expression, then lies back down, and playfully swats Riley with his forepaws.

Lily sits and rests her back against the wall across from me. "You know I'm closer to your gramps than to my granddad because he's always upsetting Mom. He told her she needed to get a man. When she said she wasn't ready for one, he told her something must be wrong with her. Granddad was hard on Mom, and she cried all the time about it and avoided visiting him. Now that he's gone, she's crying even harder because she could have been there more, for him and her mom."

She twists her hands in her lap, frowning at them. "Guess it feels bad to think you've let someone down." A gust of air empties her lungs. "What I'm trying to say, Nick, is I'm sorry I let you down. I didn't know you were having a hard time. Your mom told me what happened the other day you tried to talk to me... about what happened afterward. Chris didn't know either."

Tears glisten on her cheeks. Her shoulders shake, and she hides her face in those hands.

I scoot over to sit beside her and bump my shoulder to hers, not wanting her to hurt inside, a pain I'd become all too familiar with lately.

Riley, in the sense of a true support dog, comes over and licks Lily's hand.

She smiles. "He must smell the hamburger I ate."

The mood's already changed for the better. *Thank you, Riley!* I'd almost swear he's smiling, shaking his head, floppy ears tossing back and forth. Oh how I love this puppy!

I'd better not let this moment pass without seizing it. I clear my throat. "Lily, we've been best friends forever, literally. But I like you more than a friend. I'm sorry I checked out of life for a while. I didn't mean too, but there's something I have to do. But I wanted to tell you how I feel about you. I didn't realize it, but I have for a while."

Her shoulder's kinda stiff beside mine. I don't dare look at her to guess what she's thinking. Riley gambols around us, then climbs on my stretched-out legs. Perfect comfort and encouragement.

A deep breath pushes out the rest of my words in a rush. "That's why I was upset that day after we spoke. I couldn't face the possibility of not having you in my life and this other thing hanging over my head at the same time. I don't know why I told Chris what I did. It just came out. I was as surprised as him."

There. It's done. I fidget my fingers, not knowing what to expect.

"I... I didn't know." She wipes her tears off with her sleeve. "What did you say to Chris?"

Toby gets up and stretches, coming over, purring, and rubbing against her. It brings even more softness to the atmosphere, and one of discovery, at least for me.

I thought everyone knew about my outburst. But my family had kept most of my secrets, if there were any. Though she knows about me leaving school, she doesn't know I told Chris I wished I were dead. Should I tell her? Do I want to be seen as pathetic?

"Nothing important. Brother talk, that's all." But it wasn't, and I needed to know where things stood between her and Eric. I use picking up Riley as an excuse to shift and face her. I don't dare miss any clue as I ask this. "How did you like Spider-Man? Did you have a good time?"

She must know what I'm doing. Holding her head back, looking at the ceiling, she smiles. Then she shakes her head side to side in the quirky little way she does, which I love.

"The movie was okay. But I don't think I'll be seeing Eric again. He wasn't too happy." She bites her lip, that gesture telling me she doesn't like him. "Besides, he was like all those boys at the mall on Saturday mornings. The grabby-feely sort. He tried to kiss me, but I couldn't."

My heart pounds like it might explode or, worse, make me start perspiring, regressing to my cocoon busting. I close my eyes. She can probably sense my feelings, my deepest thoughts. After all, she knows me better than almost anyone.

"For a long time"—her voice sounds so soft—"I've imagined you would be my first kiss, one day."

When I open my eyes, she's smiling shyly, now fidgeting too, playing with Toby.

I leaned toward her, and her to me. But then hands and feet slap the ladder. Someone's coming up. So not great timing!

We stop and giggle. The kiss will have to wait. I kinda kick myself inside, though. Maybe I shouldn't have stopped. Either way, my heart's getting ready to explode. I haven't lost her after all.

CHAPTER SEVENTEEN

THE FUNERAL'S hard the next day. Lily seems torn, crying. Her mom's much worse. Not knowing how to help, I edge closer to Mom. "Kayleigh's in bad shape."

Mom gives me a soft-sad smile and rubs my sleeve. "It's mostly because of her decision not to visit them much. Sometimes we forget what's important, not judging or bossing our loved ones around, but supporting and loving each other."

Makes sense. We all have our struggles, some more than others, and we need to remember that. Nevertheless, we all need love, especially from those who are supposed to love us.

My admiration for Mom swells even more. She never came down on me for my impulsive and, at times, dumb decisions. She simply loved me and tried to understand what I needed to get through the rough patches along my way. No, I don't have a dad, but who needs one? Mom is better than three dads. That must be why she has to be so nosy staying on top of things.

I head over to Lily. Chris tags along, standing back while I hug her. There's hurt in his eyes, but he manages a smile. He's always known Lily likes me in a different way than she likes him. Still, his pain hurts my heart. Having Lily back is great, though. I hate that he doesn't have someone too. I guess that's what twins do, or maybe loved ones. We laugh with each other and cry with each other. Thankfully, we have Riley now. He always seems to know how to love us the way we need it.

Afterward, during the large dinner in the church hall, Lily sits with her cousins, but there's a telltale distance between them all. Her mom joins her siblings, and I hear them talking about their dad's struggle being over and how he's in a better place now. Something I don't fully understand.

Gramps comes over to our table to check on me. "That's the major reason believing is so important," he says. "The Helper not only helps us here, but He seals out the bad so we can have a life after this one."

Gramps calls it the afterlife, in heaven. That's the same thing they teach in Sunday school.

I squirm a bit because it's probably all a myth. At least, that's what some of my teachers teach at my high school. It's even in some of our books.

That evening, Lily and I go out to the tree house with Abbie, Chris, Riley, and Toby. Lily's not her normal happy self, which we all understand. Then Gramps climbs up and sits in the doorway. He doesn't come in because the tree house is almost full.

He hugs Lily as if she's his, and to me, she is. The rain stopped the night before, but now fall's making its presence known. Homecoming is next Friday. So there's a buzz going around school. I haven't given it any thought until now.

Along with homecoming comes colder weather. The breeze now blows leaves across our yard, covering the porch and chilling the air. High up in the tree house, the wind blows much harder and shakes the tree, making it an adventure.

With the place swaying, Gramps backs toward the ladder. "It's time for me to get my old self down and home. You guys want to come say goodbye to Granny?"

I grab Riley and hand him to Chris, then head down the ladder, following Lily. Reaching the bottom rung, I take Riley so Chris can climb down.

And now, the long day's ended—a sad and wonderful day, allowing me to see goodness all around me while teaching me the most important thing in life is love. I open the journal Gramps gave me and write:

Dear Journal,

Today, we went to Lily's granddad's funeral. It was sad. Lily wants to kiss me, her first kiss. I want her to be my first kiss too. We almost did. But Abbie came up the ladder, and that was that. I'm so happy I haven't lost Lily after all. Having Riley is wonderful too. He's such a ham. We all love him, and he helps make everything better. Help me always to remember my family's love and never forget it. Good night, Journal.

At first, writing in the journal felt kind of weird, so I didn't write much. But after finishing and reading it back to myself, making sure I'd written correctly, I like how it makes me feel. Kinda satisfied, almost like a little of the dirty water residing in my soul was scooped out, maybe only a small scoop—but it's a start. I don't know if that's possible, but I feel good.

Riley's training is going well. He doesn't bark as much, and he sleeps most of the night—and so do we, now. I climb into bed, turning out the little light on my bedside table, Chris already snoring across the room. Maybe my dreams will all be good.

CHAPTER EIGHTEEN

COME MORNING, a commotion wakes me. Chris is in the hall, speaking way too loud. Guess he can't find something and he's accusing me of taking it. Mom's trying to calm him. What is it I supposedly pilfered? I steady my breathing so he can't tell I'm awake.

"He's always messing with me, Mom," Chris complains. "He took it and hid it."

"I don't see how." Mom's much calmer voice drifts around me.

I peep open one eye just a squinch, not letting on I'm awake.

Still in her bathrobe, she touches Chris's shoulder. "He's still asleep. Are you sure you plugged it in on the end table?"

"Yes!" He jerks away from her. "Right beside your Bible."

Uh-oh, he's getting super frustrated now.

Then Abbie calls up the stairs. "I found it. Riley has it." She giggles. "Maybe he needed to make a call."

Chris sprints downstairs, leaving Mom.

Her footsteps pad into the room. Her hand shakes me.

I pretend to be waking up. "What's going on, Mom?" I fake yawn. "Is everything okay?"

"Everything's fine. Chris was having a hard time finding his phone, but it's found, thanks to Abbie. Time to get up, sleepyhead.

Breakfast is in twenty minutes." She pokes me playfully, then heads off.

Chris never apologizes for blaming me over his missing phone, but then I never tell him I heard it either.

At school, I walk into a hornet's nest first thing in homeroom, Chris three steps behind me as my witness. We're early getting to class. Bad mistake! The teacher hasn't called for everyone to be seated yet, and Peg must've had a bad weekend because she comes right over to us and lights into me.

"If your mom wasn't such a Bible-toting idiot, we wouldn't be stuck with your stupid dad." Hands on her hips, she gets in my face, only inches from me, fingers pointing, arms flailing. "It's all her fault my life sucks!"

The suddenness of it hits me. Before I can think, "the meaner" living inside me springs to Mom's defense. Peg's in my face, so I push her—just a little!—to get some space, some room.

She trips over a desk behind her and falls hard on the floor, her body entangled in the overturned desk. I didn't mean to hurt her, but she asked for it.

Her arm gets stuck in the desk during the fall. I hear a nasty pop, almost like a cracking sound. That's gotta be bad.

Chris and I gawk at each other, mouths open.

Peg screams out, and my heart screams out with her. I reach to help, but she won't accept it. The whole thing happened in mere seconds. Now, she's rocking back and forth holding herself, trying to protect her arm.

Mrs. Manning came into the room in time to see me push her. Go figure. She didn't hear Peg provoke me. She rushes over to Peg, calling over her shoulder. "Nicholas Marks. Get to the principal's office— right now!"

I skedaddle, wanting to apologize, but knowing better of it. I think Peg broke her arm. *Helper!*

I'm sitting in the reception area, avoiding Mrs. Reynolds's gaze, when the PA comes alive with Mrs. Manning calling for the principal. Soon, I'll have my time in his office. Why does trouble always come looking for me? I didn't mean for Peg to fall over the desk. She was screaming in my face. I just wanted some room to think.

When bad things happen, I play them over and over in my head. Gramps tells me it's the source of a lot of my problems. He's right. I need to stop it.

Chris texts me that Peg did break her arm. They've taken her to the hospital.

The door opens, and I peep up as the principal walks in and stands before me. "Mr. Marks, we're sending you home now. Tomorrow, I'll call a meeting here in my office with you and all the parties."

I nod. I don't know who all the parties are, but it doesn't sound good. I push from my chair, but he waves me back down.

"You can't walk home by yourself. We need a guardian on file to sign you out."

I sit back down. Mom registered our grandparents, Cara, and Kayleigh too. Gramps arrives about forty-five minutes later. He comes in quietlike, passes me, and enters the principal's office. When he exits, he takes me up and hugs me, whispering in my ear. "It's okay, Nickie. Everything will be fine."

We walk outside and slide into Gramps's old Blazer. "Chris texted your mom during the chaos of paramedics and an angry mother. He explained it wasn't your fault."

"I was just trying to get Peg to back off." Thank God for cell phones! Huh, where'd that thought come from?

Gramps pulls into the ice-cream parlor's lot. He clamps a hand on my shoulder. "Thought we should get something to cool down while we have a talk."

Seriously? Wow.

We soon settle at a corner table. Gramps with his vanilla sugar cone, me with my Star City creamsicle.

"Nick, I know you didn't mean to hurt that girl, but you have to control yourself in those situations. Other people don't know you, and they don't know what happened. We stand behind you one hundred percent, but you need to have some compassion for your stepsister. She has to live with your dad." His ice cream melts down his cone while he talks. Now, he licks it off before it can drip on him or his pants.

"Compassion?" Heat sears my chest and burns up my throat. I blink before it can come out my eyes. "*She* gets *my* dad, and *I* need to have compassion? Why? That doesn't seem right? Besides, she called Mom names."

Gramps said he understood and I didn't do anything wrong. But I'm being convicted anyway. Even the creamy treat can't cool me down.

"Having your dad isn't a picnic." Gramps pops his last bite of cone into his mouth and wipes his hands. "Your mom's going to talk to you kids when she gets home. You need to know some things, and she needs to be the one to tell you." He loops an arm around me and nudges me toward the car as I finish my treat.

Cool air blasts us when we step outside. I hustle to the passenger side and slide in. Chris's life seems so much easier than mine. "Why does everything have to be so hard for me?"

Gramps starts the car. "I believe in you. You're a good kid. It won't always be like this, I promise."

He pulls into traffic and heads toward my house.

"God doesn't have the same plan for you. Even though you were born together, your lives aren't going to be the same. No two ever are. It's how God reveals Himself to each of us, at different times and in different circumstances, using our lives along with those around us. Otherwise, the world would be a boring and unimaginative place, and He wants us to all be our own special unique selves."

I don't say anything else on the way home, but a million things dance through my head. Why did Peg have to start something today? I was finally feeling half normal again, and she had to go and provoke me. Even still, I didn't do anything but try to get by her and get her out of my face, to stop her from screaming at me. It was an accident.

Some kids at school will label me as a girl bully now. I'm not the bully—Peg is. Still, I'll be labeled for life. Will Lily believe them?

Mom goes by the school to see the principal before coming home, finally arriving before two o'clock, having to leave work early once again because of me. My brownie points are going away fast. When she comes in, Gramps is napping on the sofa. I'm lying on the floor playing with Riley. Seeing Gramps asleep, she motions me to the kitchen.

I obey, scoop up Riley, and bring him along for moral support.

Mom hugs me as soon as I get to her. "Honey, I'm so sorry. I don't know why that girl has to be so obnoxious. I guess your dad has that effect on people. When Abbie and Chris get home, we're going to sit down and talk. It's time you guys know the truth about your dad."

Her face allows that reliving those times to share them isn't something she looks forward to. But I guess the time for us all to know the truth has come. Soon, the whys and how comes, the reason we never see our dad, will be known, partially.

CHAPTER NINETEEN

GRAMPS HAS LEFT. We're waiting on my brother and sister to come home, Mom and I, curled up together like old times on the floor. It feels good. We play with Riley and watch reruns of *I Love Lucy*. I'm not a big fan. But Mom cracks up, and watching her watching the redheaded lady is fun. Riley likes it too, even barking at the screen a couple of times.

Tonight's leftovers night. Abbie will like that, Chris, and me too, and Mom doesn't have to cook. Giving her plenty of time to talk to us about Dad and our family's early years while we enjoy Granny's spaghetti and garlic bread once again.

Shortly after four o'clock, Abbie and Chris bust in talking, looking for us. Riley was asleep until they came in. Abbie picks him up first thing.

Still sitting on the floor with us, propped up against the sofa, Mom smiles. Even in this most stressful time, she still freely gives all her love and herself, no ugliness, just love. I have the best Mom in the world.

"I need to share some things with you." She pulls her knees up to her chest and hugs them. "Things about your father, things I'd hoped

I'd never have to discuss, but... After today's little incident at school, your grandfather and I talked, and we both agree you need to understand your dad better. So I'm going to explain things the way I saw and still see them."

Chris and I crawl over to sit on either side of her. Abbie's still in the middle of the room, playing with Riley, but she's frowning the deep look she gets when she's concentrating.

Mom tucks her chin on her knee. "Your dad and I were married when I was nineteen right after high school. I met him at the chili shop downtown. He was so dreamy, and I'd never dated before. Your gramps had watched over me and my sister like a hawk. Your dad misled me to believe he was a believer too, but he wasn't, not even close."

Riley wiggles from Abbie and snuffles Mom. He must know she needs him most right now.

She strokes his furry, floppy ears. "We agreed not to have children for a while when we first got married. I soon learned he didn't want any at all, but I did. After a year and a half, I became pregnant. He was furious. I couldn't believe the anger, the hate, he showed me. It grew worse and worse. But deep down, I was happy I was pregnant, ecstatic. When the doctor told me I was going to have twins, I was even more excited, thinking this may be the only time I'd have babies. I was so glad God had made it for good. I couldn't wait to meet you boys." She reaches over and grips Chris's and my hands.

"After you two were born, he was a different man toward me, nothing like the man I thought I married. He came home late, shouted at me all the time, and occasionally... hit me. My dad helped me. We got a restraining order and made Dale move out to seek counseling."

My brother, sister, and I trade shocked glances. Now we know why Mom *never* talks about Dad.

"After six months, he showed progress, even going to church with me again. I reconciled with him, eventually, and I became pregnant with you, Abbie. God's special plan for me, another gift to our family." Mom leans over and smooths Abbie's long hair back from her cheeks. Then she pushes her back against the couch again. "Your dad went ballistic, even worse than before, accusing me of trying to trap him. That night, he hurt me pretty bad. I had to spend the night in the emergency room. I thought I'd lost you, Abbie, but God's plans were better."

Abbie crawls closer and plunks herself at Mom's feet, Riley playing by jumping between Mom's legs.

Mom's shoulders hunch in as she relives the events to share them. I imagine it's almost more than she can bear. "Dale was arrested and did ninety days in prison before being released early. The last time he saw you boys was at our divorce hearing. He wore the most disgusting, disturbing look. I vowed, whether he helped me or not, I didn't care. I wanted my babies safe and happy. That wouldn't—could not—happen with him around. I imagine, after what happened today at school, his stepchildren have had enough too. We should feel sorry for them. I don't think they're believers, so it must be really hard for them."

We sit, silent, Riley licking my hand. I'm thankful, not sad. Chris and Abbie probably are too. Mom is so loving and affectionate, a supercool mom. I'd rather have my mom the incredible way she is than be fearful of a maniacal dad.

And I'm beginning to see a pattern between those who believe and those who don't. The darkness must sometimes be so intense for nonbelievers that they don't even notice it. *I have to believe!*

We all hug, crying and laughing too. The emotions feel strange, but I'm not the bad guy today. Neither is Peg. The darkness stole all goodness from her, so she lashed out at the first person who came into her circle—me.

Before going to bed, I pull out my journal.

Dear Journal,

It's been a hard day. I was sent home from school after I pushed Peg. She tripped over a desk and broke her arm, but she deserved it. She was mean, calling Mom names. Mom tried to explain why she's mean, probably our dad. He doesn't like kids, and he's abusive.

I'm glad he's not here with us. I hope the Helper, if He ever shows up, will show me how to believe. I don't want to be like Dale. Good night, Journal.

PS: I almost forgot. I hope the Helper teaches Peg and her family the way. Dad too.

CHAPTER TWENTY

THE NEXT MORNING, Tuesday, I can barely push myself out of bed. Chris is already downstairs. We're due for a meeting with the principal at nine o'clock sharp. Dressed and ready, I stump into the kitchen. Mom's standing by the sink, the water running for no reason. "Mom, I'm sorry you have to take your vacation time to go with me."

My nerves are in a ball. My heart feels like a fist two times too small, squeezing tighter every minute. My face burns as I ride to school with Mom, wondering who else will be in the room. Who are "all parties" anyway? Mom's gotta be wondering the same.

"Nickie, it's okay. We'll be all right. We need to stay calm and forgiving. Okay?"

But there's fear in her eyes. I'd never seen this look on her face. What could be bothering her? Then I see it—the blue Hummer. My heart topples to the car mat at my feet—it probably landed next to Mom's.

"Nick, no matter what is said. You sit quietly unless the principal asks you something, okay?" Mom straightens her hair and shirt going into the school. Guess we're both nervous.

Too bad, she doesn't have her work shoes on. The distraction would've done me good. I don't know what's coming, but there's probably a trapdoor in the principal's office floor, ready to suck me into oblivion. Thoughts running, I slink down the hallway close behind Mom, using her as a human shield. I imagine she feels like one too.

The office door screeches, like in those cheap horror movies, naturally. Mom tenses up and pauses before going in, reinforcing my fear. When the door opens all the way, I see Peg and a woman who must be her mom. Peg fires up her laser stare as if trying to dissect me. The woman puts her hand on Peg's stomach as if to hold her back.

Mom's breath whooshes out with the same relief I feel. Dad didn't come, so we can pick up our hearts and put them back. Peering from behind Mom, like I used to as a young boy, I realize now how brave she is, and then I step out to be brave too. Breathing deeply, I sit across from Peg and her mom. Her gaze is cold... and hard.

Soon, the principal emerges. "Glad to see you all here. This is just a simple meeting, so let's all go into my office and relax a bit as we talk this through."

Not a word had been spoken until he came out. I didn't notice much of anything until I got up, but Peg has bruises around her good arm today. Her mom does too. Mom's story must be true—I mean I never doubted her, but seeing their bruises helps me understand even more how bad a man can become.

Helper, where are You? I don't want to become a bad man.

"A good man takes no comfort in the suffering of others," a tender voice responds to my soul.

Great... Now I'm hearing voices. What would the doctor say about *that*? My thoughts have gone from survival to compassion. Gramps is right. Living with my dad was no picnic.

The principal settles at his desk, rolls his chair back a bit, and locks his hands in his lap. He looks so relaxed. Too bad it's not catching. "Let me begin by explaining that we've taken statements from other students, along with Chris Marks, so I have a good understanding of what took place. But I still want your stories. Peg, can you speak first?"

Though her eyes blaze, she's quiet. Her lips purse tight. She begins to cry, then buries her head on her mom's shoulder.

I'd never met my stepmom, but she seems nice enough. Only, she's walking the same trail Mom walked so many years earlier and finding the way hard.

Instead of Peg speaking, the new Mrs. Marks speaks. "Peg is sorry for all the trouble she's caused you, Nick. She wasn't mad at you. Her problems began at home, and she took them out on you." Her mom's brave, her voice steady, but her hands shake.

I swallow hard at the tears lodging in my throat. I think we all must.

After a few words, the principal nods to me. "Nick, why don't you go join your classmates now?"

Whew. Hard to believe I'm not suspended. I spring up so fast I nearly trip in my haste to skedaddle.

My classmates all giggle when I come into class late. They know my troubles from the day before. Who cares? All I can think about is what's going to happen to Peg.

That evening, Mom talks to us about what happened after I left, how Peg's mom spoke with her, discussing Dale and his anger issues. She got a protective order against him two weeks earlier. They are splitting up—finally. His abusiveness must've become intolerable.

That night, I write:

Dear Journal,

I feel terrible for Peg and even more thankful for my mom. I hope Peg's family can find the joy we have in our home. Even though she's always been mean to me, I can't help but feel for her. Her pain must be incredible. Today, I heard a voice inside me. I don't know what it was, eerie, then comforting too. I'll ask Gramps. He might know.

I see why love is so important, allowing for forgiveness in hard times. Like Gramps says, it's time I believe and find the Sea of Life. I must make some changes and soon.

PS: Journal, I hope Peg and I can be friends.

CHAPTER TWENTY-ONE

WEDNESDAY MORNING COMES FAST. It might be a better day. It's already starting better with the smile greeting me first thing from the window next door. Lily, waiting on me to say hi, threw a ball against my window and hit the trim. I smile to myself. The evening before we talked in the tree house with Chris and Abbie for the longest time, discussing Peg and Craig and what they must be feeling.

It's strange, but none of us want anything but good for them. I never felt that way when they were bullying me—er, what I thought was bullying. Mom says, "Hurting people hurt people."

"Your mom is so wonderful," Lily said.

Lily's such a big part of my newfound happiness. I'm going to ask her to homecoming. There's only ten days left, and I can't chance her going with someone else. Now that I know she wants me to be her first kiss, well... I'm full of confidence.

Everything's strange and exciting. I kinda know her better than myself, and since the cocoon busting is over, especially hers, I see her differently. I never thought about the future or having more than our friendship, but as we've grown, other feelings for her emerge. Like the first-kiss thing, I feel an attraction to her, a magical, almost magnetic attraction, one I can't describe or explain.

Peg's back in homeroom this morning, sitting at her desk—sad, defeated, and abused—head down. Some of the kids whisper, pointing at her. I know how that feels—I've been there. So I go over. No way will I join the kids making her feel worse about herself, not after living through it.

"Hi, Peg." I lean against her desk, trying to be cheerful, but not overzealous. Mom wants us to be kind. Today, I'll give it a try. "Are you okay?"

"What do you want? You here to gloat?" she half whispers. In the dark circles under her eyes and the slump in her body, I see pain. If only I could help!

Huh, what changed in me? Instead of making her suffer more, I want to ease it. Where has the meaner me gone?

After class, she doesn't get up to leave fast like the other kids. I wait in the hall, bracing against the wall.

Finally, she makes it outside. "What do you want?" She raises her good arm. "Want to break this one too?"

A flat stare, no emotion, tells me she's in a place I'm familiar with. If not for Riley, I might still be there.

My recovery began with love from a puppy, an unconditional love. Even though my family loves me so much, it took a puppy to get me producing an inward love, a love toward myself. Riley showed me there was good inside of me. Peg needs to find it in her heart to love herself again too.

"Peg, I'm sorry I pushed you. I was startled. I hope we can be friends." How strange to hear myself reaching out to my old nemesis, hoping to be a comforter.

Her clothes aren't as pristine today. She's wearing long sleeves, even though it's hot out. Probably to hide the bruises on her good arm. Still, she has a bruise on her face. Is it from her fall? I don't know.

Kids rushing to class cram the hallway. We only get seven minutes to go from one end of campus to the other. We can make it unless we talk too much. I'd better book it. "Well, see ya tomorrow." I start down the hall.

But she reaches for me. The look in her eyes, one of gratitude and sorrow, halts me more than her cold grip on my arm. "Thanks, Nick. I'm sorry I've been mean to you."

She lets go. Then with her head down, she shuffles down the hall. Maybe we can be friends after all. I'd be cool with that, wouldn't I?

During my lunch period, I run across campus and wait for Lily to get out of history class. Each hall lets out at different times for lunch. Mine will be over and hers starting when she comes out. After a quick talk, I can then run back across the campus to my next class, hopefully happily.

I wait, heart pounding, pulse thudding my ears. My palms sweat. And a cold chill grabs my chest. "What if she says no?" I wonder aloud.

"If she says no to what?"

Uh-oh! That's Lily, standing behind me. How'd she even get there?

I spin around, and she's smiling. I almost melt on the spot.

"Hi, Lily. I... I, um, I was wondering aloud that's all." Great, the meltdown's about to begin. I pause and close my eyes for a heartbeat —maybe two—to regroup. "I was wondering if you'd go to homecoming with me?"

Time freezes, leaving me suspended in the moment and watching the world come to a halt, my life, everything hanging on her answer. My life will forever change.

She wraps her arms around me. Then she grabs the front of my shirt in her balled-up hands, just like old times, and pulls herself to me, holding me tight. "Yes, yes! I'd love to go to homecoming with you."

Our faces almost touch, her blue-blue eyes flashing. Maybe she's as excited as I am. Looking at her this close, I feel a strange desire. I want to kiss her so badly. I think she feels the same, but the bell rings.

"Oh, I'm late. I've got to run." I give her one last quick hug, getting ready to sprint to class. "See you this afternoon? In the tree house?"

"Okay, I'll see you."

I began to sprint to class, running sideways, watching her.

She raises her hands to her face, covering a joyful smile. I almost imagine she hugs herself with her elbows as if she were checking to see if it were a dream.

Maybe she does. My confidence soars. I'll gladly face any penalty for being late to my next class.

The rest of my day drags, my heart about to burst. It's like waiting for Christmas morning as a kid, only much better. Finally, the bell rings.

I run out front to meet Chris and share the good news. Hopefully, he'll find someone too.

I hadn't thought about Craig or Peg. The Hummer isn't waiting. Instead, Peg and Craig meet where the school buses load. I guess their life must be different now. I hope it's better and they recover from their situation and are okay.

Thank You, Helper, for giving Mom the strength to face life without Dad.

I don't understand what's happening deep inside me, but this whispering to my new friend begins to feel natural—sort of.

While I'm watching, Chris comes out and pokes me on the shoulder. "Earth to Nick. Are you in there?"

I shrug. "I was daydreaming, I guess."

His brows rise as he follows my stare. "Can you imagine how Peg must feel?" He grips my shoulder and turns me to walk home. "She'll get over it."

"We talked in the hallway after homeroom. I feel sorry for her. That could've been us if Mom weren't so brave." I loop my arm around him. It feels so good to be back. "They could use a friend like Riley."

Walking into the sun, I shade my eyes with my hand, finally noticing the chaotic rush of students darting this way and that. Cars at the curb wait to pick up some. Others cross the busy street, a live game of Frogger. A few horns blare.

"Chris, thanks for warning me about those boys coming on to

Lily. I asked her to homecoming today, and she said yes." My eyes must have sparkled or something. I know my smile's big, and my heart's full with love. But I want it for him too. I hope he has his sights on someone.

"Did you have any doubt? I never had a chance with her. I've always known that—deep down. I feel stupid for even thinking that way about her." His hand's no longer on my shoulder, nor mine on him. He's found a rock to punt along again, but his kicks are lively, not angry. He's better today, happy for me too.

I'm at a crossroads in more ways than I can know. I want so badly to tell Chris how close we came to our first kiss today, but I can't. I want to be a good man, and good men don't share things about the girl they love. Peace washes over me, my soul happy again.

On the walk, Chris and I talk about everything. Better than old times. We may have been strained, I was, but we'll make it back. I still need the Sea of Life, but some of my desires have changed. I want it for someone else more than me. I want it for Peg and Craig Holland, their lives bearing the scars from life with Dad. Time to fix that.

After doing my homework, I join Abbie and Riley in the tree house. They're almost inseparable—fine with me. He has enough love for everyone. She pets him, her love spilling over. An elusive peace makes its way back into my life.

"Hi, Lily," we both say in unison as she pops her head up the ladder. She must've finished her homework too. She's changed her clothes, and her smile brightens the tree house. It feels so good to have her coming up here—to be with me!—again. We talk about homecoming until Mom calls us to dinner.

As the sun sets over the rooftops, the red and orange hues give way, and darkness prepares for the moon's next night shift. Autumn's here, and it looks spectacular.

But no kiss today. Abbie never left us alone. She's excited for us too. We say our goodbye with a long tight hug. I love Lily's hugs, but they feel different now as new sensations replace my boyhood memories of her hugs.

CHAPTER TWENTY-TWO

I HADN'T THOUGHT about it before, but now panic—fear—grips me. I don't know how to dance!

I've never needed to know. I have to ask Mom to teach me at least a little. Maybe Abbie can help too. She's a good dancer. She's always twisting and swinging while listening to music on her phone. Maybe that's why Chris and Abbie are on their phones so much. I'd never thought of that. Are they listening to music?

"Mom, I"—I tumble into the living room—"I don't know how to dance. What will I do at homecoming?"

I'd already shared the news with her. Now, she puts her hands on my shoulders and laughs, lighting up like a Christmas tree. "Well, I guess we're going to have to do something about that."

I thought she'd figure out how to help me or at least decide when we could work on it. I still had over a week, so it isn't crunch time, not yet. Instead, she leaves the room going into the kitchen, laughing, twisting rhythmically, all the way. This isn't the response I had in mind.

Abbie, having heard our conversation, clamps a hand to her mouth, but giggles still escape.

I scowl at her. "What's so funny?"

She scrunches her shoulders. "I don't know. Maybe something came to her mind."

Scooping Riley up, I look him in the eye. "Riley, do you know, boy?"

Having fun with it, he licks my nose. I take it as a no.

Mom doesn't say anything about dancing the rest of the evening, and I don't bring it back up. Even though I fear the whole not-knowing-how-to-dance thing, I'm still excited. I'm so psyched up I can't sleep. So I slip over to the window quietly so as not to wake Chris and look toward Lily's house. Huh. She's at her window too.

We both raise them, and since our houses aren't too far apart, only wide enough for a driveway and some bushes between, I admit I can't sleep. For sure, the feelings inside me are glowing on my face, giving me away.

"Me either," she confesses. "Want to practice dancing tomorrow? I've never been to a dance. I'm a little nervous. Your mom told mine you asked her to teach you." Her angelic face glows. The full moon lights up the driveway, and I felt like howling. "Could we learn together? I'd really like that."

Mom did it again, making lemonade out of my lemons.

Pretty cool how our longtime friendship allows us to be open with each other, not afraid of sharing our thoughts or feelings. I know Lily almost as well as—er, probably better than—I know myself, and she knows me. Sure, many things have changed, but our knowledge of each other makes some of those things much easier.

"That sounds like fun." I can't help laughing. "See you tomorrow." I wave and lower my window, never taking my focus off her. The love I felt from Riley rescued me from the spiraling depths of depression. But the love I feel for Lily takes me to places I never dreamed of. I lay awake for hours, thinking of tomorrow, and it comes fast.

A strange smell snakes and slivers its way to our bedroom. Mom must be trying a new recipe. She loves trying new things. I've happily performed the role of guinea pig along with Abbie and Chris. Some recipes are okay, many are terrible, but once in a while, Mom finds one that becomes a favorite. I hope today's the latter.

I follow Chris down the steps, my expectations for the day high. After all, I had hope, and I was going to learn how to dance—with Lily.

"Okay, boys and girls, we have a 'new' recipe, country breakfast burritos. I like it. I hope you guys do." Mom has that look on her face, like she's being sneaky and hiding something. She loves to play little games with us, keeping us in suspense. She says it adds spice to life.

"Okay, Mom, what's going on?" Abbie braces against the kitchen doorway, arms crossed, an eyebrow rising inquisitively. Abbie watches actresses who use theirs to convey their feelings. It's one of the things she does for fun, and it does help lighten things up.

"Nothing is up. Does something have to be 'up' before I try a new recipe?" Mom slides down beside me at the table, her hand on my shoulder. "So, Nick, how did you sleep last night?"

She's about to bust. I can tell.

"Thanks, Mom," I say sarcastically, and my face flushes. "I couldn't—at least not at first."

"Well... I had a thought. Maybe it would be fun if we had a dance party Friday evening with Kayleigh, Lily, and Cara. We'll make tacos and put on some music. Then we'll all have fun dancing. Does that sound good? After all, we have two of the most handsome bachelors and the fairest ladies in all of the town—that we can be sure of." She wiggles and twists back and forth on the bench seat beside me, bumping me in a melodic way.

Thursday goes by slowly, and the world beckons. But I'm stuck in class, studying how to cut up a frog and something called a philosophical approach to world harmony—whatever that means. I didn't hear half of what the teacher said. My mind was a million miles away and tuned to a different kind of harmony.

Finally, the bell rings. I race to the front sidewalk like always, waiting there on Chris. I didn't see Peg in homeroom, but I didn't look for her either. The blue Hummer's missing again, and my stepsiblings aren't heading to the buses either. It doesn't register much, not when I have better things to focus on.

On our walk home, I notice a few things for the first time, like how a white cat watches us from a porch step in front of a house along the way almost every day. I never paid attention before. Today, we're running later, and a well-dressed lady gets out of her car in the driveway. The cat must've been waiting on her, something he probably does every day. Little things that mean so much to someone go unnoticed by others.

Never, *ever* will I shut my eyes to the world or others again. Especially those I love.

"Hello, earth to Nick. Are you in there?" Chris elbows me. He's been trying to tell me about a girl in his home economics class.

"Yes, I'm in here. I heard you. Are you going to ask her to homecoming or what?" I'm still watching the cat, walking backward while the lady picks the cat up and goes into her home.

Chris was talking about Monica, Monica Musselwhite. She has long brown hair and a cute face. She didn't go to middle school with us. She came from Madison, a school in the middle of town. It's a rough place, or so I'd heard.

"I don't know. I might. I'll have to ask Mom. She'd have to drive us, and I don't know how that's going to work. She already has you and Lily to drive."

"I can ask Cara to take Lily and me. Then Mom would be free to drive you and Monica. Find out where she lives. I'm sure Mom will be happy to do it." I can't let Chris give up on going to homecoming. Plenty of pretty, smart girls would love to go with him. "Did you think about asking Emily?"

"Yeah, but her dad won't let her go on dates. She's going stag. She said she'd dance with me though."

"Talk to Mom, maybe Monica can come to our dance party tomorrow night if she wants to go to homecoming with you. Wouldn't that be fun?" I breathe deep, proud of myself and Chris for trying again.

"There's no time. I needed to ask her today if I wanted her to come over tomorrow night. Besides, how would she get to our house?" He hunches his shoulders. As they keep rising—all the way to his ears—he must be trying to figure out how he feels, if he even wants to go with Monica, not how things could work out. Soon, those shoulders lower. He raises his head and shakes the hair out of his eyes, and they're aglow. Yep, he loves the idea.

I reach out and stop him. "Call Mom, ask her. She can ask Cara and let you know. Then call Monica once everything is set. What do you have to lose?" It's the perfect solution. Chris has got to have a good time too. Besides, it's much easier to be brave with Chris's life than with my own. I knew how he feels, and I'll stand beside him.

By six o'clock, it's all set. Monica said she'd love to go to homecoming with Chris, and her mom said she could come over for tacos and dancing tomorrow night. I don't know if Chris mentioned the dancing, but no matter, once she's at our house everything will be great.

Tonight's pizza night. I come home to find Riley sleeping in his bed under the hallway bench. How odd that neither Chris nor Abbie scooped him up to spoil him. Riley loves it under there. He can watch three rooms and stay up on all the action or not. I rub his belly. Soon, he won't be a puppy.

Taking him outside to the tree house while Chris preps for his debate, I see Lily on the swing in her backyard, reading a sci-fi book. Reading about make-believe worlds and people is her favorite. She's a huge *Star Wars* fan, along with everything Marvel. We've spent many Saturday afternoons at the theater matinees, watching movies and eating popcorn. I almost forgot how much fun I've had with her and how I've always looked forward to going. Almost all my happy memories include Lily.

Today's a new day, and this afternoon, our relationship feels like it's at a new level. *Helper, please don't let me mess this up!* I stop in my tracks, looking around, noticing the calm all around me. Why did I say that? Who is this Helper?

Lily must've seen me talking to myself. "Care to introduce me to your new friend?" she pokes, laying her book on a table made from a stump near the swing. Our parents may not be rich, but we rarely want for anything. Partly because we know not to ask and partly because of the ingenious use of ordinary things around us, like the stump.

"Does he talk back to you? Assuming it's a he?" She laughs. Eyes sparkling in the sun, her cheeks rosy, her smile melting me like one of those laser beams from *Star Wars*. Man, I'm hooked. We met near the stump where I put Riley down, and we hug for the longest time. It feels amazing. I remember the times we hugged at church. How could I have ever forgotten or turned away? She loves to grab my shirt, and it feels like she isn't ever going to let go. Today, she shudders with excitement and closes her eyes, still holding on and hugging me. Then she opens her eyes—and I feel the same way.

We end up in the tree house with Riley where we talk until her mom calls for her. We hug good night, and I head inside for pizza. Again, I want to kiss her so badly, but I don't do it. Will I ever get the chance and courage?

CHAPTER TWENTY-THREE

THE NEXT MORNING, Friday, I rush downstairs to get breakfast and head to school. I don't think I touch a step all the way down. Abbie and Chris are almost ready to leave, so I've gotta hurry. After gulping down two of Mom's blueberry pancakes and bacon, I finish my milk and load my dishes in the dishwasher.

Mom leans on the counter, smiling. "Hey, don't you forget to kiss your mom goodbye. Nickie, keep your mind on the teachers today. This evening will come soon enough." She hugs me and kisses both cheeks. Then her eyes probe mine as if searching for my thoughts. "Take a deep breath. Don't overload your brain with Lily, okay?"

I hope I never get too old for her mothering. "I won't. Bye, Mom. Love you!"

Out the back door, Lily's waiting for me. My feet can't touch the ground today. Somewhere in the last weeks, I've grown up. My thoughts no longer only about becoming a good man, but a good man *for Lily*.

I hold her hand on the way to school for the first time. It feels wonderful and natural.

Abbie smiles and giggles. She loves Lily too.

Walking to school never was this much fun before. I can't wait to learn to dance with her. We drop Abbie at her school, and the three of us continue on, talking about dancing this afternoon.

Lily doesn't know Monica, except to know what she looks like. She says Monica's pretty. I don't say anything. After all, Chris and I discussed it the day before.

Passing the white cat's house, I see it coming out the door, the lady following close behind. She pets the cat and puts down two bowls, leaving to go somewhere. Strange I never noticed before. I guess my eyes are wide open now. Where have I been for two years?

Getting to school, I let go of Lily's hand. We hug and go our separate ways. Chris makes big eyes and smiles knowingly toward me. "Looks like someone is back in Lily's heart again." He drapes his arm around me, and we run to homeroom.

The bell rings as we entered our homeroom door. Our teacher studies us as we cram in, wearing Kool-Aid smiles and laughing. I can't remember ever feeling happier.

Then I see Peg, cast and all. My heart sinks. Chris's must too. There's such a chill in the room.

She's bruised up pretty bad and still wearing a long-sleeve shirt to conceal her bruises, her sleeve rolled up over the cast. Dad must've been at it again. Her once proud look's now a distant memory.

After homeroom, she remains seated while everyone leaves, humiliated, like the day before. Her embarrassment obvious, her pain uncovered. We hurt for her.

"What kind of monster is that man?" I sit backward at the desk in front of her.

"The kind that's going to prison. That's the kind," Chris chimes in. He's stayed behind too, his compassion like mine—must be feeling almost like guilt.

"How are your mom and brother?" I look around for our teacher, but she must've stepped out to do something. I set my recent joy aside. Peg may have been mean to me, but I have O'Hanahan blood in my veins, and we care about others. "Are they okay?"

Tears stream down her face. She tries to cover it with her hands. Her shoulders shake, and she sobs. I don't know if it's because of her beating or because we care. Either way, I ache for her. Chris hugs her to console her, so I try that too.

We talk about Dad, about his abuse.

"Mom's in the hospital." Peg gulps out the confession. "Craig's more or less like me."

Which means beaten, but okay.

"What happened?" Chris asks.

"Dale got all drunk and came by, despite the court order."

I'd heard of that in other people's cases.

"The order only made him angrier." Peg shudders. "He... he held off the police for *two* hours, finally giving up when the alcohol wore off."

I can't imagine it, but here it is—the truth. My dad's the worst of men, a wife and child beater and a drunk. I have to find the Sea of Life now. I *have* too. I don't want his curse falling to me or Chris—something the pastor talked about on more than one occasion.

Though I can't wait to see Lily, my happiness and Chris's has been tamped down. We have to run before the bell rings, but man, I'm so thankful our mom's strong!

Finally, the school week ends. Chris and I meet out front. Lily joins us as we leave to pick up Abbie. She reaches for my hand as I reach for hers. We tell her about Peg and her family and our dysfunctional dad.

Her eyes get big, and all joy leaves her face. "Wow, he's a monster. Your mom had to deal with that?"

The color drains from her face. Did she remember the pastor preaching on curses too? Could I be a monster one day or Chris?

After we pick Abbie up, our conversation turns happy. She has that effect on things. But the question lingers: Will Lily ever think I can become a monster? Guess I'll find out soon enough. At home, we hug goodbye, but it doesn't feel quite right. We plan on her coming over around six with her mom.

I trudge inside. Did our hug and goodbye only seem strained to me, or did we both feel it?

Mom comes home around four thirty and begins putting things together right away. I haven't seen Mom like this for quite a while, all happy and bubbly. She has her oldies playing on our television—well, old to us kids. The house smells awesome, like a Mexican restaurant. Abbie helps, but she's dancing around with Mom and Cara more than prepping food. Then Cara leaves with Chris to pick up Monica.

I go out back and sit on the porch with Riley since he's constantly seeking fun and companionship. I hold him close and whisper a promise into his floppy ear.

"Riley, I'm not going to be like Dad, not in a thousand years."

But I can hear the preacher's words, even as I hold my pup tight. I need to feel Riley's special love, but I can't. What happened? Has the curse already begun? Was my mind playing tricks on me? I shake off that thought and head back inside, wishing I'd never gone out.

Kayleigh and Lily come over right on time. Lily looks amazing. Her mom must've helped her get dressed—with makeup. I nearly trip over myself. She smiles, almost laughing when she sees my reaction. Since she's the first girl I've ever liked, I'm not smooth, but I know what I think.

"You are beautiful, Lily." I gawk.

Her face flushes, and she wraps her arms around me to hide her thankful embarrassment. She does look beautiful with her long black hair up in curls, and her eyes, always beautiful, are breathtaking tonight, blue as blue can be. My gaze skims her white shirt, jeans, and, um, *heels*. She's taller than me now. Will she think differently about me because of it? No. I push the thought aside.

Mom and Kayleigh gush, admiring her, us, but longing glosses Mom's eyes. She must be sad to see her kiddos growing up. Looking at Mom, I wince at a twinge of regret before it vanishes.

Chris and Monica arrive, and we dive into Mom's awesome tacos, rice, and all the things needed for a taco party. Then Mom and Kayleigh help us slow dance. Doesn't take much apparently, except not stepping on each other's toes too much. It's mostly me stepping on Lily's. She has rhythm. I sure don't.

Monica going with Chris allows me and Lily to sneak out to the tree house for some private time. As I nudge her to the door, though, I catch Chris staring at Lily. Not knowing what to think, I keep mum, take her hand, and lead her to the tree house, no Riley this time. Somewhere, somehow, our relationship's changing, and my excitement's undeniable. My whole being—body, mind, and soul—is alive, electric. Does she feel the same?

She climbs up first and clicks on the light, a battery-powered contraption Gramps helped us with. When I follow and edge through the door, all I can do is gape at her, the moonlight now shining on her brightly through a window. She's not the little girl I grew up with anymore. She's the beautiful young woman living next door, the one I'm mad about. Self-doubt causes me to wonder. After all, what does she see in me?

"That was fun. You're a great dancer." She captures my hand. "I'm so glad you're back, Nick. I've been crazy about you forever. I've dreamed of evenings like this for two years. I hope I always feel like I do tonight, here—with you—just the two of us." Her soft voice soothes me. Her beautiful face glows. Then she leans toward me.

We kiss. *Finally!*

I step back, still holding her hands, and she blinks up at me, those blue-blue eyes all glazed and glossy. I *have* to be a good man. I won't believe what the pastor said. Curse or no curse. I love Lily.

Mom and Kayleigh give us a few minutes to rest, then come out looking for us. My feet never hit the ground the rest of the evening dancing—well, except to step on Lily's toes. I don't think hers do either. Monica laughs, joshing Chris and enjoying herself. Mom and Kayleigh cut it up too, dancing a lot, even Abbie joins in. Mom has a special glow about her, one I haven't seen in years. Maybe she's finally ready for a special friend too.

Then I walk Lily home, her hand soft in mine. She frees her hand and loops it through my elbow. "Nick... things feel different."

"They *are* different."

"Happy different." She hugs my arm to her and rests her head on my shoulder.

Happy different. Good words. True words. Our lives forever changed. Our cocoons busted.

CHAPTER TWENTY-FOUR

THE SUN SHINES through my bedroom window early Saturday morning, now hanging lower in the sky as fall rolls through. I won't see Lily again until church Sunday morning. What a long day!

In the surrounding counties, they've harvested the apple orchards, and many smaller churches began making apple butter.

I follow Chris into our kitchen.

Abbie hands us each bowls of steaming oatmeal. I don't like oatmeal, but she's sliced peaches into it, so it's okay, I guess. "Guess Granny and the ladies will begin quilting today." She carries her bowl to the table and drizzles in too much honey. "I should join them."

Granny makes such special heavy quilts for Mom every several years or so. My granny is the best, but we all feel that way.

"Today's Nickie's day." Mom settles in with bland cereal.

Today marks the first of three Saturdays the church and community come together where they live. The men will begin making apple butter in batches over a wood fire in copper kettles, working from dawn till dusk. And today, Gramps is taking me.

"It'll be a good experience." Mom points her spoon at me. "The guys have such a special camaraderie, neighbor helping neighbor, friend helping friend. You two will get your turns over the next Saturdays."

Abbie kicks her feet back and forth. "Then, on the last weekend, we all go to the shindig, right?"

The church sponsors it each year to raise money for outreach in their community. Apple butter and quilts will be for sale with all the proceeds going to help those in need.

Mom winks at me. "Maybe Lily will come too."

I shrug. "Too bad, she can't come today."

Abbie twirls her spoon through her oatmeal. "She'd just go inside with Granny to work on quilts like the two times she came with me." Abbie stops stirring. "I should go today. Think of all the stories I'll be missing."

Chris reaches across the table for the milk, then splashes some on his oatmeal. "You always say their wild tales can't be true."

"Doesn't mean I don't like listening to them tell about their children, homes, and menfolk."

Telling stories must be what older people do.

Mom pats Abbie's hand. "It does make life sweeter, giving us more hope and more promise. But you'll go next week. Finish up, Nick. Your gramps will be here for you soon."

He honks shortly later, and I gulp down my milk and sprint to his truck.

When we arrive, wind whips up smoke and flames from raging fires. One of the dozen or so men standing over the copper pots waves us over. "Come give us a hand. Gotta keep these kettles stirred."

The guys rotate around each kettle. Gramps picks the furthest of the six pots and nudges me into place. "Goal's to ensure the fire doesn't burn too hot and the kettles are stirred just right."

Smoke stings my eyes, and I swallow down the urge to cough.

"Otherwise, it can burn the insides of these pots." The guy beside me uses his elbow to wipe sweat from his brow. "And you don't want to know what these beauties cost."

Gramps points at a man and woman in jeans sitting on a bench nearby blowing steam off their coffee. He waves to them, and they nod back. "They belong to the Cranwells, so the church needs to take special care of them. We borrow them every year, then take them to another church next week."

I try to peer into the big pot. "I'm surprised I don't have to help peel the apples." I'd have enjoyed working with a knife like that.

"Some older couples always do that the day before." A guy hands me his paddle and gestures for me to have at it.

Gramps wraps a handkerchief around his nose. "They don't *have* to be peeled, but the finished apple butter tastes a lot better if they are."

As the hours pass, my arms ache from working beside Gramps, stirring the pots, or carrying cases and cases of glass jars, bags of sugar, and spices for canning. A few teens help by water bathing the jars, getting them ready, or stirring the kettles. But, man, I can see how much good we're doing, giving the needy things they wouldn't have, bringing the community together, and helping people get to know one another. My favorite's gonna be selling everything, then seeing the eyes of people it might go to help. Their appreciation and love for their community shining through their humble smiles and grateful thanks.

Oddly, through it all, I enjoy the older folks. The boys my age are all distant, even adversarial. I didn't know any of them, nor they me, but it's like they're judging me. The girls are okay enough. Maybe the boys see me as competition? Who knows.

Around five, some others come to finish the day's work. After a nice meal at the church, we head home to my grandparents' house. "Guess it's good Riley didn't come." I lope over to pet Butch. I miss Riley though. "He'd have been hard to entertain while making apple butter."

"I heard you've asked Lily to homecoming. I'm proud of you, Nick." Gramps lowers himself to our spot with a grunt. "She's a special young lady. I can see how much she cares for you. We all can."

I leave Butch alone and ease myself up onto the bench beside Gramps. I feel like grunting too. *Everything* hurts. Even my eyes from all the smoke. But as he drapes his arm around my shoulders, I feel so at peace. Kinda hard to imagine how only a week earlier my turmoil burned so hot, hidden deep inside. Still, I remember what Gramps said about the moon. Even though it isn't shining, I can still see it in the sky. It hasn't left. Nor have my problems.

"Did Mom tell you about our taco party last night? They helped Lily and me learn to dance. We had such fun, and Chris danced with Monica." I stretch out my legs, crossing them at the ankles, every bit of me relaxing. "I hope they get to like each other and have a great time."

"Yep, your mom did. She shares just about everything with her mom. It's a special bond most mothers and daughters share, kind of like the bond fathers and sons share—or in our case, like you and me." He dips his head against mine. The smoky smell from the day still wafts from him. "I enjoy my time with you. Chris too, but he doesn't seem to need me as much right now. Of course, if I remember what being young was like, then I know that can change at any minute."

Butch pads off toward the house. After being outside all day, he's probably ready for a nap at Granny's feet, or maybe he likes watching *Star Trek*.

"Gramps? Lately, I feel different around Lily, and I can tell she feels different around me. We held hands and kissed last night—it was both of our first kisses. I didn't want to leave her." Telling him might feel strange, but I need some guidance, man-to-man guidance. Things are different, like a magnet's attracting me to her now.

He slides around on the bench enough to face me. Good. He's smiling, but his arm on my shoulder feels kinda heavy, like the weight of his serious gaze. "Well, it was just a matter of time. Things are going to be different now. When I fell for your grandmother, we didn't kiss until we got married. To some, that sounds nuts—nowadays. But I respected Helen and God. When you shared that kiss, you probably felt something inside you that didn't want to stop. That's how God made us, how He made everyone. When we kiss someone, we're sharing a piece of ourselves with them, and them with us. Our bodies are made special, to desire each other. You have to be careful, Nick."

A shadow of a smallish animal flashes across the path going down the hill.

Gramps points it out. "Probably a raccoon." He rubs his hands together, probably sore like mine. "Lily has grown into a beautiful young woman, and I can see how you two connect. So you need to talk to her about how you felt, and don't brag to your peers about kissing her or about anything between the two of you, okay? You must protect her from people talking about the two of you, and they will talk." He jostles my shoulder with his. "Most importantly, don't look to kiss her all the time, or else your love might spill over to more than kissing. You are too young, and that shouldn't happen until after you're married, and then only with your wife."

Gramps scrunches his brows in his way—the way that says he's trying to see if he missed anything. "You already know about the birds and the bees, right? Where babies come from?"

"Yes, sir. Is this what Mom meant about cocoon busting? I feel so different around Lily now. I can't take my eyes off her, and they want to see her, all of her. Sometimes it's like the first time I've ever seen her. She looks so... so different—beautiful, I guess."

"She is a very pretty girl, a real sweetheart." Gramps exhales, closing his eyes for a moment. "Yes, this is one of the things your mom meant by cocoon busting. Now your body has matured, but your mind... well, it still has a lot of learning to do."

A dog bark carries over the hillside, must be seeing the raccoons too.

Patting my shoulder, Gramps seems refocused. "This is that time the pastor was talking about, the age of accountability. If you want to be a good man—from now on—you'll have to take account of all your actions. You can't simply react no more. You have to think and reason your actions first. More than ever, if you want a good girl like Lily, you need to believe, to believe in God." Gramps's stern face shares the seriousness of our moment and everything he's passing on to me.

"The boys at school are always talking about the girls." Like those at the mall. "Why is everything so different for me?"

Gramps shakes a finger at me. "You don't do things because other people are doing them. *You* need to make your decisions based on your beliefs, not someone else's. Before, you made your decisions based on what you wanted. Now, you're beginning to feel like a young man, and that brings with it different decisions, responsibilities, and being able to control yourself." His shoulders rise and fall with his deep breath. "That's something your dad's never learned. It's why he's the man he is. You must take things slow, okay?"

"Yes, sir. I think so." I scuffle my feet in the dirt. Am I ready for this grown-up stuff? I get what he's talking about. I'd already felt it, and it scared and excited me.

Thinking on that, I try to listen as he tells me stuff about needing to trust the Helper, to believe in Him, and to follow the Lord. It's a lot to take in. Then he prays for me. I understand, but I'm confused too.

Now the wind's blowing harder, more powerful as the night pushes in. It's whistling through the barren treetops. The river below is quiet, probably because of the wind. The sun has gone down, and all that remains is that faint glow shining only briefly, a reddish hue, like a wave goodbye from daylight to the night.

Before going inside, darkness coming fast, I hear a whisper, though faint. It sounds like "Come to the river."

I stop.

Gramps goes in. The screen door shuts behind him.

I stand listening. The crickets are loud now, the moon hiding halfway behind a cloud. The air seems alive with a sense of purpose. It began cooling as the sun moved further away.

Listening, I don't hear it again. Did I hear it at all?

Leaving my curiosity, I go inside. Granny has an apple butter jar open. "Wow." I let out a low whistle. "Hot homemade biscuits."

She winks at me. "I thought, after all your work today, you boys deserved a special treat." She pats the sofa cushion beside her.

"What a delicious reward." I drop onto it, and we sit together. I breathe in deep, sniffing the spicy sweetness and eating the fruit of our labors while watching *Star Trek*.

I'd have to be crazy to think I heard something out there. Right?

CHAPTER TWENTY-FIVE

SUNDAY MORNING, Granny fixes another terrific breakfast. Laughing, I rub my stuffed belly. "I eat so much when I'm here."

Gramps's knife scrapes his plate. "I'm going to get fat if you children keep coming over every week." He cuts into her tenderloin. Eggs and more homemade biscuits with more of the apple butter wait alongside it. "Who knows, maybe I'll get a gig as Santa this Christmas."

I point a loaded fork at him. "You're kidding, of course."

He winks at me. Granny and Gramps have mixed feelings about the whole Santa thing. They only went along with it until Abbie turned six. Since then the truth has been celebrated—goodbye, Santa.

Granny hums a song from church as she cleans up after breakfast and ushers us out to their Blazer. She turned sixty-six in May, and if not for her fear of falling, she'd still be in good shape. She says the shape of your soul is the most important thing. For sure, her soul and Gramps's are in great shape. God must be proud of them. I am too.

Rushing into the church ahead of my grandparents, I join Mom and my siblings. Lily isn't around. Right. She plans to sing with the youth choir this morning. She won't be out and about until after the service.

Chris loops an arm over my shoulders. "Forget to shower this morning?" He gives an exaggerated sniff. "You still smell like campfire."

"Wait till your Saturday manning the fires." I wrestle free of his hold. Despite the shower, dirt and maybe soot still lurk beneath my fingernails. "Those old folks sure work hard, and they work you harder."

"What did you learn in Sunday school today?" Mom sits beside Abbie, waving to a friend in front.

"They taught us something about how all things work together for good of those that love God, those called according to His purposes." I push by Abbie's legs, and she scrunches in for me, Chris following close behind.

"The teacher talked about how even bad things, things that hurt or cut deep, can act as a catalyst and work for your good. How God uses them to change things or make them better," Chris chimes in, leaving me no room to follow-up.

I hope that's the case for me too because I have a lot of bad things that need to work for my better, or else I'm in for some trouble. "She used stories about someone named Paul. She said if he weren't in prison, he couldn't have written all the letters that became part of the New Testament, what she called the prison epistles. Whatever that is."

Chris pokes at me. "You know what that is! Think." He shakes his head. "That's what your brain is for."

I elbow him back. "I didn't think you could take all that as real." I don't know. It sounded like Paul suffered a lot, but she said he counted it all as gain. People talk differently when they talk about the Bible. Maybe I'll never understand it. I guess it's something I need to ask Gramps about.

"What was that you asked? Did you ask about the Sea of Life? You know Gramps made that up, right?" Sliding over, Chris cranes around, probably trying to find his friends.

"I asked her about the Sea of Life, if she'd ever found it." Note to self, don't ask that again. The other kids laughed. "She said she didn't know anything about it, that there wasn't a Sea of Life in the Bible."

We sat as close to the stage as possible to hear Lily sing. She always dresses nice coming to church, so she'll definitely look pretty. Little did I expect a short musical skit with all the singers dressed as trees and animals. Lily's a tree. I can hardly tell it was her, except for her voice.

After the initial song and introduction, the scene comes alive, starting with Tree Lily. "I was grown for such a time as this, to become the boat that carried the King of heaven and earth across the sea," she says. "I gave it all for the good of the world. Now, I'm part of mankind's history."

"I proudly carried Jesus on my back. Over the palm fronds, I went into the city of Jerusalem," the colt replies.

Another tree chirps in, "I became a cross for all man's sin."

Then they sing about the rugged cross. At the end, everyone stands and applauds. I must admit, it was good. Then afterward, Pastor teaches about gladly receiving the sacrifice.

When the sermon's over, I find Lily, or she finds me. She walks down the same hallway where we often meet, smiling, only prettier than I can ever remember.

"You were great. The best tree of all." I hug her as tightly as I can. It feels so wonderful. I don't know why, but I want to kiss her so badly. But I don't try it. Later, I'll ask if she felt the same way. I want to know exactly how she feels.

People pass by, sliding to the left or right, watching us, watching our young love blossom.

"Thanks." She fiddles with her blouse collar. "I felt dumb in the tree costume. It was tight around my neck too. I wanted to be the bear, but they let Tim do it since he was the largest. It was fun, though."

She grabs hold of my jacket's front pockets, kinda turning them the wrong way, and slips her hands into them. "I missed you yesterday. Did you miss me?"

"Of course, I missed you! Want to go and sit out on the swings?" We've always gone to the swings. Since there's only two seats, we usually can be alone.

"I'd like to, but I can't." She wads up the pockets' liners. "We're going to my grandmother's house for lunch and to help with chores. She's struggling since Granddad's gone. They were married over forty-seven years. Mom's been sad, so I doubt it'll be a fun day." She sways with me side to side. She's gotta be as happy with our "new" friendship as am I. "But we can meet in the tree house later if you want. I'll call you on my way home, okay?"

"Sounds great—I mean meeting up later, not you saying it will be a sad day for you."

Her mom's calling her, so we go our separate ways. My mom's taking Abbie, Chris, and me to lunch at the new deli near the church. We each order different foot-long submarines, saving half to take home for Monday's leftovers.

I pivot my diner stool to face Chris. "Did you have a good time Friday night with Monica?"

Steely cool, he keeps eating his sub. Then he wipes his mouth and takes a sip of water. "She's nice. Homecoming's going to be fun." He kicks against the deli bar enough to nudge his swivel stool to face me. "Thanks for the needed push. How's everything with Lily?"

With his gaze so somber, he's gotta be measuring me, wondering how serious it's becoming. Fair enough. I'm wondering it too. He still likes her, though, doesn't he? I mean how could he not?

Mom leans around Abbie toward us. "I need to talk to you, Nick, at home—in private. I have something to ask." She flashes a quick, fake smile, nothing like her normal smile as if something isn't quite right. What's up with that?

The minutes become a dizzying blur. Ever since Gramps gave me Riley, everything seems to come and go so fast. Back at home, Abbie stows our leftovers in the fridge while I go straight to Riley's bed. He always stays there when we're not home. He stretches out his fluffy paws, then tail wagging, runs to me. Nice to have him as happy to see me as I am him.

"Bring Riley if you want, but we need to talk." Mom's voice is serious, stern even. This doesn't seem like something she's looking forward to.

Whatever I've done must be important. I trek after her to her room and close the door, turning and leaning back on it.

CHAPTER TWENTY-SIX

I STIFFEN my knees to keep the wobble out. Mom's bedroom door pushes hard against my back, supporting me.

She crosses her arms, her gaze drilling me. "Lily told her mom you kissed her Friday night in the tree house. Nick, do you know what you're getting yourself into? Lily is crazy about you. She has been ever since she finished the eighth grade." Mom's way intense. "How do you feel about her? Have you considered how serious things become once you kiss?"

Whoa. This intensity scares me. I've never had a conversation like this with her. And she wants answers—not just answers. The *right* answers. I guess I do too.

I cuddle Riley, grateful to have something warm and steady to hold onto. Especially when it's hard to grasp just how I feel and what I want to say. This needs to be big-boy talk. "Gramps and I talked, some." I fiddle with Riley's fluffy ears. "I tried to explain it to Gramps, to myself too. I like Lily a lot—I always have. Only now there's some kind of magnetism, you know? Something attracting me to her, especially after we kissed."

As if he understands that word, Riley yips, then stretches his neck, lurches upward, and licks my cheek.

I set him down. I can't be laughing and distracted right now. "She's been my best friend. Now, when we hug, I feel like I'm walking on air. She's so different, so grown-up. I want to talk to her. I loved our kiss, but Gramps said he didn't kiss Granny until they were married, that kissing could lead to other things, more serious things. I love her hugs and holding her hand too. That's enough for me right now, but" —I've got to admit it—"her kiss was amazing."

My ears heat up. My pulse races. Amazing doesn't describe the kiss I'm remembering and how she made me feel.

Mom must sense it. She wobbles to sit on the bed, eyes closed, maybe visiting her happy place. I imagine she'd rather have been anywhere other than here. It's not only me and my feelings—it's Lily's too. We all love her. This is uncharted territory.

A deep breath raises her chest and maybe brings her back from that happy place. Those eyes focus on me. "I was happy when you invited her to homecoming. I guess I was wrapped up in being happy for you, not realizing what all this could lead to." She holds up a hand. "Don't get me wrong. I'm still happy you two are going together. You've played together since you were babies, and I think you're an amazing young couple. But I didn't think you'd be kissing so soon."

I can't say she looks mad—or happy. Maybe surprised? Shocked, even. Like she's trying to figure it all out.

"I dated your dad in high school when I wasn't much older than Lily. I guess this brings back some of those memories. I know you're not your dad, but you need to take this slow so you can figure things out ahead of time."

Riley noses around my feet, then lifts himself onto his hind legs, his forepaws padding against my shins.

Good boy. He knows I need him right now. *But give me a minute, boy. I need to get through this first.*

Okay, time to retrace my steps. "When I asked her about her date with Eric, she said it was terrible, that he tried to kiss her, and that she'd always dreamed I'd be her first kiss. That got me thinking. I didn't want to not kiss her when the time came, and I wanted her to be my first kiss too. It was magical, Mom."

I scoop Riley up. I need him now. No way can I get through the rest of this without him. "I'm going to talk to her, tell her how I loved kissing her, but I don't want things to turn into something far too serious. I'm happy with her hugs and hand-holding. I already planned the speech on how she means too much to me and we have the future to think about. Is that okay, Mom?"

Her shoulders sag while her lips curve upward. She grabs me and holds on tight. "Didn't I tell you you're a great son? You're going to be the best husband one day, more than any girl should hope for—but not now, okay?" She rubs my back, her powdery shampoo scent as comforting as her touch. "I love you, Nick. I'm proud of all three of you. How did I get so lucky to have you guys? It's surely God." She holds me for a long time, rocking back and forth.

My mom—I'll never get enough of her hugs. She's perfect.

"You won't say anything, right, Mom?"

"Never in a million years. Your secret is safe with me and Kayleigh." She opens the door so Riley and I can join Abbie and Chris in the family room. They're watching *Guardians*—again.

I stop. "Mom? Why does Lily grab the front of my shirt in her balled-up hands when she hugs me?" I've wondered.

She ruffles my hair. "That's so she can hold you as close as possible, but not so close you can feel her pressed up against you. It means she really likes you and is trying to have self-restraint. Why? Does Lily do that?"

"All the time. For the last three or four years at least."

"There, that should tell you something. She's crazy about you." Mom nudges me.

"That's amazing." I take Riley to my room instead of going downstairs. I stretch out on my bed, everything good in my world.

I barely shut my eyes before the phone rings. Huh. It's five o'clock, and Lily's home. I must've fallen asleep. I swipe to answer the ringing.

"Hey." Her voice comes through supersoft. "Mom and I finished dinner at a restaurant not far down the street. Do you still want to meet in the tree house?"

"Sure I do. I need to talk with you. See you in a couple of

minutes?" My heart races, and my palms sweat like I'm cocoon busting all over again. It just was fear, the jitters. But I gotta do this, tell her how I feel about her, about us, and discover her thoughts too.

I gotta focus on Lily and me, so I hand Riley to Chris before I head out the back door. Mom gives me a thumbs-up as I hurry out. Lily must've run because she's already there. After dozing, I probably should've brushed my hair or something, right? I paw at it before I climb the ladder and peep inside at her. She laughs, doing her little headshaking thing, while saying hi. I know she's good. I hope what I have to say will please her.

We hug, balled-up hands and all. I feel her love, and she feels amazing. I might as well be dreaming.

"Is your grandmother and all of you okay?" I ask. It's gotta be tough on them, even though they weren't as close lately, not like me and Gramps.

Letting go, she sits down, but her gaze roams. She's probably trying to think how to put words to her feelings and how it was going with her mom. "As good as can be expected, I suppose. We weren't ready for it. I wish things had been different. That's all."

"I'm sorry. If you need to talk, I'm here, okay?" I reach for her hand.

"Thanks, Nick. That means a lot." Her eyes appear to be awash in tears, the blue making them look like deep oceans.

So I dive into them and out comes the rehearsed speech. Maybe it was even coherent. All I can hear is my thoughts screaming: "There, you've done it. No turning back."

She giggles, grabs me, and hugs me. "Nick, I'm *sooo* glad you said that! I feel the same way. Our kiss was *perfect*. I feel it too when you seem to want to kiss me. I want so badly to kiss you. But what you said is also perfect. Let's hold hands and hug for now. When the time comes for more, we'll both know because you're all I think about too. I can't wait till homecoming to show you off to all my girlfriends."

She squeezes me tight.

Man, I want to kick myself. All I can think of is wanting to kiss her. Our friendship has grown into a romance overnight. One kiss changed everything. How is that even possible?

Not a clue. But now I know this is years in the making, all the afternoons together, the laughs, the tiffs, everything. That's why it's me—and not Chris.

CHAPTER TWENTY-SEVEN

COME MONDAY MORNING, Chris leaves an hour early for his debate team practice or something. So Abbie decides to ride the bus. I think a boy she likes rides it. Since Lily has to go by her dad's house first, I walk by myself. This gives me a chance to refresh my thoughts and take in the things around me.

"Do you want to believe?" someone asks.

I turn around but don't see anyone. Great, now I'm hearing things. I keep walking.

"Do you want to believe, Nick?"

There it is again!

"Is this the Helper?" I ask myself.

No, it couldn't be. I hurry on, afraid to stop.

When I get to the house with the white cat, the lady's standing at the bottom of a tree, trying to coax the cat down. In her nice red dress, probably dressed for work, she looks professional.

She waves at me. "Son, can you help me get him down?"

I'm already close to being late, but how can I refuse? Our pastor says we're supposed to help others, something he calls "being a light."

"I'll try, ma'am." I walk under the tall walnut tree and crane my neck to find the fluffy white cat. About fifteen feet up, he starts to inch his way back down.

"Mr. White's timing is terrible. Something must have scared him. He never climbs trees. I have an important meeting this morning, and I'm running late. I'll make it up to you—I promise." She tries to smile, but it flattens. Then she sprints to her car, shouting out a thank you while leaving me to Mr. White.

"Great. Now, I'm *really* going to be late." I scowl at the cat. But a promise is a promise.

"This is a nice thing you're doing, helping Esther like this." A stranger sidles up. "She must appreciate your taking care of him. Mr. White's been with her for years and is her pride and joy. How can I help you?"

I try not to gawk, but he's dressed in some strange white linen pants with a colorful robe that hangs down nearly to his feet. Something like people in the Middle East wear, I guess.

"Yes, sir. Make sure I don't fall out of the tree and catch Mr. White when I drop him down." With the wind calm this morning, climbing's much easier. By now, Mr. White has backed halfway down. Whew, because time's ticking away. I needed to get to school—and fast. Soon, I hand the cat down to the man.

He pets Mr. White, then puts him on the porch where Esther placed two bowls for him.

I drop out of the tree and pick up my books, ready to run to school. "Wait, young man. I have something for you. Please take this coin. It's not worth any money, but if you want to believe, you won't want to lose it. It may help you when you need it most." He plunks a heavy coin into my hand. "Have a great day at school, Nick."

I pivot to run, only glancing at the funny-looking coin. Probably some Arab coin or something. Strange, though. I didn't tell the man my name. I turn to get a better look at him, but he's gone. He must have left fast. I'd better do the same. I push the coin into my pocket as I run. About the size of a silver dollar, only three times thicker, it thuds against my leg with each step.

I reach my class a minute after the bell rings.

Our teacher frowns at me as I run in and slide under my desk quietly, trying to go unnoticed. "Mr. Marks, you do realize the goal is to be in class *before* the bell rings. It would appear this is becoming a trend among some of you in this class. So, beginning with you, Nick, I'm going to have the tardy students come to the front of the class and share their reason for being late. Please come and do so." Only her voice shares a hint of sarcasm.

"Um." I clear my throat. "I'm sorry. It won't happen again. It's my first time. Do I have to?"

Everyone's watching. They'd never believe me.

"Come. Let's get this over so I can call the roll—unless you have some earth-shattering story we need to discuss." She snickers. No doubt, she'd been scarred in a similar fashion when she was in high school.

Should I tell a white lie, saying I left my books and had to go back and get them, or should I tell the truth? Maybe, if I stretch the truth out, she won't ask anyone to do this ever again. Maybe.

Afterward, she rolls her eyes. "I think there is a moral to this story. Make sure to give yourself enough time to get to class *before* the bell rings, especially if you're retrieving cats from trees in a fairy tale."

Yep. She didn't believe me. But she applauds, and the class bursts out into laughter. I should've told them the book thing. Sometimes the truth only gets you into trouble.

"Nick, you may be seated. Thank you for that clever tale. I'm sure it inspired your classmates to have a clever story too... if they should ever be late."

As I return to my desk behind Chris, he gives me a look. "Really?"

"Yes, Chris, really." I tap my pocket. The coin's causing it to twist from its weight. I pull it out and look at it during roll call. It's not money, more like a token or something. I put it back in my pocket. I'll show Lily later.

The day drags by. I guess because homecoming's only ninety-eight hours and twenty-four minutes away, not that I'm counting or anything.

Chris joins me on the school's front steps. "I don't get you. One minute, you're taking on the world. The next, you're roped and quartered. Where did the mean Nick go?" He pushes me, laughing, and waves his arms around, pretending I'm some kind of madman. "Oh, and where did you come up with that ridiculous story this morning? I can't wait to tell Mom."

"I didn't make it up. That cat sits on the porch every day. You'll see." I jut up my chin. "We pass right by there in a couple of minutes. I'll show you the tree I climbed." Maybe the meaner me needs to come back—if only for a little while to take care of this.

We walk on. My mouth dries out as we approach the house. You've got to be kidding me!

"It was right here. You've seen it. The white house with yellow shutters—it was right here."

This isn't the same house. Its shutters are black, and the house is brick. I pivot left, then right. Where could I have been? I've walked this way going on two years. This morning's route was no different from any other.

I grab the top of my head. I must have turned around in about four circles trying to figure out what had happened or where I was this morning. I couldn't come up with anything.

"Great story, Nick." He slaps my back. "Like I said—Mom's going to get a kick out of it." He shakes his head, having fun at my expense.

If he doesn't believe me, what's Mom gonna think?

"Don't say anything, Chris. Mom might ground me. I don't want to miss the dance." She only grounded me a couple times in my life, but this was a grounding offense, making up a story and telling it to my teacher, *lying*, wouldn't be high on her list of commendable things to do.

"Oh no." He smirks and shakes a finger in my face. "I'm going to watch you squirm! Like you've done to me in the past. I told you I'd get you. Maybe I'll go to homecoming with Lily after all." He puffs up, like getting to stick his finger in my eye, his payback so sweet.

I fist my hands, twitching to knock the smug look off his face. But I know better. I'm already in too deep. "Where did that house go?"

Head down, I trek after him. I gotta come up with an angle for Mom. Only I *didn't* lie, so there's no angle.

Where's Lily, anyway? What will she think of all this?

We join Abbie at her school, and Lily's waiting with her. She grins at me and waggles her fingers at us. "My home economics class had a field trip to Abbie's school. We helped cafeteria workers prepare the day's lunches—you can't imagine what goes into feeding over five hundred middle schoolers!"

She hugs me, and I can feel the tiredness in her body. But she smells like Aunt Rachael after a day in the kitchen baking bread. I breathe in deep before she scoots away.

"I've never seen so much food. I hope your day was better than mine."

"I'm pretty sure yours is going to finish better than mine." I glare at Chris.

"Why? What's wrong?" She's standing almost nose to nose with me. Minutes earlier, it would've been hard for me to resist kissing her. Now, it wasn't something I considered. Chris had me—and I knew it. Time to fess up to Lily.

"Why didn't you just say you had to go back to get your books, anything?" she demands after I explain. Her face goes red, her mouth open. "What about the dance? If you get grounded, what then?"

"But it was the truth. I'm not making it up." I *did* see the cat. I did. *Didn't I?*

CHAPTER TWENTY-EIGHT

UPSET, Lily runs home ahead of us. When I try to go after her, Abbie grabs my arm and shakes her head. And my hands clench tighter. Oh how I want to pound Chris. What changed him in just one day? If he'd left this alone, I wouldn't be grounded. Does he have secret ambitions?

I whiz through my homework and whisk Riley to the tree house. We hide there even after Mom gets home. Chris'll be having a good time now. I snuggle up to Riley. He's so easy to care for and has added so much to my life. Gramps is a wise man. Someday, I hope I can be wise too. I should have told the teacher I forgot my books or something simple. I didn't think about the consequences of telling the truth and no one believing me, at least not enough.

Mom comes out to the tree house before supper. Today's Monday, Abbie's favorite leftovers night. Mom doesn't have to cook tonight, but I know I'm cooked. She climbs the ladder, talking already. "Nickie, are you up here? There you are! Kayleigh called and said Lily is all torn up over what you did today." She eases into the tree house, her face red and unsmiling. Yep, she seriously thinks I did something wrong. Chris! He's going to get his—twin or no twin. I don't deserve this.

"You can't keep playing with Lily's feelings." Mom glares in a way I've never seen. Maybe she thinks I'm following in Dad's footsteps.

"Mom." I hug Riley closer, his warm body a shield. "I didn't do anything to Lily. Chris told her I couldn't go to the dance because you were going to ground me. Then she ran home before I could say anything, and she wouldn't answer my calls. I didn't do or say anything." *Thanks, cat lady. Thanks for nothing.*

"Oh, we're getting to that young man. What were you thinking, making up such a crazy story? Being a minute late isn't a big deal, but lying to the teacher? Chris is right. You're grounded unless you can come up with a good reason I shouldn't." She takes Riley from me and climbs down the ladder. She's mad, fighting mad. I haven't seen her this mad, not in a long time. "Dinner is in ten minutes."

"But, Mom... I didn't lie. I did get the cat down!" I close my eyes. *Where is this Helper?*

She doesn't believe me. I wait until the back door shuts before climbing down. I've been branded a bad guy, even though I've done nothing wrong. Being someone's hero isn't always easy. Is this how it started for Dad? Did he get blamed for something he didn't do? *Where are You, Helper?*

Lily's sitting on her swing. She must've been listening to Mom let me have it. I start to go over to her, but she sees me and hurries inside. I don't know whether to be heartbroken or mad. Maybe I'm both. But why won't she give me a chance, at least listen to my side?

Abbie and Chris have dinner on their plates, Mom making them wait on me. I don't have an appetite, so after washing my hands, I figure I'll watch.

Mom shakes a finger at me. "You're not going to make me feel guilty, young man. This is all your doing. Now get your food and eat."

"I didn't lie," I insist.

"Eat. I don't want to hear another word about this!" She purses her lips, her eyes no longer soft beacons of light but steely daggers. She's gotta be flashing back to her time with Dad. She's too furious, and this isn't passing like most times.

I pick up a quarter of a sub and nibble at it. The rest of the meal, I don't look up. When it's over—*finally!*—I head to our room, not saying a word. I check out my window, Lily nowhere to be seen.

What am I going to do? I haven't done anything wrong, but I feel guilty. Why?

I return downstairs to feed Riley and take him out for a bathroom break.

Mom rushes at me. "You're grounded. That means no Riley. Abbie and Chris will take care of him. Go back to your room."

"Gladly," I lie and stomp up the stairs.

The emptiness I felt before getting Riley climbs into my soul. Only now, it's twice as dark. I'd had Riley's and Lily's love snatched away—for nothing. But unlike how, I've felt after my rash decisions in recent weeks, this time I've been betrayed by those who are supposed to love and support me—Mom, Chris, and Lily too.

When Mom took Riley from me in the tree house, a lifeline unplugged from my heart. The love I received from him vanished. Only an icy shell remained. I hurt so bad, but I couldn't cry or get mad. I was too empty. Is this what bad men feel like? Dead inside? Did she take him as an attempt to get back at Dad?

Tuesday morning after breakfast, I excuse myself, but Mom takes hold of my arm. "Come straight home. Don't go to the tree house. Don't play with Riley. Go straight to your room and do your home-work. Do you understand?" Her voice emerges hard and cold from a jaw set like stone. Deep red circles lurk under fiery eyes. I've never seen Mom like this, especially for this long. Usually, her love over-flows every boundary. "And leave Lily alone."

All I can do is shake my head. Words won't come.

And leave Lily alone...alone... alone.... The words play on repeat. All our years together, all our tiffs and squabbles, Mom's never said that. Her reaction now makes no sense.

My world is crashing down, over—at least, as I know it. *Helper, where are You, or are You just something Gramps made up?*

But my mind isn't on the Helper. He's been no help. I'm torn between what I can see and what I hoped for.

As I walk by the place where the cat was, my shoulders slump.

What happened? Where did the house go? I can't believe it isn't still there. Was I daydreaming, checked-out again? Even I began to doubt my own story. No wonder everyone thinks I'm a liar.

A voice inside me says, *"Step 1 to becoming a bad man almost complete—lie unapologetically to those you love."*

How could this have come this far in so little time? Lily won't even listen to me. If she won't believe me, then she doesn't know me or trust in me like I do her.

Gramps lied all the time about this Helper and that stupid Sea of Life. So why shouldn't I do what helps me?

Then I hear the voice. *"Step 2—disavow those who love you and those you love."*

I stiffen my spine. "I am the oldest of the Marks boys. That counts for something. I have Marks blood in my veins, and we look out for ourselves."

Temptation tempts me to skip school, but as the bell rings, I slink into my seat. Not daring to make eye contact with anyone. I loathe myself, but I didn't do anything wrong. Maybe I can't escape the blood in my veins, my destiny. With the good feelings from having Riley around gone—undone—I'm unplugged again.

After homeroom, I head to my locker to get my books for my next class. Chris doesn't speak to me, nor I him. I open my locker to a note from Lily:

I don't know why you said that stupid story. Especially knowing how your mom feels about people lying. Since you're grounded and can't go to homecoming, I'm going with Eric. I hoped we had a chance, but my mom is mad at you too. She doesn't want me to hang out with you anymore. ~ Lily

I ball it up and toss it into the bottom of my locker. My face flushes, and my heart sinks like a lead weight. I'm a mess. Outwardly, tears won't flow. Inwardly, they've all been spent. Why is Mom making such a big deal out of this? The teacher didn't get mad or punish me. I can't make sense out of it all. Most of all, how could Lily discard our friendship and give up on me so easily?

It seems as if a spirit, or demon, has magnified everything.

CHAPTER TWENTY-NINE

IN ONE DAY—NO, one tardy minute—my life changed. But I survive Tuesday and myself. Wednesday looks like another hard day coming. I walk to school, alone, just me and my thoughts, thoughts that for some reason loathe me.

In homeroom, the other kids watch me, even Chris. He's still not talking to me. Why doesn't he, of all people, believe me? He wants this for me, maybe. I don't know. After class, I open my locker, but the balled-up note from Lily lurks there, reopening a mortal wound. Someone taps my shoulder. I turn. Peg? *Oh, great.*

"What do you want?"

She hugs me. "I believe you, Nick. You have a good heart. You cared about me when no one else would, even though I'd been mean to you. If you need to talk or anything, let me know, okay?" Her hair's back to being impeccable, her clothes too. She must've picked herself back up. Maybe I can too—with a little help.

The world blurs in her arms. How could someone I had disliked so much come to my rescue? "Thanks, Peg. I needed that. Friends?"

"Brother and sister." She hugs me again.

As I absorb her love, the ice in my veins begins melting. *Oh, Helper, where are You?*

"

Apparently, my soul's ready to begin the search it gave up.

We walk down the hallway toward our next class. I'd taken the coin the man had given me out of my locker, sticking it in my pocket.

"Maybe you'd like to go with me to see our grandfather Marks?" She tucks her books to her chest and scuffles alongside me. "He's nice, not like Dale. He hasn't seen you or your brother and sister, at least close-up, since you were born, so he'd like it. You could come after school, maybe. We can give you a ride, maybe for a minute or two?"

Her smile's amazing. I've never paid attention before, but Peg's pretty. I guess, when you think someone's mean or something, you paint them in an ugly sort of way. That's probably how Mom, Kayleigh, and Lily paint me now.

A voice inside says, *"Step 3—it doesn't matter to me. I didn't do anything wrong."*

I nudge her shoulder. "Thanks, Pegs. For being nice and for the invite. I'd like that."

"Cool. How about you meet us at the blue Hummer after class?"

I nod, my day brightening. What would it be like to meet my other grandfather?

The brightness stays until I see Lily walking with Eric. Am I dreaming? Is this someone's twisted plot to hurt me? How can she turn off her feelings so easily?

Once, Cara told Mom the best way to get over one man is to get with another. Is that what this is?

The sight still haunts me now as I wait to meet Peg. Why's it so hard for people to believe I'd help get a cat down? Am I that bad? Do people think I'm mean? What do they think I could gain by making the story up, making the teacher look bad?

Peg scoots out front soon after the final bell, and her mother drives us toward my home. "Seriously?" I whisper as I gawk. "All these years I never knew I had a grandfather living in the same area?"

Does Mom know?

We pull up in front of a nice brick house, not nearly as big as ours, but well kept. The yellow Volkswagen in the driveway looks familiar with its black convertible top down.

Peg pats my hand and undoes her seat belt as her mom parks. Then she hurries out, and I follow her up a cement walk onto a tidy porch. I hang back while she rings the doorbell.

Mr. Marks answers the door. He blinks a few times. Then a smile crawls to his face, his arms go wide, and he steps forward and hugs me. He smells like bologna. Strange. But I accept his love and return it. I don't have any reason not to. It's not his fault Dad's a jerk. Yet, I still don't know what happened to Dad to make him so bad. Does Mom know?

After seeing Granddad Marks, I remember where I saw the car. He's taken pictures at a lot of the neighborhood events and sports teams. He must be a photographer.

I step into his home, then nearly trip. Everywhere I look are pictures of my family, including Mom. They span my lifetime from the time I was old enough to go outside. Abbie's are there too.

Since I'm grounded, I gotta keep our visit short. He won't have time to explain things. But the pictures and his hug tell me one person loves me unconditionally—at least for now.

"Can I get you kids lemonade or something?" he asks.

Man, I'd love that! I shake my head. "I have to hurry home now, but I'll stop by again. Maybe we can talk then if you want?"

"I'd like that very much." He scoops me into another tight hug, holding me like I was the most precious thing in the world. Bologna aside, it feels nice.

Peg and I run and jump back in the Hummer. Then her mom drives me home. I don't know where her brother is, and I don't ask. A peace rests on me, for now. "Thanks, Peg. I appreciate it." I unbuckle and reach for the door handle before spinning back to her. "We'll talk tomorrow, okay?"

"Sure. Granddad was happy to see you. I hope we can all get together soon. I'm afraid he doesn't have much time left." She waves as I step out. Then her mom drives off.

We'd passed Chris on the way home. I duck inside, hoping he

won't know I rode home with Peg. Just what did she mean by "he doesn't have much time left"?

I clomp upstairs as instructed. In our room, I grab my journal. I haven't written much lately, but I gotta write about today, my much-needed break from being fingered as a bad boy.

Dear Journal,

For the first time, I met my dad's dad, Grandfather Marks. Thanks to Peg, someone I never considered a friend or stepsister. Somehow, because of—or despite—everything happening to us, we've become friends, family. I like it.

Then that familiar voice grates me. *"Step 4—replace those who hurt you with those you won't let get close enough."*

I won't be going to the window or the tree house. Lily has moved on, and so will I. My heart's crushed, betrayed. No love remains for her. Or so I lie to myself, trying hard to believe it.

CHAPTER THIRTY

THURSDAY MORNING COMES WITH A THUD. I wake to find Chris playing with my special coin. He flips it and lets it flop to the ground, scoops it up, and drops it again.

"Stop that. Give it to me." I spring out of bed. Great. Before I even have my feet on the floor, the morning's starting off wrong. Plus, I must have slept on my neck wrong.

"Where'd you get this? It looks like some kind of token." He turns the coin over and over, reading the inscriptions, feeling the weight.

"From the man you said didn't exist, at the house that didn't exist, getting the cat that didn't exist from the tree that doesn't exist. Now— Give. It. Back."

My anger must've been more than enough to make him comply. Normally, he wouldn't have. I guess my coldness toward him has become apparent. I won't ever give him a chance to hurt me again.

"Step 5—complete the process."

I bite my tongue to keep from telling the voice to shut up. Instead, I take the coin and dress, not speaking to it or Chris. Then I go to the bathroom to get ready for school. Someone knocks. "I'll be out in a minute." I finish combing my hair and brush my teeth before opening the door.

Mom frowns. Her eyes are even redder, the circles under them darker. "What has happened to you? It's like you've become someone else, someone I didn't think my sweet son could ever become."

I don't say anything. There's nothing to say.

"Step 6—move on."

She hugs me, but I stay cold and unresponsive, simply standing, arms limp. I hurt so badly. I hadn't done anything wrong. I guess I've followed the voice.

"Okay." Her lips quiver. "If this is how you want it, this is how it will be." She heads to her room. I hear a sob.

But I can't move. Every fiber of my being shakes in agony. How did it get this far? Should I take responsibility for something I didn't do or trash my entire life? My soul screams for the Helper.

"Shut up, soul," the ugly voice says. "There is no Helper!"

I'm still frozen when Chris pushes by me, almost knocking me down, never mind the turmoil inside me. He doesn't care, but this is all his fault. Abbie comes down the hallway, then stops, and gawks as I have an internal meltdown—good versus evil, light versus darkness, an all-out war wages inside me, my soul and life hanging in the balance.

Instead of attacking me, Abbie does what I need the most. She hugs me and hands me Riley. I haven't held him for three days, part of the grounding. It helps some, but I can't stand here forever. More attacks await me, and I know it.

"Put that dog down." Mom half shouts, half growls, coming out of her bedroom. "You're grounded from all friends, and that includes Riley. You know better. What has gotten into you?"

Yep, now Mom's my worst enemy, something I'd never have given any odds on four days earlier. It's like a switch has been turned off.

I bend over and drop Riley to his feet.

"Mom, it's my fault." Abbie jitters from foot to foot. "I thought he could use some cheering up."

Great. Now, Abbie's gonna be in trouble too. Yet, I stand there unable to speak or move, my only advocate now being attacked.

"Well... don't let it happen again. He's got to face up to his mistakes." Mom walks by me, now colder than an icebox. "Get ready for school!" Down the steps, she goes.

Coming down the steps, I hear muffled voices as Mom talks to Abbie and Chris. She stops when I enter the room. She goes over to the counter, her back toward me. So I leave, no goodbye, no nothing. The door slams behind me.

I begin finding more and more effective ways to burn bridges to those I love. Why do they keep setting me up for failure? It never was like this in the past. Instead, Mom even gave me Riley to comfort me, after refusing to let us have a pet all our lives. But taking him away—that was going too far. He'd never mean the same to me again. I'd make sure of it. I wouldn't be hurt that way again.

"Now you're talking," the voice cheers.

I take off running. I don't want anyone to see me like this, hurting so bad. "I haven't done anything wrong!"

I don't go to school. I head to my grandfather's house. I don't know why. At first, I sit on his steps. Then getting hungry around ten o'clock, I knock.

In a few moments, he opens the door, eyes me, then looks around as if to see if anyone came with me. "Nick, aren't you supposed to be in school?"

The dam bursts. A wave of anxiety, frustration, and yes, tears top it, then crashes over me. I'm unable to do anything but blubber under it.

He takes me inside and leads me to the sofa. "Peg told me how got you grounded and your girlfriend broke up with you." He squeezes my shoulder and sits us both down on brown corduroy cushions. "You've been kind to Pegs. She believes you, so I'll believe you too. But that means we've got to get to the bottom of this."

Wow. Finally, I get a fair shake—unlike with Mom and Lily.

I press a hand to my leaden guts as they rumble like a rusty machine. "Granddad, I'm hungry. Can I have a cookie or something? I left home without breakfast."

He smiles a smile as big as Texas. He must've liked me calling him granddad. "Sure, son."

We spend an hour talking about the man, the cat, and the lady. Then he drives me over to the place where it all should've happened. We sit there. No matter what I want to see, this isn't the house I described.

"I've got this coin he gave me." I pull out the heavy token or coin and hand it to him. "Mom believes I found it somewhere."

"You hold on to that tight, Nick. Don't let anyone have it." He winks. "It may be the very thing that saves you."

He's right, of course. At that bit, he takes me to school. I finish the rest of the day and came out to find not only Chris but also Mom waiting. And, yep, she's steaming mad.

"Where have you been? Why weren't you in homeroom this morning or here for two of your classes? The school called me at work. Nick, this has to stop."

She's probably wishing I was never born.

"Step 7—give the pain back."

"Didn't you hear? I held up the 7-Eleven." Whoa. How'd those words find their way out of my mouth?

For the first time, Mom swats my rear, and good. Then she covers her mouth with her hands. Like me, she must realize everyone around saw that, including Lily.

I run, I run, and I run. This is more than my soul can handle. And I did nothing wrong.

Panting, I slow. I'm not just out of breath. The panting comes from something deeper—fear.

What's happening anyway? Why didn't Gramps come to my rescue? Surely, he believes in me.

Is this why some people become bad? There's no one to believe them, to love them?

No, that couldn't be it. My dad had all those things. He still became a bad man.

I have to find the Sea of Life, or else.

"Forget that stupid fairy tale!" the voice shouts this time.

Wandering the streets, I don't know what to do, skipping dinner, skipping everything. Who knew you could ignore your bodily needs when you hurt so badly inside? Guess I'm discovering a lot of things, all things I don't like. I wander around for three hours before ending up back on my newfound grandfather's steps. Mostly because I have nowhere else to go.

I don't even know where I'm going to sleep, not wanting to go any further. So, this time, I huddle against his door to stay warm, too scared, too unsure to knock.

I guess I doze off. Then a siren wakes me, and a bright light shines in my eyes. A police car's spotlight captures me leaning against the door. My grandfather comes to look as two police officers approach.

He opens the door and helps me to my feet before they reach me. "I didn't hear you knock, son." He drapes an arm over me, enveloping me in bologna aroma, and faces the officers. "It's all right, officers. This is my grandson, not an intruder. I'm afraid these old ears didn't hear him."

Whatever they say, I'm not listening. Then he takes me inside and eyes me, brow upraised, arms crossed. Guess I'd better explain.

After I do, he pats my back. "Nick, you must go home soon. This has to stop. It's gone from a simple grounding to reaching a point of no return. You've got to stop this, and now."

His words are a noose, but they're also true. I could lose my family forever. Would they even care?

CHAPTER THIRTY-ONE

WHILE I WAIT for him to dress to take me home, someone knocks at the door. The police have returned. After he talks to them, he comes and takes my hand. "Your mom called the police when you ran away. They want to take you home. You should let them." His cold fingers squeeze mine. "We'll talk soon. I love you."

I trudge to the door and leave, a police officer on each side of me like I'm some criminal. When the car pulls up in front of our house, the whole neighborhood's watching. I even glimpse Lily at her window. Great, now my humiliation's just about complete.

The officers walk me to the door, one in front, one behind. Only the handcuffs are missing.

Mom opens the door and speaks to the officers while I stand on the porch, unsure. Do I still belong here? She grabs my hand and pulls me inside, none too happy. She takes me straight to her room, shuts the door, and leans her forehead against it, her back to me. Then her body starts shaking, and sobs squeak out.

I love my mom. I don't want to see this. I did nothing wrong, but nobody believes me. Was I that bad of a person? I'd never been one to tell fibs or make things up. Why won't she believe me?

My feet scuffle side to side. I fidget, unsure of anything.

Finally, she turns around, her face tear-streaked. Her eyes tell me she's afraid too.

I stare straight ahead. I won't let my gates down. All the steps are completed, my emotional state sterile.

Then I hear the voice again, not my soul, the one that beckoned me to the river. *"This is your mother. You love her, remember? You said you never wanted to forget."*

The dam burst, but I can't cry. I simply stand there, shaking violently. Then we make eye contact. Can she see the fear in my eyes? Maybe. She hugs me, rocking back and forth. She cries. I can't.

Minutes pass.

"Nick." She sniffles, causing a long pause. "I'm sorry for hitting you at school. If I could take it back, I would, but I can't. I don't know how we got to this place, but we have to stop before we lose each other forever. I don't want to lose you. I love you and need you too much. Nick, please... talk to me."

"I didn't lie." My emotionless voice squeezes past my lips, surprising me.

"Can we forget that? This is out of control." She cups both hands on my cheeks and leans closer as if trying to look into my soul, but I think it already left.

I don't like feeling this way. Something keeps pushing it, reminding me—the steps are complete.

"You don't believe me or believe in me. How can I forget that?" The monster inside me is alive and well, fighting my every attempt and effort to love Mom back.

She slumps against the wall, studying me. Finally, she opens the door and sends me to bed. I won't want to go to bed in the same room as Chris. He made this whole thing happen. After she goes downstairs, I sit on the steps. Finally—tears come. I didn't realize I made any noise until Abbie sits beside me. She hugs me, no words. I couldn't have handled any, and somehow, she knows that. After a few minutes, she pads back to bed.

I haven't held Riley for any amount of time in four days. Oh how I miss him! He got me back on track. Now, he's being held from me. I guess I shouldn't blame Mom. My story can't be verified, but I never lied to her before. Shouldn't that count for something?

I fall asleep on the steps. Mom finds me leaning against the wall, wakes me, and guides me to my bed. But I can't sleep well. At five o'clock, a full hour before I normally get up, I go downstairs and pet Riley—just once. I don't want to get in even more trouble. Mom said I couldn't go to the tree house, so I sit on the back porch. It's cool now. Fall sometimes gets into the low thirties, so I pull my knees to my chest to stay warm.

Soon, footsteps pad down our gravel driveway. I scoot back against the house to stay in the shadow until I see who it is.

Lily holds out a blanket.

Somehow, I mumble a thanks. She looks pretty. I've missed her, but we're over.

"What is going on with you, Nick?" She stands over me. "Mom says you're turning into a troublemaker. She doesn't think it's wise for me to spend time with you. I thought you cared about me."

The blanket warms my shoulders, but her words bring a fresh chill inside. "Does it matter? Everybody thinks I'm lying, and I'm not. There's nothing I can do. I can't explain what happened other than what I said and this coin." I toss it to her. "Mom thinks I found it on the road or something. But the man I handed the cat down to gave it to me and said not to lose it. No one believes me, though, so what does it matter what I think?"

She sinks to sit beside me and turns the coin over and over in her hand, not talking.

"So how about you, Lily? I've never lied to you. You've been my best friend forever. Do you believe me?"

She keeps frowning at the coin. "I don't think you'd lie, but my mom said—"

"She thinks I'm becoming like my dad." I hug the blanket against the chill, but it's inside me now. "Mom must've told her because she feels the same way. Mom always told us we should love the people we're supposed to—love and support them. It's funny though. I don't feel any love, not from Mom and not from you. I wish you'd believe me. It would make all the rest bearable."

She gets up to leave, no hug, no nothing. "I'm sorry... I can't." She lobs the coin back to me. The sadness in her blue-blue eyes can't help us.

I lean back against the house, snuggled under the blanket. Why'd Lily bring it to me if she doesn't care? I *know* she cares. She's just doing what her mom and mine tell her to do. *Thanks, Mom.*

"I wish I was God. I'd fix things for good. Where are You, Helper?"

The summons goes unnoticed, no longer holding any power. Why should it? My soul's given up, checked out.

I toss the coin into the air. It begins to glow and spin as it climbs higher and higher. I expect it to fall back into my hand, but it keeps climbing, even faster. I scramble to my feet to catch it. Shouldn't it fall back down? It's a heavy coin. As I stretch, jumping, reaching for the coin, out of the corner of my eye, I see myself still sitting on the porch, staring upward.

The coin becomes a light, flashing brilliantly. Then the world tumbles each time the coin spins around. It becomes so dizzying I close my eyes.

After a few moments, a voice intrudes. "We're glad to see you didn't lose the coin. You can only get two or three of those in a lifetime. Well, some get more and some less—the Helper decides that. But I wouldn't want your fate to rest on a lost coin."

CHAPTER THIRTY-TWO

I OPEN my eyes to the coin man from Monday who helped me get the cat down. A glow surrounds him now. Its bright white light almost hurts my eyes. I gasp.

"You can help me! My mom thinks I'm lying about getting the cat down." I reach out for his arm to take him inside to Mom. But wait. I'm hurling through trails and streams of light at a terrifying speed.

It feels like we're standing on a plate of thick glass, the universes streaking by us.

"That's exactly what this is." He seemingly answers my thoughts. "We're going to the Sea of Life. Didn't you say you wished you were God?" He takes my arm, steadying me. "The Helper is expecting us, watching out for us like He always does."

"Who is this Helper? I hear something inside me crying out to Him sometimes, but I don't know any Helper—and who are you?"

About time I get answers, the ones Gramps wouldn't or couldn't give me.

"Surely, you remember me. From your dream? I was with Angelo." His infectious grin comforts me—at least, as much as one can be comforted with all those lights flashing by. Lights and voices.

"Where are you taking me?" The breathtaking sight dazzles—so eerie, all colors and shapes I've never seen. At times, our speed becomes so dizzying and fast that the colors seem to be pouring, almost becoming a liquid. The sounds are even more extreme—moans, laughter, and screams all combine with a roaring wind that darts in and out. I can't tell where it comes from or where it's going. It's all too weird, supernatural.

"We'll be there before you know it. Then you'll get your chance to be your own god. I'll explain everything. First, I have some things to talk to you about."

How's he doing that? Talking as calmly as if we're standing on my back porch where my body apparently now sits waiting on me?

"Nick, you've come to the point and time where you're becoming accountable for your actions—*all* your actions. You must make the right choices from here on. After all, you'll never know how long you have to set things right. You said you wished you were God. If you choose wrongly, you might think you are, and that would be sad in the end—for you, me, your mom, *and* God. He's giving you this revelation to help you understand, learn, and choose."

I guess I'll know very soon, but I still don't understand. That scares me even more. What if I decide poorly? I try to be calm, but now and again, a larger light screams by too close. Sometimes, it carries a terrifying sound—like people screaming in anguish, others more like joy.

The guy shields me from those lights. Now, they're becoming dimmer as they flash back toward earth. Their life streams are all white and black.

"We are traveling through the Sea of Glass before the throne of God, heading to the Sea of Life. Everyone who has ever been born has their beginning here. Here, all God's people come or leave through, like the darkening stars passing us by, but that's another story."

His voice is melodic, almost tangible as if I could grab onto it.

"Since you are coming into your time of accountability, it's time for you to believe or not. It's your choice. The longer you wait to believe, to decide if you want the Helper to remain in you, with you, the harder it becomes, the heavier the obstacles to faith bear on you. Tonight, you get a chance to see what being your own god will bring with it, besides eternal darkness after this life passes from you."

Shivers track over me at the darkness of those words. His countenance no longer glows quite as brightly.

"The Helper is blessing you so you can see the Father's love for you." He nods ahead, so I look. Something's far in the distance, something like a large looking glass. And we are in it.

"What's that?" I point, frightened even more. Gramps said he became scared. Well, so am I.

"Here you can see every life stream, every dream, and every death. Babies being born, and folks moving on to their final destination, each making their decisions on what to believe, as you will too."

He's even darker now, cold, almost lifeless.

I'm spooked. "What's happening to your face? The light, where did it go?"

"I might be like this for forty-eight hours after you make your changes or maybe forever. That all depends on you. I'm one of your guardians. But, if you choose not to believe, I'll be like this until the end of this age." His color's completely gone. Even the melodic tangible quality to his voice vanishes. So does his emotion. Now, he's little more than a robot.

"I don't understand. This is *my* fault?" Great! I'm getting blamed again.

"Nick, it's not your fault. It's simply the way it is. My honor has been to care for you and look over you since you were born. I was forever before the Father's throne. That's where my light comes from. I soak in the Father's light, all for you. I only hope we can continue our journey together, but only you can decide that."

He reaches up, holding his hand out. We stop moving, and then I'm standing on the Sea of Glass. An amazing throne towers not far away. With it so massive, I'm little more than a tiny bug, inestimably small.

"Do you see the lights coming from everyone? Those are the life streams they have chosen. The clear streams are to children who haven't come to the accountable place yet. The red-black streams are those who decided to believe. They have redemption connected to them forever. The red stream carries life and forgiveness to the people. The black stream carries hate, crime, and death from each person back to the cross. See? There, it is." He points to a wooden cross. Someone's there on it, their streams flowing freely. "It's a transfusion of love."

That seems cruel, hard, and real. I have to look away.

"It's okay, Nick. He chose to be there, He chose you, and now that you know, He asks you to choose Him." He smiles in his first show of emotion in minutes. I guess even darkness can't stop the love from flowing from the old wooden cross like the one in the church skit.

"What about the white and black lights? What are they?" Thousands of them lead to one of the lights getting ready to leave. Amazingly, it isn't as bright as those arriving.

"Those streams don't carry any light, even though their colors are lighter than the life-giving lines from the cross. Instead, they deceive people, eventually taking away all their light. Those are the people who chose not to believe, who want to be their own god. Their line comes from the accuser. He fills them with a false light through the white streamer. But their black streamer is hatred, and it doesn't flow to the cross of forgiveness. Instead, it flows to them from their accuser. It makes them insensitive to God, to love, and to good, eventually. Some may still come to believe, but the longer they wait, as I told you, the darker they become. Like the father of lies."

"Father of lies, is that Dale, my father? Is he the father of lies?" I want to know everything. I have a big decision to make, changes to take care of, and I dare not mess it up.

"Your accuser is the father of lies, not Dale. Thankfully, the accuser's days are numbered. But when his fall comes, those with the white and black light streams will fall with him. That's forever, Nick —forever without hope, peace, and above all, without love, without God."

CHAPTER THIRTY-THREE

WE'VE TALKED FOR HOURS, or so it seems. Now, my time has come.

"I want to warn you." He touches my arm. "If you make any changes and it doesn't work out the way you thought it would, you only have forty-eight hours to change it back or change it to something else. Once the forty-eight hours are over, you won't be able to switch it back or change anything around. You will have chosen to be your own god. He allows everyone to make their own decisions, but as your own god, you must live with those decisions. If you make your changes, you—and only you—will be responsible for any cost due at the end of the age."

Those words in that robotic voice sound so final, daunting!

"The coin you have will become a timer. It starts counting down as soon as you pull this lever to make the changes you choose. Be careful. Many have chosen to be their own god. Most can't get back to reverse their decisions—not after they've gone too far." He turns and slowly disappears into the distance. But one last set of words reaches me first. "I hope to see you again. It has been an honor and privilege."

Mom has always taken us to church. I know a lot of the things Pastor talks about. Yes, some had hurt me. Still, I remember one particular story, or at least the punch line. It went something like "I set before you life and death." Now it comes back to me, inside me somewhere. That's scary. Even scarier are all the streams. Only a portion have the red-and-black streams coming from the place the coin man mentioned—Calvary.

He instructed me on how to find the things I want to change. So I won't waste any time. I have to find my dad and trace his timeline back to his point of no return. If I can fix him, I can have a normal life, and Mom can have her husband back. Life will be perfect then.

Even though I know how to find Dad, sorting through billions and billions of lives and streaming lights becomes a daunting task. It sure takes time. No wonder the world needs God. This is too complex, even for only saving my dad, much less the world. I keep at it, seemingly for hours, though that can't be true. I find his life stream —all white and black like I thought and entwined with hundreds of thousands of other lights the same color. One stream wrapped around his when he was in his early twenties. It's a deep dark red-and-black line. Out of it comes three other streamers, all clear black. A voice in my spirit says this is Mom and us kids.

I see the day Mom marries Dad. It should've been great. Instead, Mom cried for hours on her honeymoon after finding out a burden had been placed on him and he couldn't—or wouldn't try to—shake it. Dad's stream was white-black at that point.

I go further down Dad's timeline until it changes to clear black, the beginning of the time of his accountability. I give a mental fist-pump. Now I'm getting close!

The Sea of Life allows me to slow down the timeline and watch Dad's major decisions and the things causing his choices. I pause at the day Chris and I were born. Mom's so happy, but Dad's irate and even meaner toward her. She cowers in a corner after coming home with us, and then—he hits her.

I grind my teeth. I must continue on. So I do. Until the Sea stops at a place where he was young, only eleven. His dad beat him badly— to the point of bleeding. His dad had the same white-black stream attached to him. That's when my dad's streamer became white-black. It remains that way today.

But wait. This isn't the first time. It's only one of many beatings he received, his dad becoming crazed.

I shiver when I see his mother leave their home. He's only nine, and she goes, unable to cope with the beatings, leaving Dad behind to endure it all. Alone. What if my mom had done that to us?

Maybe if I stop these beatings, Dad's light stream will turn, and everything will be better. Mom and Dad won't be divorced, and I'd have my dad.

I pull the lever.

The glass floor begins to shake, cracking into chunks. Wave after wave rocks the heavens. All the streamers move—the liquid colors change and pour—more being added, many being erased. Then the glass welds together again. My changes are done.

The glass stiffens under me, freezing solid.

Everything in me jitters as if rent in pieces like the glass was. But I have forty-eight hours to undo anything that went wrong. I shiver, feeling like a weight has been dropped on my shoulders.

I fall back down to join my body. Super weird. I fall through the liquid light again, the sounds far more disturbing this time, no one with me to shield me now. I guess I'm in a light that's going dark, heading back to the porch. Somewhere inside myself, a voice cries out.

Is it the Helper?

"Nick, this is your test. I'll never harm you but work all things to prepare you. Remember you have O'Hanahan blood and a great life ahead. Nothing great ever comes easy, so you have to be tested to prepare you for that greatness. I will always be with you until you choose otherwise. But remember what your brother told you—not choosing is choosing."

Then the voice falls silent. Actually, it feels more like it leaves.

The last thing Coin Man told me rushes through my head again: "Don't expect your feelings to be the same. When you become your own god, you remove certain loves from your heart. The Helper can't help you. You will have total accountability for all your actions. Don't act rash, or you'll lose control."

He said more, something about knowing I was right and I did nothing wrong. "But remember how you said you never wanted to forget your family's love, how they've supported you? Yet, you've chosen to forget, to forget how much love you've had in your life, simply because you were right. It's not too late—not yet. But the time's coming. If you don't choose to remember and forgive them, you might lose everything."

He'd gone on then, saying there's more to life and eternity than being right. There was forgiveness and love. "If you never forgive others who hurt you when you're right, you'll be alone sooner or later without their love and without hope."

I heard all this in my spirit, somewhere deep inside, before a coldness settled in. I wasn't sure at the time, but I almost suspected... my life stream became white-black as soon as I pulled the lever, choosing to be my own god. Everything would—*had*—changed.

My spirit returns to my body, but it feels different. Like a piece of sand's between my body and soul. I feel mean, maybe because of the sand or whatever it is.

Then the coin tumbles toward me. It flips over and over until it hits my hand. The numbers 47:59:45 flash on one side, ticking down. I must've fallen for fifteen seconds, through all eternity, to get back home. The other side has the words *admission void*.

A chill slithers up my spine. What does *that* mean?

CHAPTER THIRTY-FOUR

I TOSS the coin back into the air, already ready to undo my choices. This time, it falls harmlessly back into my hand. What have I gotten myself into? Tired, I huddle against the house. I can't find the blanket Lily gave me, but I fall asleep anyway.

Until a rough man's voice wakes me. Dad—easy to recognize after prowling through his life streams—hovers over me. "Are you going to sleep all day?" He smacks my face twice, shouting curse words. "Get downstairs, now!"

He leaves.

I press a hand to my stinging face. I'm not on the porch. And this isn't my bedroom. Where's Chris? He must already be up. I dress and hurry down to the kitchen and join Mom and Chris. Dad's already left for work. But... are those bruises on them?

I grab a banana. "Abbie's going to be late to school if she doesn't hurry."

Mom's not acting anything like herself. Her shoulders hunch in on herself, and her head seems ducked in permanent submission. But when she peeps up at me, her eyes blaze. "Who is Abbie?" she mouths. "Did you do something stupid again, Nick? Don't you dare bring trouble on us, you hear?"

When I saw the lights, Mom's was red-black. How'd she get this mean?

And what's she mean by asking who Abbie is? "Abbie, your daughter, my sister. *Ab–bie*."

Chris gawks at me as dumbfounded as Mom.

"Have you been next door with those wild boys again? I told you to stay away from them. They're mean, troublemakers. If you aren't careful, you'll be one too, and I don't have a daughter." Mom rubs her forehead, eyes closed. This isn't the happy, fun-loving Mom I know, the one who raised me. She's frowning, probably wondering where that came from. She slumps forward at the table, chin braced in her hand, curlers bobbing with her movement.

"Mom, aren't you going to be late for work? You're not dressed yet."

She's just sitting there in an old faded yellow robe. Or at least it might've been yellow. The dark circles under hers and Chris's eyes tell me something's very different now, very wrong. Gone are Mom's khakis and shoes that sounded like clackers.

"Work? You *have* been next door. You know your dad doesn't allow me out of the house alone. Are you all right?" I don't hear any love in her question, nor feel any in my thoughts about her. It's like a vacuum sucked my guts out. If I hadn't known Abbie and that I was the one who changed things, I might've been like everyone else. Dad beat the love out of Mom, Chris too. Coin Man warned me. I didn't know about it at the time, but now I know it. Hate is ugly.

"Are we going to Gramps's this weekend, Mom? I gotta talk to him."

Chris jolts, scowling at me.

Mom comes over and puts her hand on my forehead, checking to see if I have a temperature.

"What has gotten into you? Do you feel okay?" She studies me for rashes and bumps on my head. Maybe thinking Dad did more than just smack me around this morning.

"I'm fine. I need to talk to Gramps. That's all." What's the big deal? They reacted like I broke a glass or something.

"We haven't seen your gramps for more than fourteen years, and *now* you want to go talk to him?" Her face twists. "Why?"

Things inside me are also twisting up. I can't imagine Mom not going to see her mom and dad.

I didn't know what to say. For sure, I messed things up. Gramps lives more than ten miles away. If they still even live in the same house. The way things changed, I can't be sure about anything. What about Lily? Does she still live next door? I'm too scared to ask. Mom might become even more suspicious. I'll interrogate Chris when we walk to school. He'll help me.

"Chris?" I nudge him. "Are you ready for school? We'd better hurry. We don't want to be late."

When I get up, Mom grips my shoulder, stopping me in my tracks. "What has gotten into you? Stop this nonsense right now. We'll start your studies like always at ten o'clock. Now sit down and eat your breakfast before your oatmeal gets cold." She slides the bowl closer to me. I hate oatmeal, but I didn't dare buck again. I glimpse two small desks with laptops and notebook paper. So that must be our school.

I slide the coin out of my pocket and grip it under the table. The counter's ticking down. Only forty-six and a half hours remain. I gotta find a way out of the house. But how? They've got the place locked down tight like a prison, and now, Mom'll be watching me even closer, making sure I don't hang out with the neighbors.

As ten o'clock comes, Mom tells us to open our laptops and begin the day's lessons. We work until twelve thirty, stop for lunch, start again afterward, and work until four.

Mom yawns. "You can go outside now. But, Nick, you be sure to stay away from the boys next door. You go play or whatever until Dad gets home at five thirty."

By now, there'll only be thirty-seven hours left on the ticker. I gotta come up with a plan, and soon. I head out back to go up into the tree house and concoct a plan. Only it isn't there.

What have I done?

CHAPTER THIRTY-FIVE

I SPRINT next door to Lily's house. Her mom hasn't gotten home yet. I try to get her to come out, but she shakes her head, looking at me through the window. I hadn't considered the effect Dad living at home would have on Mom's friendships or her relationship with other parents. Dad managed to sever or prevent them all, forcing her to homeschool us, isolating all of us. Homeschooling seems the only thing remotely Christian in our lives, and he means to keep us that way—hidden away from family, friends, church, and God.

Oh, Helper, why did You let me do this?

The soul-deep silent scream bounces back, hollow. There isn't a helper with me anymore. I'm my own god now.

Confused and desperate, I must take action before this becomes our reality forever. Worse, before I never see Abbie again. I search out my old bicycle and unearth it from a blue tarp out behind the carport. Good thing, it hasn't changed too. The tires are almost flat, and it probably hasn't been ridden in quite a while. Still, it's all I have, and I've got to get going. I must get to Gramps's house. He's the only one who can help me now.

Chris must be in the house, so I rummage through the carport for anything to help and find Dad's portable air pump. I don't dare plug it in until I'm far away from the house. It'll be loud and draw Mom's attention. I'll see if I can plug it in at the convenience store, maybe a quarter of a mile away.

Riding the bike's out of the question. With the tires so low, they might burst off their rims. I can't chance that.

The wind picks up, a cold front coming in. Soon, it'll bring rain, an icy October rain. After laying the bike against the house and hiding the pump underneath it, I hurry inside for another hoodie and a baseball hat. It'll be a long ride, so I head into the kitchen where Mom's making dinner. "Can I grab a snack?" After all, I'll be missing our meal. But I don't dare tell her *that*.

She frowns at me, then slaps together three peanut butter crackers and wraps them in a paper towel. "Take them outside and don't get any crumbs in the house. We don't want to make your dad angry again."

Happy to oblige, I grab a water bottle along the way, then hug her. "Mom, I love you." As I turn to leave, I catch a look I'll never forget. Telling her I loved her took her by surprise, giving her immense joy. Apparently, even in the harshest of circumstances, love can change things—for good.

I shoot a glance into the living room as I leave. It's nothing like our lives without Dad. Here, there's no open show of love. The house is dimly lit, the curtains and blinds drawn tight. It's repugnant compared to what was. Gramps was right. Mom is a fighter and a great mom. Even when she makes mistakes, she admits them. Living with Dad wasn't a picnic, just like Gramps said.

Outside, the wind blows at me, hard and steady. Leaves tumble around as the heavier, cooler moist air moves in. I push the bike as fast as I can, going by Lily's house. Eric's car's parked out front, and she's sitting on her porch swing. I almost can't see them with how Kayleigh's wisteria hides their front porch. In the spring and summer, the blueish blossoms droop down like bunches of grapes. Lily doesn't look happy. I wave, but she won't wave back, only a cold stare returned.

How could changing just the one thing in dad's childhood effect the entire neighborhood, not to mention Mom's relationship with her family?

Apparently, hate's an ugly thing, something I'm coming to understand. I have to get back. I have to fix this and stop playing god.

Now I know I need to be more restrained, at least until I get things changed back to normal. I need a low profile to keep from becoming suspicious. The convenience store on the corner below our house has an electrical outlet on its outside wall. I pray under my breath, asking that the compressor works and the tires hold the air. It springs to life and soon inflates my tires. I hide the pump under a shrub and take off riding, thanking the Helper. Why? I don't know. He left, hasn't He?

Time rolls by. In my mind, I picture how the Sea of Glass froze again, and with each passing minute, I know it's becoming even more fixed. At first, I struggle to pedal the bike with the chain so stiff and the wheel hubs so rusty. But soon, they spin freely, becoming easier to power.

I pass the grocery store on Main Street. After turning left, barely a moment goes by before I see my dad on his way home. He sees me too and hits his brakes. He tries to turn around in the middle of the street and come after me. Good thing traffic's heavy, and he can't make a U-turn.

Still, I glimpse how fast rage came upon his face. I ride behind a house while he turns around. *Please, please, please, don't let him see where I went!*

If he does, I'll be in for it. Mom and Chris will get it too. Worse—all hopes of getting to Gramps and resetting the timeline will be gone.

Oh, Abbie, I'm so sorry!

Peering around the corner of the house, shaking, scared almost to death, I watch his gold Charger prowl past, engine roaring like a race car. The cars behind him wait as he cruises by extra slow. My heart beats wildly, like a stallion on the open range running for its life, nearly mirroring the engine's rumble.

It's begun getting dark, so I eat the peanut butter crackers Mom made me.

Eventually, our car comes by again and turns toward home. What a reprieve. Plus, the crackers calmed my nerves and quieted my rumbling belly. I start out again after about five minutes, getting up the nerve. Only this time, I ride one block off Main Street, hoping not to be seen again.

Maybe he went home, maybe not. Either way, he'll beat Mom again and maybe Chris too.

"Why—*how*—did I think I could be God? Look what I've done!"

Hot tears mix with the cold steady sprinkle falling, streaming together down my cheeks. This is *not* going to become our reality. No matter what I have to do or what I have to give.

CHAPTER THIRTY-SIX

I DIDN'T REALIZE, though, how long the ride would be or what obstacles or who might lie in my way. I've never even been past the corner convenience store outside of my dad's car or ridden my bike in the dark of night, much less in a strange neighborhood. What makes me think I can pull this off? Is this part of my playing god?

The neighborhood becomes darker in more ways than I could've imagined. And harsher. Nightfall slides in with a bang, a hard reality check coming with it. Shadows begin making the men sitting on darkened porches look like criminals, and the lack of light adds to the blank hopeless stares on some faces. A few might want to come after me, so I pedal faster, not knowing and not wanting to chance it.

I didn't realize the poverty of the neighborhoods here, being trapped in my own home. Had I, I might have looked for another way. Some tough-looking kids roam around. A few years of this, and all hope could vanish, I suppose.

With Halloween only weeks away, some yards and houses are already decorated for the pagan night. The trouble is, some or most of the homes are dark, not a light on inside them, but people moving around in yards and on porches make every house appear frightening, like they can't wait for the witching hour.

I pedal faster as the sprinkle morphs to a steady rain. The only money I have is the five dollars and fifty-two cents I busted out of my piggy bank to buy food and water on my journey.

I'll have to suck it up. This is all my doing. I must fix this, Helper or no Helper.

But why'd He leave me? It happened as soon as I pulled the lever to play god. Was He from God?

I must find out. Maybe it will help me believe.

The rain pounds my face hard now, pushed by a driving wind. Its coldness bites into my skin, the hoodie not enough protection. At least the hat helps, keeping the water out of my eyes. And pedaling warms my body, but it sure is slow going, riding against the wind. The downhill stretches help, but for every one of those, there's gotta be two uphill climbs. Already, my unaccustomed legs ache and throb. I didn't realize how little I rode—until now.

As I pass a McDonald's, I smell the burgers in the air. Fatigue, more than hunger, urges me to stop. I almost do. But if I eat a burger, I'll get lazy, colder, and struggle to start again. I can't risk it.

I pedal on.

Thirty-five hours remain when I make it to the Sheetz on the truck route. Having left Roanoke's city limits, I'm in Salem now, and it's seven thirty. I'd traveled a little over a mile past the restaurant, and I hadn't seen Dad again. I must be a quarter of the way, only having a crude map I made from Gramps's last-known address. Maybe I can risk a quick and much-needed break, seeking refuge from the cold, rainy night. But I won't chance sitting, in case I can't get going again.

The busy store makes it easy to blend in. I begin warming up while buying muffins, one for energy and to quiet my now angry stomach, the other for later. In the men's room, I use the hand dryer to speed up the warming process, especially on my numb hands and face. Holding the handlebars with the wind blowing the rain became almost more than I could stand.

I refill my bottle from the house with water. I'll need to conserve my money, now down to three dollars and twenty-nine cents. Who knows how long the journey will take. I'm still a long, long ways off, so I'd best stretch every penny. Since I'd never been to Gramps's in this reality, I hope they still live there.

Strange. I'd never thought about reality in that way. I was beginning to understand there were many realities, each of us living in our own perceived way, true or not, some believing, others not. Could it be that simple, belief and unbelief? Gramps once told me God reveals Himself differently and at different times to everyone.

Reluctantly, I leave, pushing on. I'd been inside for fifteen minutes, long enough for my body to warm and my legs to rest up. I head out into the cold stinging rain. Only now, it's falling much harder, the drops bigger, and it restarts the cooling process all over. I begin to shiver, pedaling with every ounce of energy I can muster. But the wind seems more determined than before to slow me.

Thinking about Abbie renews my fire to keep pedaling. The darkness grows heavier, but I won't—can't—give up. Abbie needs me.

Maybe out of sheer desperation or plain loneliness I began talking to the Helper. In my dream, before I played God, the angel Angelo told me: "He's where He always is. With you, for now."

Does that mean He would return? Even after all this nonsense?

Mom brought the three of us kids to church every week, some weeks three times. I've heard all the Bible stories and all the pastor's teachings. Some helped. Some didn't. Now—here in the cold darkness with the rain and wind beating down on me—I recall it all. Something inside keeps revealing little things from the past—nuggets whispered to my soul.

Is it possible to hear your soul? I hear mine. It feels like it's searching, calling out for help. It admits I'm too naive, too young to know. Then something inside begins comforting the worldly me, instructing me what to do and how to do it.

"Help me, God. I need You!" I cry out, not knowing where it comes from. *Please save us, Helper.*

It's like this is the last battle for my family, for my soul.

"Why did I change things? Who do I think I am?"

Only a week earlier, Mom patted my chest and told me I had a good heart and she was proud of me. Where did that boy go? She's not so proud now.

A car horn bellows, startling me.

Somehow, I must've drifted off while my internal battles raged. I veer back to the side of the road, and the car speeds by, horn still blaring.

I'd gotten lost in self-pity. If I don't focus, I'll never make it. Abbie, Chris, and Mom—our whole world depends on it. I alone changed it. I alone can undo it. Like Gramps said, I have to walk in my own shoes in this life. No one else can do it for me. I need to believe.

CHAPTER THIRTY-SEVEN

BY NINE THIRTY, I make it to another Sheetz. This one is on Salem's Main Street by the Roanoke River. With the rain pouring down and the wind blowing even harder, the cold front cuts through our valley. Cold air races down the mountains, kind of like at Gramps's house. The rain seems to be falling sideways. Why does it all have to be against the wind?

I didn't take a moment's break except for these quick stops at the Sheetz convenience stores. I stay inside until I warm up, using the hand dryer once again to speed the process, then head back out, pushing on.

Before leaving, I try my first-ever cup of coffee. The caffeine and warm liquid should help in my struggle. I try the breakfast blend, almost gagging before putting in some milk and sugar in to take the bitterness out. I won't be drinking coffee again for a while. But since I have to pay for it, I'm doctoring it up as best as possible.

If only I'd remembered Gramps's telephone number, instead of programming it into my cell phone back in my other reality. I didn't even think to see if I had a phone in this one, probably not. Dad's a control freak. Everything in our lives screams that. I'm glad my mom left him, but now I have to get back to that us, back to that brave Mom.

In Dad's life streams from the Sea of Life, his early years showed his dad beat him, sometimes brutally. Is that why he's the way he is? Mean beyond reason because there was no reason for the way his dad beat him? Grandfather Marks didn't seem like a bad man. Why did he beat Dad so cruelly? Was this something that happened to him too? What did the pastor call that, a generational curse? Was the pastor right, and if so, did it pass to me or could it?

Somewhere inside me, something is changing, growing up. I sure realize how strong Mom is. She broke free from Dad, raising three children without their father or financial support. I love her more and respect her for it. She didn't deserve my behavior. Whether I was right or wrong, I should've been kind to Mom. She sacrifices so much.

I love my mom! Why was I so foolish?

What about how I told Mom I didn't want Chris as my twin any longer? I felt cruel inside just saying it. I knew it was wrong, but I still said it. I love him too. He's a part of me, and I him. For good times or bad, we'll always be twins. I have to be kind, even when it doesn't feel good or feel right. Mom says we're always to love those we're supposed to love. I guess that means always being kind too. It'll be hard, but I'm going to try, even if it doesn't get returned.

"Helper!"

My mind rolls through memories, one by one, person by person. I didn't realize how many people love me or how many I love. When I come to Lily, my heart skips a beat. My cocoon-busting days are about over. Somehow, until Monday, I managed to have her heart. Now, I'd lost it. Our night together at the homecoming was supposed to be our first actual date. Instead, she's going with Eric of all people. I only hope I'm not going to mess this up with her.

Gramps always led me to the right path in my other reality. Will he have the same wisdom in this one? Will he care enough to help me? This me has never been to his house before. Why do I think he'll help?

Great. For every positive thought, another opposite pops into my mind, like a matching set.

By playing god, had I given my mortal enemy access to my thoughts? If so, he isn't wasting it. He knows every button to push and each thought to crush.

Once, the pastor said, "There's nothing new under the sun."

I didn't know at the time, but I guess, people are going to be people, each of us with our insecurities and problems. My enemy simply knows mine.

Maybe I should turn around and go home, leave things the way they are. Something or someone reminds me how tired and achy my legs and body have become, saying I should nap or something.

Soon hatred burns inside me, toward him, toward the world, even toward life. Each time I'm ready to give in, though, the Helper gives me just enough encouragement to continue. That's when I know I must fight this battle the rest of the night until I change things.

Every scenario plays out in my mind as the pedaling becomes harder and harder. Memories of Abbie roll through my mind. My legs ache. The wind won't ease. I have to take a break. With my adrenaline empty, my legs start to cramp. Cold, wet, and starving, I stop under a bridge to eat the other muffin. Is my self-pity or the pain in my aching legs mixed with the cold rain and falling temperature draining me?

The wind whistles off a nearby street sign, stirring empty packages and leaves, making it feel much worse. I lower myself to the cold concrete, then freeze at a growl.

It gets louder, coming closer. I can't see what's lurking in the shadow, but my heart tightens. I brace for an attack.

Hoping for the best, I throw the muffin toward the growl. I see a reflex in the shadow. Then something bangs like a gun fired. The animal runs the other way, whimpering, leaving my muffin. And I pivot toward to where the shot came from.

Steps approach me.

CHAPTER THIRTY-EIGHT

"YOU SHOULDN'T BE OUT HERE in this weather all alone. Besides, isn't the timer still ticking?" The intruder enters the light. It reveals his pants, then a robe, and finally his face. "Do you believe yet, Nick? What's it going to take to win you over?"

His cloak flaps in the wind, but he isn't fazed or distracted.

I thought it was my guardian. I'd never seen him before, but Coin Man described him, said the Helper would send him when my time had come. If he's here now, this must be my time.

"What's your name? Who sent you?" I gotta know this is the real one. I've been warned. Coin Man said my enemy will do anything, even fake being the Helper, whatever it takes to stop me.

"I'm Angelo. Your grandfather sent me to bring you to his house. We must hurry. There mustn't be much time left." He holds out his hand. It isn't normal looking, and he doesn't look like the Angelo from my dream.

"First, I need to rest. I'm tired. The Helper will be here with me. Thank you for taking care of the animal."

Did he *bring* the animal? Was it my enemy's creation to get into my comfort zone? The enemy of my soul is reaching for me. I can feel it. Is this him?

When I mention the Helper, he slips out the other side. I hear my lips whisper, "Thank You, Helper."

It's time for me to believe. The enemy is right on that. Either I take that stand and believe, or I could lose all, my soul included.

"The pastor was right," I say aloud. "'Bring up a child in the way he should go, and he will return to it.'"

Just like that, my cocoon finally busts. I pray, asking for God's help, for Him to save me.

I don't know what to expect. I've always been told angels rejoice over every saved soul. But I don't see anything. Everything is the same, except me. And this new confidence in something other than myself.

I'm still scared, and I don't know what the Helper wants of me. But under the bridge—alone—I've never felt more love.

Picking up the muffin, I dust it off. Should I eat it? Hunger pushes me. I can't be fussy. I need the energy and strength to push on. I take a big bite.

More eyes are watching me. I *feel* it. Then comes a low growl, then more growling, then a whimper. It's over. The enemy runs off after trying the same test again. I don't know why he leaves, other than something in a name.

My energy renewed somewhat, I check the coin. With where the countdown is, it must be half past midnight. The ticker's winding down, furiously now. I still have a long way to go with only thirty and a half hours remaining.

I climb back on the bicycle, but the back tire's flat. Something slit its sidewall. Maybe it was dry rot, maybe not. No matter what damaged the tire, I can't ride it, and that's that. I begin my walk, leaving the bike under the bridge. There's just a couple of miles left. How difficult can that be? I know about my help now.

I think about Abbie, about our life together, about how much she means to me. Sure, we've had some arguments. What siblings haven't? But she's my baby sister, and her heart is as pure as gold. Think of how she handed me Riley after Mom had grounded me, even telling Mom it was her fault when Mom caught me holding him.

"I have to get back. I have to change things back!"

Does the Helper hear me?

Ever since I can remember, Mom taught Chris and me to be Abbie's protector. She's our only sister, and according to Mom, she needs our love and help to become the woman she can be someday. Now I let her down. If I don't get back, I'll never see her again, and worse, Mom will never get to hold her little girl. How I ache thinking about it.

I will get back or die trying.

People often say God told them this or that. Tonight, I hear nothing. The only thing I have is my belief, but what if my beliefs aren't real? What if I don't actually believe? How can you *know*? It felt real, but now... I can't be certain. I feel like I believed, but nothing is changing. If anything, the wind's blowing harder, and the rain pouring more. Things might be worse, and my legs still ache.

Walking is easier, but much slower, allowing my mind to race even more.

The Helper sent the enemy away, didn't He? Then I hear something. Not an audible sound, it comes from within, down in my body. My spirit hears someone say, *"Pick up a stone, put it in your hand, and call it faith."*

Now that feels stupid. But I do what I think I hear. I pick up a smooth, flat stone, the kind that skips good across water.

In my gut, I sense the Helper say, *"The rock of faith is useless until you throw it. Your faith is useless—unless you use it. Trust me!"*

My thoughts whirl. Could it be that easy, simply trusting? I walk quickly now, almost unaware the wind is calm and the rain a sprinkle. The clouds begin breaking up. I glimpse a star, then the moon. I'm wet and cold, but hope has found me.

Taking the rock called Faith, I squeeze my fist around it and close my eyes. I renew my hope in the Helper, in my new beliefs, and in my destiny. If I fail, it won't be because I don't believe. Thanks to the times Mom dragged us to church, the lessons come to memory as each new temptation pushes the boundaries of my imagination.

I put the rock in an imaginary slingshot of hope and shoot it at the giant each time he lies to me, over and over.

And each time, he falls in my mind.

CHAPTER THIRTY-NINE

BUT EVERY TIME one giant falls, another rises up—fast. Still, I hold tight to my new hopes and push on toward Gramps. I'm beside the river now. The deep waters roar through the lowland. The dam upstream must be opened wide, releasing excess stormwater through its channel gates. I better not need to cross the flat stones. Surely, they're a foot or two under water by now. Would there still be magic in them?

I check the coin. Only twenty-three hours remain. My trip's now taken over twelve hours, and it's almost five a.m. Why is it taking so long? It doesn't seem far riding in Mom's car. At least I can see Gramps's house now. Once I cross the small bridge, I can walk up the hill to their home. Will he let me in when he hasn't seen me in years?

After crossing the bridge, I climb the hill. Something rustles in the tall field grass and brambles beside the road. Fear jumps into my throat. Is it the foxes? Even though I didn't think they'd attack me, I'd rather not have that thought. Instead, I sight a buck. Their rut has begun, and he's active, something I hadn't seen much of.

My imagination has tortured me all night, probably more than my enemy. I squeeze the rock tight and continue uphill—which feels like a mountain. My legs, aching and cramping, refuse to carry me much further.

"Is anyone ever prepared for a journey like this?" a voice asks from behind the white oak, no swing dangles from the tree branches, but the speaker, a man, hides, halfway.

"Who are you?" I step sideways, away from him. My breath feels like steel daggers as I force oxygen into lungs burning from the uphill climb, and a cold grip seizes my heart from constant anxiety.

"The better question is who are you? I live here." He steps out from behind the tree. He's enormous, like Beast in the Disney movie.

I freeze.

Then something inside me says, *"Keep walking."*

I follow instructions, walk faster, willing myself along, half dragging my legs.

Then comes another voice. This time, it's feminine. "Hey, Nick, stop walking away. Let's have that first kiss."

Huh? That sounds like Lily. But it can't be, can it?

I peer over my shoulder. I might see Lily, but my eyes blur.

I fall....

When I recover after what must've been a couple of minutes, a dog barks in the distance. My head pounds, and chills shake me to my core. How long was I out, exhaustion having its way?

Getting to my feet, albeit slowly, I sight Butch behind his doghouse.

He barks more like a deep-throated howl than a bark. He barks again, getting up and rushing me.

Funny, I've never seen Butch as a guard dog, but here, he is.

"Shh, Butch. You're going to wake everyone up. Quiet, boy." I kneel, showing him I'm his friend, not his foe.

He doesn't bark again. He even slows and stops after hearing his name.

I reach and pat his head. His glossy eyes inspect me, unsure, but he keeps quiet. Good. I don't want to wake them, not until the sun rises.

After the storm finished pushing through, the temperature

dropped dangerously fast and has been nearly twenty-five degrees cooler for hours now. I need shelter and fast. It'll be near freezing soon, and in these wet clothes, that can't be good. I pull on the shed door. It swings open freely. Inside, I search for the sackcloth Gramps stores to cover his crops in early spring and save them from a late frost. I find the lantern we often use while sitting on the old bench. At least Gramps hasn't changed his habits.

Bundled in the cloth, I sleep in an old rocker that used to inhabit their front porch. Now, it's worn and ready for the scrap heap, but far better than sleeping on the cold dirt floor.

I've never hurt more. My legs couldn't have taken another step, though cold causes most of my pain now. After I pile on five large blanket-sized sackcloths, warmth still doesn't come. I might have a burning fever.

Still, I fall asleep as soon as I sit. It's restless, though. The feverlike symptoms keep me shivering, my mind running wild. Maybe because the clock's ticking or because I'm too tired or because it's outright cold now.

Around ten in the morning, a car door slams. Yikes! Otherwise, I may have slept the whole day. I jump up only to see their car pulling away, both Granny and Gramps inside. The coin's ticking off the time. Only eighteen hours remain.

I gotta get going.

I can see my breath in the sunlight streaming through dirt-stained windows, even my shadow on the floor appears frail. Shivering uncontrollably, I can't warm up in the shed. I must get inside the house, even if I have to break a window or something.

Their house has the windows with those small glass panes interlocked into a larger setting. I could break one and reach through to open the window. After poking and prodding every door and window, I remember their old bulkhead basement door can't lock. If he hasn't fixed it...

I run as fast as I can, limping, half dragging my feet and legs, then step behind Granny's large azaleas hiding the bulkhead. Sure enough, the same old rusted and wobbly doors secure their basement, or not. Gramps called it his escape hatch when we were little and often sneaked out through it before Granny could put him to work in the house.

How great that not much had changed here, Granny and Gramps as predictable as the morning sun.

I scramble and shuffle down the steps and shut the doors behind me. They're loud and squeaky, but no one's home to bother. I make it to the parlor before collapsing on Granny's sofa and curling up under a quilt she's working on. I can smell her familiar perfume, all sweet with a hint of flowers. One of my favorite fragrances in the world.

Sleep overtakes me once my body begins to warm. Then I hear the door opening. Yikes, it's been almost *eight* hours?

I don't want to startle them, so I slide down on the floor to hide. Not sure why I think that'll help.

Granny comes in, sees me, and screams.

I hold up my hands and push myself up from the floor.

Gramps runs in, then gasps. "Helen, it's Nickie!"

He comes over and helps me up. He squeezes me as tight as ever, then kisses my face and forehead.

"Oh my!" Granny bustles over too. It's the most love I'd felt in days.

Telling the story and then having them believe it is unlikely, but so's my being here. I've never been to their home that they knew, and yet I made it all the way across the valley. Maybe that's enough.

Then I see pictures of Chris and me, none of Abbie. Until I fix things back, she doesn't exist.

I check the coin. Only ten hours remain.

My heart seizes up. I must have been visibly shaken because Gramps takes me into his arms. I'm blubbering, the excitement and danger rendering me almost speechless.

Someway, somehow, almost forty hours have slipped by. I still have to find my way back. Only the Helper can get me back, but He's been quiet since I began to believe and picked up the stone named Faith. What am I going to do?

"The Sea of Life, Gramps. How can I get back to the Sea of Life?" I beg, my arms and hands speaking just as fast.

"How do you know about the Sea of Life?" He furrows his brow.

Right. He's never told me or anyone, that he knows of. I'm gonna have to explain.

"Gramps, I've been there. I've made changes. I wish I hadn't, but I *did*. I thought if I tweaked one thing on Dad's life stream, it would change things for the good. Instead, it's changed everything for the worse. Our home's a prison, and Abbie—oh, my sweet sister, Abbie! She doesn't even exist anymore. I have to get back, and I only have eight hours to put everything back to the way it was. Will you—*can* you—help me? It can't wait until morning. Our time will be up."

My pulse runs like that stallion again. Only this time it's not from a fever, but from sheer fright. How much more can my heart stand? I'm trying not to be too excited, but there's no hiding the urgency.

CHAPTER FORTY

"COME ON." He waves me to follow him and leads me out to the bench, a crazy grin on his face.

I'm not wild about going back out into the cold again. My clothes are still damp, but I'll endure whatever's needed. I must get things back to normal. I have to return to my real reality.

"Helen, I have some urgent business with our grandson. Don't wait up on me." Gramps calls over his shoulder as he takes my arm, then grabs his truck keys. Just what's he thinking?

We walk out to his old Blazer.

"No need to freeze our butts off. We've got to do some real deciphering. I'll pull the truck over beside the bench, and we'll get to it." He must know the seriousness of my situation. Maybe because he's been there. Now, I only need to find out what he did.

I never stopped to consider why in horror movies the weather and surroundings all scream out, making the scene seem even more chaotic and desperate. Guess it's that way in real life too. The elements have stirred again. Only now, there's no rain to tamp down the flying debris or quiet the wind's roar as the river below rages.

Gramps's Blazer rocks back and forth, side to side, pushed by the wind. I'm glad he's wise. I can't imagine trying to figure this out sitting on the bench.

"Nick, you have no idea how much your grandmother and I have wanted to be part of your life. But your dad wouldn't allow it. He beat your mom, and finally, she couldn't fight back. She was too scared for you and Chris. He told her he'd beat the two of you unrecognizable if she didn't obey him."

Gramps rubs a hand down his face, pulling his eyelids down with it. "I wanted to help her, but every time, it seemed to make things worse. So your granny and I watched you from a distance." The tear rolling down his cheek and his smile tell me how happy he is to see me, even in this dire situation.

A stick slams the windshield, startling us both, reminding me why we were here.

"Now... let's see." Gramps taps his steering wheel. "When you crossed the flat stones, was the water high, like now?"

"I didn't go that way. Coin Man gave me this coin." I recount the way it happened when I lunged after the coin. I shiver over looking down and seeing myself on the porch. "It was eerie."

I fiddle with the gearshift, tracing the *D* engraved on it. "After a while I came to the Sea of Life. It was just as you told me. I found Dad's and Mom's life streams, going back past the time he first beat her, thinking that would change things. Oh, was I wrong—so wrong."

More flying debris strikes us. This time a large reed blows across the windshield.

Gramps grips my jittering knee to calm me.

"Gramps, I never knew how much Dad beat Mom. He's a monster. Mom is so sweet. I've got to get back there. I've got to get her back." My hands fist, but there's nothing to fight. I cannot do this on my own. Just knowing that starts my insides quaking again.

Gramps puts his arm around me, and we sit there. He's probably thinking about the stones, the coin, and the changes I gotta undo. Then he lets out a breath and tightens his grip, squeezing my shoulder. "I've always wondered about that. I didn't know whether He revealed Himself the same way for everyone, or if it was only that way for me. You know I don't know what I've told you, but I didn't make any changes. Once I was there, I realized I couldn't be God. There were too many unknowns, and only He see's tomorrow."

Gramps wags his head side to side, eyes closed. "I guess I should have told you that. If I didn't, I don't know what I would've been thinking." His eyelids appear heavy, and his lips purse.

Easy to read regret on his face. "That's okay. You were only trying to get me to believe." I smile quick to reassure him things are good between us. "But now what? How do I get back?"

"Do you, Nick? Do you believe? Do you even understand what that means?" The Blazer's warm now, so he switches the engine off and cut the lights.

"I do now. The Helper saved me under a bridge. He told me to pick up a rock and name it Faith while holding it tight in my fist. When I did, the bad guys ran away." It was the scariest thing I'd ever seen or been part of.

"That's fantastic. Your granny and I pray for you and Chris every day and night. Sometimes, you have to hit rock bottom before you can see the mountains." His eyes renew their shine and sparkle. Guess, he's seeing his prayers being answered. "How about your mom? Does she still read her Bible?"

"If she does, it's in hiding. Dad won't let a Bible in the house. He says it brainwashes people into mindlessness." I don't know how I came to know that. It seems I'm beginning to forget my other reality and facts. Information from this one is replacing those thoughts altogether. What's gonna happen to Abbie? If I can't change things, will I even remember my sweet little sister?

"Well, we'd better get you back to the Sea of Life. Let me see that coin."

I hand it over. Only seven hours and fifteen minutes remain. "We better figure this out quickly."

Time keeps ticking away.

"Did you learn anything, Nick?" He rolls the coin around and around in his hand.

"Yes, sir. The Helper told me God has a set of rules He uses, but man, when we want to be God, we don't go by any rules, just what is good in our own eyes. I guess that's what I did. Now, look at what I've done." I swallow hard, pushing words out as raw emotion cracks up my voice. "I don't ever want to try to be God again. There can only be one God, and I'm never going to be Him."

"That's a lesson we all could use." He pats my knee. "I've tried hundreds of times to control things myself, only to find out I can't. A friend once told me he couldn't even control when he went to the bathroom, much less others in his house. Yes, that is a good lesson to hold onto." Gramps rubs a finger over the coin, frowning at it, still searching for clues. But there aren't any to find. Are there?

Wait! "Gramps, do you think my rock has the answers? He told me to name it Faith and said that, like faith needs to be used, the rock needed to be thrown—if I didn't throw it, the rock couldn't help me." I pull the smooth skipping stone out of my pocket and drop it into Gramps's palm.

"This is a nice skipping stone." He turns the rock in every direction. "Did He give this to you?"

"No, I found it. You know how—well, you will know how—I love to skip rocks across the river. I saw it lying on the ground and couldn't resist." I scoop the stone from his palm. "You don't think I should go down to the river and try skipping it now, do you?"

He studies me. "How about we pray together about it? I'll pray if you want. You exercised a lot of faith in me, what with coming all the way over here by yourself and all. We must have a special relationship for you to trust in me so much."

"We do, Gramps. I can't wait to get back there again, to where everything is good. I don't ever want to do this again, having a dad would be nice, but not the one I have." I bow my head, and Gramps prays. It seems he knows exactly what to pray for.

"Come on." He ruffles my hair. "I'll walk down to the river with you."

We tramp down the worn path to the river. The wind picks up again when we reached his garden as if trying to guard the river from us or something. A low growling rumbles like before, and chills seize my heart.

"Do you hear that growling?" I turn in a circle as I walk, watching behind us.

The giants push me even harder now.

"Nick, trust in the Helper. He won't lead you astray. Something's always trying to stop us from using our faith, our destiny. Don't pay any attention. You've got things you've got to do. We don't have much further to go." He looks around too. Maybe trying to see what causes my fear. "I don't hear any growling, so I guess there isn't anything for me to see."

We reach the river. It roars now along with the wind.

I take out the stone. It's a good stone, solid. If I throw it, I'll never see it again, and it might not work.

"That's a nice stone." Gramps winks, guessing my thoughts apparently. "But it's just a stone to throw."

I let it skip. Five times, it skims over the raging river before sinking out of sight. Nothing happens. I gawk at Gramps, and he at me.

Minutes pass.

Still, nothing happens.

"What do I do? It didn't work. How will I get back to the Sea of Life?" I clench my fist, holding onto nothing now. If only I'd held onto the stone!

We wait a while longer. Then, after looking at each other, we walk back up the hill to the house.

My fear grows deeper with every step. "What am I going to do? It didn't fix it."

"We must trust He heard our prayer and saw you throw the stone. It's up to Him now to show you the way. You can only do what He allows. But it's cold out here. Let's go inside and warm up."

He takes my arm, and we join Granny in the house. She has a pot of beef stew warming on the stove and loads us each up a big bowl.

The coin keeps ticking down the time. Now only six hours remain.

Six measly hours.
I've got to do something!

CHAPTER FORTY-ONE

SOMEHOW, even in my fear and anxiety, between my aching body and the long cold journey, with my belly full of beef stew, I fall asleep leaning against Granny. Like always, she's watching her favorite show again. The last thing I remember seeing or hearing was, "Where no man has gone before..." It's a good sound that always comforted me in the past.

The stone and prayer must've worked. I awake and see Coin Man again. He still looks lifeless, so I have to hurry.

But everything looks different, and the way to Dad's timeline is twisted now and entwined with the rest of my family. I search and search, but I can't get back to that place where I had made the change. Is it gone?

I call out to Angelo for help. Lightning flashes. Then thunder rolls in the distance. It sounds closer and closer each passing second.

Still, no Angelo. "Helper," I cry out. "What can I do to change things back to the way they were? I don't want to be God. I'll never say that again. Please, Helper—I believe in You—please help me."

I slide down onto the Sea of Glass before the throne, scared, afraid I won't make it to the place to change it in time. I'd resigned myself to this new reality, but instead, I find myself on my back porch, accosted by a ruckus. Doors slam. Angry voices scream.

Somehow, the Helper brought me back. I'm not at Gramps's house any longer. God answered Gramps's prayer. Seeing me throw the stone, for real this time, He heard my cries for forgiveness—my repentance and put everything back to the way it was.

Except me. Now I believe.

Then I hear my name called out. I slip inside the back door, carrying the blanket, *Lily's* blanket.

Abbie sees me and calls out to Mom. "He's down here, Mom." She rolls her gaze toward the ceiling. "Mom's mad. She thinks you ran off again."

I run over and hug Abbie. I missed her terribly.

"I didn't do anything. I was outside." I wasn't making good decisions, but my choices were limited.

Mom enters the kitchen. "What were you thinking? I've torn this house upside down, looking for you. Why weren't you in your room? This nonsense has to end—and I mean *now*." She stops and breathes deeply, then closes her eyes to calm herself. But her face is still beet red.

I've never seen Mom this worked up. Why's she so hostile?

"I didn't want to sleep in the room with Chris. He started this whole thing, and I don't want to be his twin anymore. On the way home, he claimed he'd get even for things in the past, and he did. So he can go find another person to be his twin." It sounds nuts coming out, but it's all I had to say. I guess I was already forgetting the lesson I'd just learned.

"Chris didn't do anything wrong. You're the troublemaker. Now stop it." Her shouting summons Abbie and Chris again. Maybe it rouses the neighbors too.

"Is that what you told Kayleigh?" I dare ask. "Lily was crying when she gave me the blanket earlier. I'm beginning to think it wasn't her decision not to go with me anymore."

"I–I didn't mean to," Mom stammers. "I was just comparing this to how your dad acted at times. I guess she decided Lily shouldn't chance it." She frowns at her shoes as one of those clackers taps the floor.

So, maybe she didn't want to compare me to Dad, but she did.

I sink into my usual chair, my heart breaking. So that's it. Mom thinks I'm going to be like Dad. She's ashamed of me.

It doesn't matter anymore. Even though I haven't done anything wrong, Mom's given up on me. I put my head down, ashamed to know she's ashamed of me. I became like Granny said the boys at the mall were, making their moms ashamed. I was no different from the boys who don't go to church.

But I *am* different now.

Mom puts her arms around me from behind the chair. I feel her shaking. I hurt so bad inside for her—and me. I never wanted to hurt her—or anyone.

Abbie sniffles in the doorway.

Chris stands there, probably gloating.

He's going to the dance, and I'm not. Lily's going too. With Eric.

Mom tells me I'm suspended for three days until Wednesday. Then she'll take me back to school and talk with the principal. She doesn't mention the grounding, so I don't ask.

Soon, I'm alone, once again. Everyone else goes on with their lives while I'm stuck in this. Mom at work, Abbie, Chris, and Lily at school, and me here. But at least I have Riley. I go through my dresser drawers, taking out things that don't fit and things I don't like anymore, just to have something to do. Then I write in my journal.

Dear Journal,

I told myself I never want to play God again, but already, I almost want to reconsider that. I guess life can be that fickle. Words can be said that aren't true, actions taken that shouldn't be, the human element.

This has been the worst week ever. Everyone thinks I'm a liar, that I'm going to be like my dad. Mom even told Kayleigh she was afraid I was turning out like him. It must be true if Mom believes it. Still, I didn't do anything wrong. I love Mom, but I hate myself. Does that make sense? Things always go wrong for me, despite my best efforts.

I know the Helper now. He fixed everything back, things I broke. I'm going to be okay one day. I have to trust Him and learn about faith. That rock must have had some power, but I need to learn how to find the Helper all the time, not just when there's trouble. Maybe He'll be someone to talk to when trouble comes. He's much wiser and knows tomorrow.

Gramps told me that was the secret to believing and really having faith, talking to Him and reading His letters of encouragement and instruction. Funny though, he said it was the Bible. I never knew that was supposed to help me. I thought it was a bunch of rules to take away all the fun. I'll give it a try, though. I need all the help I can get, especially now.

PS: I need to forgive.

CHAPTER FORTY-TWO

AROUND ONE, I go out to the tree house with Riley. He's getting so big, and his magic brand of love is as effective today as the day Gramps gave him to me. I'd vowed not to let him back into my life, not ever chancing the pain of losing him again, but I can't do it. I love him too much. Besides, he never left my heart, neither has Mom. In a way, Chris hasn't either, even though he seems to be on a mission to destroy my life.

But what about me? What about how I've been toward Mom and Chris? I cringe, soul hurt that I could turn so cold toward them, even if I was right. How could things go from being so good to this, that fast? I don't understand. I'd seen earlier how ugly hate is, like the way Dad became when he beat Mom or us kids. It's hard to believe some of that same seed began to grow in me, not because I was bad but because I chose it.

Gramps comes over a little later—to check on me, I suppose. He comes straight out to the tree house, climbs up the ladder, and pops his head in the open door.

"I knew I'd find you out here. Can I come in?" It's so good to see a smiling face again.

"Sure, Gramps." I ruffle Riley's fur, making him look funny, and chuckle.

"I see Riley is still making you smile. I heard you've had a rough week. Are you okay?" He drapes his arm over my shoulder and kisses my forehead, like the past fifteen years. His love so dependable, so needed. He doesn't say anything about the river or the stone. I guess it's just as well. But then the Helper told me I'm the only one who will ever know.

"I don't know if Mom wants me to hold him. On Monday, she said I couldn't take care of him while I was grounded." I hug my pup closer. "I didn't do anything wrong, other than being late to class—one lousy minute. Now I'm a liar and a troublemaker, and Lily doesn't want to have anything to do with me because Mom said I was becoming like my dad." Did I leave anything out?

"Whoa, slow down. Everything'll work out. Your mom called me crying this morning. She didn't mean to tell Kayleigh you were becoming like your dad. She hates that Lily won't go with you, hates it almost as much as you do." He slides his arm away and rubs his hands. His joints must be flaring up again.

My soul hurts as I then gush out how everything snowballed. At least, Gramps is understanding. I guess from a hindsight perspective everything appears much better than it does at the time.

"Your mom's gonna wipe the slate clean. You're not grounded any longer, and we want you to come stay the weekend. We'll go down to the river and fish. Then I'll take you to the overlook on the parkway where we can have some man-to-man talk. What do you say?"

"What about Chris? It's his turn to come over." I didn't want more strife with him. I trace my sneakered toe along the line of a floorboard. Years of our play wore smooth the woodgrain. Stick-men drawings of our family mark it and the walls. Mostly by Abbie's hand. She loves to draw.

"Oh, I don't think he'll mind. He's going to homecoming and will probably be too pooped Saturday morning. Your mom said him taking Monica was your idea. I doubt Chris thought things out when he got you in trouble." He pats my leg, then stands up. "I'll come by for you around ten, so pack some things for church. I love you, Nick, and I'll always believe in you. It's time you start trusting in God."

A tear wiggles free of Gramps's eyelid, and he's from a time when men didn't cry. "The abuse your mom took was heartbreaking. That's why she's scared now." He swipes the tear away. "It's not that she doesn't love or believe in you. She's more afraid of losing you. I love you, and so does your mom. You've got to meet her halfway, and you have to believe."

I reach for Gramps's arm. "I love you too. I do believe." When Riley wriggles, I plop him on the floor. "I went there... to the Sea of Life. I saw everything, how Dad beat Mom, how Grandfather Marks beat him. I'm not making excuses for him, but he didn't get much of a chance to become a good man."

Gramps blinks at me. "You found it? The Sea of Life? You were there?"

"Yes, sir. I messed everything up, but I got back in time to fix it back—just in time, thanks to the Helper." I tell Gramps everything.

"I'll *never* go back. I don't ever want to play God again." There, we can put this behind us once and for all.

"See you Saturday morning." Gramps climbs out, patting Riley's head on his way.

"Bye." I push to my feet and move to the window overlooking our yards. Somehow, I keep from looking at Lily's house. At least, the weekend will be better.

Then my phone rings. I hadn't even realized I'd brought it with me. I fumble it from my pocket and gawk at the caller ID. Whoa. Peg?

I swipe to answer.

"Nick, are you okay? What's been going on? I didn't see you in class this morning? Granddad said the police came and took you home last night. Wow, I'll bet your mom was mad." She rushes on so fast I can't get a word in. Amazing, the one person I'd never figure to be my friend still wants just that.

I slide down the wall to sit cross-legged. "I'm getting better. My mom's dad is taking me fishing Saturday. Besides Mom, I can always count on him. I don't know about Mom anymore, though. Chris fixed that." I rock my head against the wall. "I love her, and she's amazing, though. I guess she slipped up. Like me." I say it aloud so I can hear myself saying it. Something inside me—some kind of thorn—wants confrontation, not forgiveness.

"Eric is taking your girlfriend to the dance. I'll bet that makes you mad." She's still so super gushy, her voice all girlie and high pitched. "What are you going to do? Would you like to go with me? We can go stag and dance together as friends. Are you still grounded?"

I don't think anyone asked her, and everybody wants to go to the dance, especially the girls. "Okay," I hear myself say. "But I've been suspended. Do you think they'll let me in? It could be fun if they do. Can you pick me up?"

Did I just say yes? Peg is nice and pretty, even though she's my stepsister. Besides, she introduced me to my grandfather, and now my life will be better, maybe. I still haven't told Mom. I could use a friend too, who believes in me.

"We can try. All they can do is keep us out. How's eight thirty? I don't want to go to the football game, just the dance. Is that okay?"

"It's perfect. See you at eight thirty—and, Peg, thank you for being my friend." I put the phone down. How nice to have more family. I don't know her brother yet. But she's a pleasant surprise.

What will the night hold? Will I see Lily dancing with Eric?

I shudder. That will break my heart. But I'm not staying home either. I don't want to stay on this road to isolation forever. I'd better ask Mom.

CHAPTER FORTY-THREE

FRIDAY EVENING as Mom dresses to take Monica and Chris to the dance I knock on her door and edge it open when she calls to come in. She's standing by her dresser, all fancy in black slacks and her favorite brown blouse. The doorjamb steadies me as she opens her jewelry box. "I was, um, wondering if I could go to the dance tonight with my stepsister."

She drops the gold cross necklace she was fiddling with. "Are you serious? After everything you two have been through?"

At least she doesn't mention my suspension.

"Mom, this is a big night. I don't want to get upset over the past again. Do you mind if I go for a little while? We just want to dance and get to know each other as brother and sister."

She scoops up the necklace. "Okay, but how will you get there?" She threads it around her neck and fiddles with the clasp. "Cara isn't planning on driving since Lil—do you have a ride?"

"Peg's mom is going to take us if that's okay." She's still fiddling with the clasp behind her neck. I cross the room and take it from her. It's so dainty that it's hard to do even when I can see what I'm doing. How'd she think she could do it behind her neck? I step back, mission accomplished.

She puts on a shawl, then gets ready to usher the traitor, Chris, to the car. "Have fun."

Peg's mom comes right on time. She still has some bruises but looks happy. "I think it's great you two have put the past behind you." She backs the Hummer out of the driveway as I buckle up. Then her glance catches mine in the rearview before she pulls onto the street. "Your grandfather was tickled to spend time with you. He's been alone for over sixteen years. I hope you get to visit him more."

I twist in my seat to Peg beside me. "Have you ever been to a dance before?"

"A few times, but mostly in dance class." She fiddles with the pretty beads on her aqua gown, and they clatter against her cast. "Don't worry. We'll have fun. I'll show you some easy steps we can do together." Bows on her sleeves bounce when she can't sit still, and a string of blue pearls gleams around her neck, matching her earrings. I didn't even know there was such a pearl. Her green eyes sparkle in the passing lights of oncoming traffic. Seriously, why wasn't this girl asked to the dance?

"Easy sounds good. Mom tried to teach me and—well, Mom taught me a few things the other night. I hope it helps." Great. Now, my thoughts drift back to dancing with Lily. What a magical night. I guess that's what magic is all about—here today, gone tomorrow.

At the school, a line of cars waits to drop off their passengers, and the parking lot's crowded. "Wow, everyone in school must be here." I check my phone. It's around nine o'clock.

"Yeah, it was like this last year too." Her eyes get big. Her uncasted hand covers her mouth, probably hiding a smile.

Hadn't she said she'd only had lessons? "You were here last year?"

"Oh, that. I volunteered to help decorate, and all volunteers got to come. I didn't have a date." She reaches for her door.

"Please let me." I get out and go around and open her door.

"Thank you, kind sir." She curtsies to me.

Walking in, her left hand on my right arm, feels strange. She's my stepsister, so how does this work? Is it merely the act of a gentleman?

She all energy beside me, craning around. "Isn't it so cool, seeing your friends all decked out? That's why I didn't want you to miss it. It sort of shows you what's to come in just a few years." She tugs at my arm, her left hand straightening her massive curls.

The band has begun playing. Peg grabs me and hauls me along, her steps perky like she's dancing already. The large disco balls flash, casting reflections all over the gymnasium. Silver and gold streamers and glitzy banners hang everywhere.

"Did you help this year?" Most of the girls are in dazzling gowns that shimmer, and the band pumps out great tunes. This must be how all those Hollywood galas feel.

"Yes, I love it. It's like getting ready for Cinderella's ball." Peg laughs, releasing my arm and squeezing my hand. "The homecoming committee always goes all out."

No kidding. I can only nod.

Soon, we swing to the rhythm. "Wow." I try to follow her moves. "You're quite an accomplished dancer."

She beams, all aglow under the twinkly lights strung across the gym. "I've had lessons for four years."

"Hi, Peg. How's your arm," kids ask, crowding us. Apparently, she also has quite a few friends, only from a different circle from mine.

She holds up her cast, decorated with a lightweight wrap. "It's healing. I had to get me some payback. So I brought my stepbrother to the dance to punish him." She laughs, shaking her head in a teasing way again, reminding me of days earlier. Only this time, it seems it's with love, not hate.

I try to be low-key, wanting to stay in the shadows, unnoticed, but with Peg so pretty and popular—all news to me—no way can I blend in. "Peg, I just want you to know, you look beautiful."

"This is super fun. I'm glad we're here." She's able to talk now, having shown me the steps enough to stop instructing. "After I called you, Mom and I had a girls' day together, getting ready for the dance. She took me to the beauty parlor and shopping. I got the full do-over, and that wouldn't have happened if you hadn't come with me."

Her long red hair loops down her back in big, bouncing curls— probably the work of that beauty parlor. I knew she was pretty, but now, she's the talk of all the guys and a few girls too. I guess money has privileges like beautiful dresses and do-overs as Peg called it.

"You look amazing. I wish I wasn't your stepbrother right now." Whoa! How'd that slip out? My face flushes. Hers does too. Now, I have nothing left to lose. "You could have your pick of the guys here. How come you came with me?"

"Thanks, Nick. You're sweet." She swooshes a curl back over her shoulder. "Actually, I didn't have a date because the boy I used to like is with your ex. I'm glad to be rid of him. He kept trying to get me to do things I won't do. I hope Lily knows what she's in for. He's probably planning to take her outside soon." She rolls her gaze toward the door. That's when I see Eric roughly leading Lily on the dance floor.

"He wouldn't try anything to hurt her, would he?" My heart pounds, not only out of jealousy but also from fear Lily won't be able to defend herself. "I know he tried to kiss her a couple of weeks ago before Lily and I sort of got serious."

"Sure he will. He hangs out with those boys at the mall. It's all they talk about. He's not very nice—handsome, but not nice." She shivers a little. "I barely saved myself. He reminds me of Dale, you know? In it for what he can get and not caring who he hurts."

"Hey, let's forget about all that and have some fun. We all make our own decisions." I take her hand and spin her. She giggles, remembering what we were here for, which is to have fun. We dance for maybe a half hour or more before I get tired. "Would you like to take a break and get some punch?"

"Sure. Those are your friends over there, right?"

Several of my friends stand over by the refreshments.

She nudges me. "Will you introduce me to your blond friend? I'd kind of like to get to know him. He's cute."

Yep, she likes Tony, a shy, introverted kid with long blond hair and broad shoulders. A lot of the girls like him, but he's so shy he won't put himself out there.

"First, I have something to ask you about our grandfather. The other day you said you were afraid he doesn't have much time. What did you mean?" I don't want to get too deep into it. Still, curiosity gets the best of me.

"He's not well—hasn't been for years. I'll let him tell you about it, okay? Let's just have fun." She shrugs me off, walking over toward Tony with a purpose in mind, I suppose. Anyway, it obviously isn't good news.

"Sure. I'm sorry. I didn't mean to—"

She touches my arm. Her smile assures me we're good. "It's okay."

Peg's the type of girl who lets you know things up front, whether or not she's interested in you. That's what Tony needs. At least, I think so. Whatever the case, my mind's no longer on Lily. I want to forget this last week.

On our way over, Peg's brother comes in with Terri. She looks pretty too. She must've also had a do-over. I'm beginning to notice most of the girls are grown-up. I guess, maybe I'm finally getting there. Only my low self-esteem holds me back now.

Peg runs over to hug Terri, gripping Terri's waist and leaning back to take a good long look. She beams her approval, causing Terri to smile and hug her again. Some sort of magical pulse surges through me, not a romantic thing, but more like something is wakening, as if a new me is born.

Something inside me was changing. I felt different. I thought different, and I think... I want different.

Peg turns Terri and Craig loose, both looking like they've stepped off some magazine cover. Definitely intimidating. Then Peg leans in and whispers in my ear. "You're still the most handsome boy here."

She must've sensed my nosediving self-esteem.

"Thanks. You're sweet. But it doesn't have to be about me. I'm enjoying getting to know you. Come on. Let me introduce you. Tony won't pull the trigger tonight if we don't go over to him."

I grasp my stepsister's hand and lead her over. The other boys all gawk, and a few mouths drop. Seeing me with Peg was probably the last thing they expected, me too—once. She's not the type of girl I could approach if not for our history. She's from a different circle, a circle I had put up on a pedestal, thinking they were untouchable.

Tony smiles as I introduce Peg to everyone. Good, he must like her back. Seriously, though, who wouldn't? But after that, he looks more at his feet than at her. Like he's afraid he'll melt if their eyes meet.

I retrieve two glasses of red punch from a table nearby, returning to hand one to Peg.

"Tony, would you care to dance with me? It seems my date is fresh out of breath." Peg steps toward him, offering her hand.

He glances at me, so I nod my yes. It's kinda strange, but she's my sister, not my date.

"You two go ahead. I gotta rest for a while." I take the fruit punch glass back from Peg. Okay, so yeah, I'm jealous of Tony. She is a pretty girl, forward, but pretty.

Brad, a friend from church, comes over and puts his hand on my shoulder. "Sorry to hear about Lily breaking up with you. Big mistake. That Eric's a player."

"There's nothing I can do. Besides, it's not the end of the world." I think I wobble out a smile. It's hard to be upbeat when you've been punched in the gut—and secretly, you *do* think it's the end of the world.

CHAPTER FORTY-FOUR

"YEAH, well... try to have a good time," he says. "A lot of pretty girls are here without dates. You should dance with some of them." Brad slaps hands with me, the male ritual in my neighborhood, then approaches where the girls who came stag stand. They're all waiting for the opportunity to dance. Several even dance with each other. He speaks with each, then pairs off. Looks easy. I gotta give it a go. Somehow, I work my courage up on the way over, his example boosting my confidence.

"I'd never have figured you to end up here on the stag line."

I spin toward the voice. Emily, the cute little blonde down the street, smiles at me. She's holding a glass of punch.

"Hi, Emily. You look pretty. Are you having a good time? Who'd you come with?" Ugh! Dumb. Her dad's strict and wouldn't allow her to come with anyone on an actual "date."

She dips her head and closes her eyes, lips squeezed tight. Then she blinks up at me. "You know my dad. He's afraid I might 'fall in love' and get confused about my future. Like I'm going to get married on the first date." She shakes her head, sarcasm shielding her pain.

I always forget—though Emily is smart, she's attractive too. It's just not what she's known for. She's the class whiz with the best grades and all the accolades. One day, she's going to be someone important, maybe a scientist who discovers a new fuel source or a doctor who invents a vaccine.

"Would you like to dance? I'll *try* not to step on your toes." I reach for her hand, surprised when hers reaches back for mine. I glimpse Lily standing near the restrooms. I guess waiting for Eric. She's watching me with Emily. In that glance, I imagine she doesn't like me with Emily.

"I'm sure you'll dance fine. Lily told everyone how you two danced all last Friday night, your mom and hers teaching you." The disco lights flash over sequins splashed along Emily's pink gown. Her dad shouldn't have let her wear that. She looks like a movie star, her smile dazzling, her blonde hair long and flowing. How come so many beautiful girls are without dates? Whatever the reason, I'm thankful.

As pretty as Emily is, my heart broke with its glimpse of Lily. But I promised myself—I will have a good time. Soon, we're dancing alongside Peg and Tony. I'd have never thought about Emily in a million years. But here we are, and I'm glad.

"So, Nick... what happened to you? I heard you and your mom were fighting over something. I've always thought your mom was the coolest."

Emily, more than several inches shorter than me, looks intently into my eyes in a way that tells me more than I'm ready to know. She likes me more than I'd previously thought or was ready for.

"It's a long story. Somehow, my mom stopped believing in me, thanks to Chris." I try not to frown, but it isn't as easy to control as I thought.

"Sorry. I don't mean to bum you out. Forget about it." She takes my hand, spins around and around, and giggles like she just discovered something new.

Her beautiful smile is contagious, so I smile too.

A slow-dance song begins. I'm ready to walk off the floor, but Emily wraps her arms around me and flashes that smile. "Don't go."

I freeze at her desire to dance, to dance *close*. My mind stutters, all confused. But how can I resist, even though I never thought of Emily in this way? Tonight, that could all be changing. She's no longer the little girl I'd known, but a young woman, beautiful and grown. It's almost too much.

A voice inside me says, *"Be careful. There may be no way back."*

I recognize it. I have to heed it, or things might get crazy. I feel Emily rise up on her toes against me, but my eyes are closed as I enjoy our closeness and rhythm. Then she kisses me ever so softly. Without thinking, I kiss back.

"I've been wanting to do that ever since I was twelve!" she gushes. Her gaze dances to and from mine, searching, full of hopeful excitement. "But you were always glued to Lily."

"Aren't you afraid I'm a troublemaker like everyone says in our neighborhood?" I gotta cool the situation. The truth is I liked her kiss. It felt electrical, almost like playing with fire. Unlike Peg's long curly red hair, Emily's blonde hair is shiny and straight, classic looking.

"Of course not. I've known you for years. You're one of the nicest, kindest guys. Besides, sometimes we all get out of sorts. Right? You need to figure out what you want in life. That's all."

I'm not used to such a matter-of-fact approach, and she's right! I do need to decide what I want my life to be. It's time I start making decisions about me, about what I want, and about what I want to do. And those decisions need to be better than those I made in the past.

A cold stare chills me as we dance. It's gotta be Lily. I don't need to look. I keep dancing, and Emily and I move in a slow, melodic rhythm, pressed together, smiling, talking, laughing. The little girl from down the block makes me feel so good about myself, and I know she feels the same way. Her dad would never guess in a million years who his little girl was dancing with. Neither would I.

But I remember the voice. I didn't want to get too deep, too fast. I reach behind me, eyes wide open, take her hands from around me, and lead her off the dance floor. I hadn't planned it, but we walk toward Lily and Eric. Lily's eyes are like laser beams. If she could, I believe she would've cut us both in half.

I veer to the right, leading Emily to a table in the other direction.

Emily doesn't let go of my hand. What should I do? I don't want to lead her on, but Lily made it clear we were through. So why worry?

So many thoughts crowd my mind, enough to bog me down again.

Peg and Tony come over and sit with us. At least Tony looks at ease. Peg has that effect when she wants to.

"Emily, you know Tony. Peg and her brother, Craig, are my stepsister and stepbrother. Peg, Emily lives down the block from us."

Emily laughs. "I didn't realize you had a stepsister and brother. That's kind of cool." Relief comes off her in waves. "I'd have never guessed it, though. You two were so natural on the dance floor together."

"Yeah, we've finally decided it's cool," Peg says. "You guys looked like you're having fun."

"Far more than I thought possible tonight." Emily winks, then squeezes my hand.

Things are moving way too fast. How can I slow them down? I can't hurt Emily's feelings by rejecting her now that I kissed her, and I do like her. Not like Lily, but I don't know her that well either. Maybe time together can change that?

But Emily and her family aren't believers, so our values are a little different. Maybe the kiss means much less to her than it means to me?

I glimpse Chris and Monica. He's all over her. I don't think she minds too much, but it might be more than she wants. I'd never seen Chris with a girl, other than at our house last Friday. Why's he so aggressive? It's almost like the boys at the mall.

Peg frowns at them too, probably thinking the same thing. "They have the wrong Marks labeled as the troublemaker."

I hope, hope, hope I'm wrong. He probably doesn't know better. But... did he make trouble for me just so he could get Lily? That's something I gotta wrestle through soon enough.

Although they don't go to church, Emily's home is one of the few on our block with both parents. Tony lives a mile up the street in another neighborhood. We all begin getting to know each other better, discussing things we like to do. Surprisingly, both Peg and Emily like to fish.

When I was younger, I noticed that, as the boys older than me started dating, they seemed to be in pairs, doing stuff with each other as couples. "You guys might like to come to my gramps's house and go fishing with us this weekend."

The girls grin at each other and nod. Peg high-fives Emily. "Let's do it."

Emily's nod jostles her hair over her shoulders, strands catch on her sequins. "I'll have to ask my dad first, but if I can, count me in."

Tony's shoulders slump. "Can't. I have to work."

Right. He's sixteen and has to pay for gas and insurance on his car, so he works the weekends.

I'm not sure who suggests it, but we head back to the dance floor, dancing lots more, taking an occasional break. Emily is a great dancer, with a true sense of fun. She has a natural, sweet humility, even though she's pretty much the classic all-American girl, or what I would imagine that is.

I glimpse Lily and Eric again. She looks sad—angry—as he takes her hand to lead her outside. Peg and I eye each other. Trouble's brewing.

"We better go help her," Peg says. "He looks pretty determined."

I stop dancing. "Emily, I've gotta run outside with Peg for a minute."

"Who looks determined?" Emily cranes around, probably wondering why we're heading outside.

But Peg and I take off, so Emily follows.

I point to them heading out the door where Lily's struggling against Eric. Out of the corner of my eye, I catch the disappointment that flashes across Emily's face. She probably wants me to stay inside with her and let Lily answer for herself. I can't, not if she's being bullied.

Is Peg doing this to save Lily or to get Eric back? Either way, I don't want Lily getting hurt or worse. True to what Peg said earlier, he's parked in the last row in the lot, near the fence. I hear them arguing as we approach the rocking vehicle. Someone's definitely struggling inside.

"Leave me alone, Eric! I'm not going to do that."

We race to the car, running. Scared for Lily, I become far too brave. I open the passenger's side door at the same time Peg opens the driver's. "Lily, are you okay? Is he hurting you?"

He glares at me. "Get out of here, Marks, if you know what's good for you. This is none of your business. You too, Peg. You had your chance."

He twists around in his seat, getting ready to climb out, still holding Lily's left arm in his right hand like he's trying to keep her from scrambling out as he slides past Peg. Peg, protecting her broken arm, pushes him down before he can get out.

"Help me, Nick. He won't let me go, and he's hurting me," Lily pleads. Terror flares her eyes wide, and her lips tremble.

Since Peg's handling Eric from the driver's side, I reach for his hand on Lily's arm to free her. I slip and lose my grip.

CHAPTER FORTY-FIVE

I WAKE TO A POUNDING HEAD. Where am I? I blink at my surroundings. I'm at home. How? For some reason, my first memory is of me being only able to lie, unable to move, to talk—to anything.

It was like being unplugged from my body and then returned to it. It's like connecting a charge to something electric. My body had to reconnect to my brain again. Now the healing is progressing in patches of revelation. Thankfully, it's a slow process because an aching in my back and shoulders feels as if I've been beaten, or worse.

Thank You, Helper. Thank You for saving me.

Kayleigh and Lily arrive. Lily leans over me and kisses my forehead while Kayleigh looks on. "Nick, I'm so sorry. Please forgive me."

Peg comes in with her mom and brother and a guy who looks like her mom, overcrowding the living room, all of them wanting good for me—at least that's what I think. But I still don't know how I got here. The last thing I remember is dancing with Emily and her kiss.

Peg explains everything, how my accident happened. I listen, trying to learn too.

"You opened the car's passenger door," Peg says. "Then, when you pulled on Eric's hand to get him to release Lily, you tripped on a gaping hole in the pavement."

Lily nods. "That sent you toppling backward where you busted your head on the ground."

"It knocked you out cold," Peg takes over again. "Once you went down, Lily got out in a flash and at your side."

I grin at Peg. "After I fell, did you get a good whack on him?"

"Nah." She shrugs, her smile sheepish. "He was scared, leaving as soon as Lily got out of the car. We were afraid you were dead. I gotta tell ya you took a nasty fall. We got there just in time for Lily."

"Where's Emily? Is she okay?"

Lily's shoulders droop. Now why'd I ask that?

"She's fine." Mom sits on the foldout bed, stroking my face from one side of the bed as Lily cares for me on the other. "She realized you still like Lily. She was upset, but she'll be okay. That was a brave thing you and Peg did. Eric wasn't going to take no for an answer. I'm so proud you helped her, even after everything that happened."

"Am I dreaming? I felt like my thoughts raced, and I was unable to move. Like I was trapped in a body that's not working." I wiggle my finger. Or, at least, I fight with all I possess to move a finger. It moves.

"You've been pretty groggy for an hour or so." Lily pushes the sheet up on me and pats my shoulder. Pain glows in her eyes.

I hear my soul cry out. What's that all about?

"I don't remember anything." Still, a peace I can't explain comes over me, even as wave after wave of pressure rocks my head, the peace comforting. Whatever happened has short-circuited my memory too.

"Peg's uncle, Dr. John, said he'd watch over you." Mom holds a glass of water to me. "Are you thirsty? You need to stay hydrated."

"No thanks. You can set it on the table. I'll drink some in a moment." I try my arms. They seem to work fine. My toes wiggle too.

The stranger leans over me. "I'm Dr. John, son." He flashes a penlight in my eyes and asks silly questions. "I'm going to be staying here to watch you for signs of concussion overnight."

I can recall my trip over to Gramps's on the bicycle. The Helper guided me and saved me from evil and, most importantly, from myself. Time drags on—or so I think.

"Mom." I grip her hand. "I'm sorry I was so cold and mean. Please forgive me." She's gotta know how important she is to me and how much I love her.

She holds my face in her hands. "I'm sorry too, Nick. I shouldn't have taken Riley from you. Will you forgive me?" In the sweetest smile, the softness of her love shines through. She hugs me.

Chris slips out the door, probably thinking no one saw him.

I especially hope Mom can forgive me. I've caused her so much pain simply because I was too stubborn to take some lumps. I may not have deserved them, but Mom has always been so good to me, better than I deserve. How could I have gotten so wrapped up in being right, forgetting everything, ready to trash my entire life because of it?

After an hour or so, everyone goes their way, leaving me to ponder what took place.

"Helper, please let me wake up remembering. I need You, Helper. Teach me. I believe in You."

The blood pulsing through my head makes my skull sore. I move my head to a different position. Then I begin to feel a coldness on the back of my head, as if it's on ice. Good. My senses wake more and more. Well, not all of it's good.

The next hours or such pass in both relief that my nerves begin to respond and agony from the pain of it. Who knows how long I'll have to endure it?

Saturday morning, everyone goes to church after checking on me. I try to rest, the television helping at times. My headache is gone, mostly. Now with Riley on my lap, I sit up, trying to figure everything out. The kiss with Emily and Lily wanting me back. Time for some decisions, but that can wait a few days.

Around afternoon, Pastor visits me. He winks as he settles onto the chair beside me. "Bet you're surprised to see me?" He pats my leg. "I often visit church members and their families."

"That's nice." I *guess*. But I fiddle with the sheet spread over me. I've never really talked to him alone before.

"That was a selfless thing you and your stepsister did for Lily. The whole congregation is proud and thankful you stood up for her." He crosses one leg over the other and latches his hands on the upraised knee, settling in apparently. "Nick... some people sometimes take my sermons and turn them around to cause harm. Your granddad told me about some using my Father's Day sermons to do that. But that's not how we see you or your brother, nor does God. Jesus said, 'Greater love hath no man than this, that a man lay down his life for his friends.' That's what you and your stepsister did for Lily. I'm so proud I am of you and Peg for that." After about fifteen minutes, he prays for me and leaves.

His nice visit helps me deal with the past somewhat. But now that I believe, it's time for me to start looking forward again, not back.

Chris and Abbie come in, letting the screen door bang shut, waking me from a short nap. I look around for Riley. Abbie has him. He must've heard them coming.

Chris nudges me. "Emily is super disappointed Lily wants to get back together with you. She said she really likes you—ever since the seventh grade."

"Wow." I rub the back of my head, remembering the fall now. "That's kinda sad. I mean I know what it's like now, wanting to be with someone who can't or won't be with you." Even though we're young, I know her pain. At least it's a temporary thing. After all, we only danced for an hour Friday night. But the kiss—my soul reminds me—changed things for all three of us.

Abbie frowns at me. "Emily says you kissed her. Did you? Do you remember?"

I nod. Unfortunately. "My memory has returned." The kiss was sweet, and I enjoyed her tremendously, including the intimacy we shared, dancing so close. But this is an image I don't want to remember. Or forget.

"Are you going to tell Lily?"

"Not sure. I mean she probably saw me." But how do I explain to Lily that I could so quickly move on? Do I need to? No... "I'll leave that for her to deal with. Besides, she broke up with me, not me with her."

The doorbell rings, and Chris lets Lily in. She gives me a little wave as she enters the living room and drops onto the couch behind me

. Then she scoots off the couch to sit beside me. Her fingers tug at my sleeve. "Listen, I'm sorry I ever doubted you. Everything kinda went crazy. I wanted to believe you, a part of me always did, but Mom didn't want me to get hurt again."

Chris heads upstairs, humming.

Abbie must've grown tired of petting Riley, or her phone buzzed. "Here, Riley will help." She drops him on the bed and scoots outside, leaving me alone with Lily.

"It took a long time when you sort of went into a shell and we stopped hanging out to get over how bad I hurt. My feelings for you had changed, somewhere." She leans over me, so close I can feel her breath. "I didn't want to be friends playing on the porch or in the tree house. I wanted to be your girlfriend." She leans in even closer, and I close my eyes. Then she hugs my neck for the longest time. Finally, she stands back up. Rats.

I shrug. "I'm sorry about that, Lily. I kinda really struggled with the whole dad thing or cocoon busting."

"Yeah, your gramps told me." She picks up Riley and brings him close enough to cuddle, then giggles when his little rough tongue laps at her nose. "Gramps said you were heartbroken when you realized I had moved on. But I could never move on that easily. We've been together forever it seems.... I want that to continue."

Moving on brings me to the topic I don't want to bring up. I tickle Riley's belly. "I guess you saw me kiss Emily?"

"Yeah."

It's quiet for a bit, Riley soothing the awkwardness.

Then Lily sighs. "I don't blame you. She told me she kissed you,

you simply responded. I promise I'll never push you away like that again. You're my hero, you know. I'll always be thankful for you and Peg saving me. Can we put this all behind us?"

Her breath tickles me as she leans in and kisses my forehead. Man, that feels good. Like sealing up the past and promising good things to come. I grab her hands. "You don't know how badly I want that." I squeeze her hands tight as if I can push my conviction into her. "I didn't mean to kiss Emily. You've always had my heart."

Glad we both emptied our souls, I relax. Sometimes the unknown can be more deadly than the known.

I squirmed to sit up straighter. "I found it, Lily, the Sea of Life. I know it sounds crazy, but I believe now. The Helper showed me what faith is all about. I know why Dad was a bad man to Mom. I saw it."

She squinches her eyes and tilts her head in a questioning way. I try to read her mind, but that's useless.

"That's gotta sound strange, but you never know how belief comes for some of us." My gaze rolls up to the ceiling, and my smile widens. Yes, my story sounds crazy, but don't a lot of stories about people coming to faith sound odd, especially to someone who didn't experience it that way?

"Okay, well... I'm glad you finally believe. It took you long enough." Her words poke at me. "Want to get baptized together?" Her eyes sparkle like beautiful deep oceans of blue, and her smile's brighter than I remembered.

Did I want to get baptized? Together? I couldn't poke back too much. I didn't want to be too aggressive and cause my head to hurt again. Instead, I reach out and hug her to me. She grabs my shirt in her balled-up hands, just like old times. Good. We're back, only this time so much more, my world so much better. Thanks to the Helper and believing. He restored everything to me, and even more.

"I think I would, yes. I'd love to get baptized with you. It'll always be something extraordinary we've shared." I close my eyes, inhaling deeply.

A different peace, one I never knew before, comes over me. I hug

Lily even tighter, feeling her holding me. I've found my place, busted my cocoon, and made it home.

Thank You, Helper! I believe.

The End.

Dear Friend,

Cocoon busting, as I've fondly called it, played a vital role in my youth, especially being a late bloomer like Nick. Unfortunately, I didn't realize I was experiencing delayed puberty and I would eventually grow, although not until twelfth grade. Millions of kids experience it. As I shared in the story, up to 3 percent of all kids will endure it.

Recently, many—especially educators and health care workers—are taking advantage of this confusing time in our children's lives to exploit them, confuse them, and convince them to change their sexual orientation. I urge parents and children going through puberty not to fall for the deception. Give yourself time to become the wonderful young adult you are. Give God the opportunity to guide you through the difficulty and the excitement of becoming an adult.

The Sea of Life is a fictional place, albeit, we all have wanted to play God. As Nick learned, believing in God, receiving Jesus into your heart, is far better than being your own god. I hope Nick's story will bring you joy, give you a glimpse of God's love, and an understanding of how to help those experiencing the difficulties of cocoon busting (puberty) or late blooming (delayed puberty).

Some of the inspiration I received to write Nick's story came from my own experiences, only not the rescue of Lily. God doesn't use the same model for all of us, having different ways and plans for each of us. He reveals Himself to us at various times throughout our lives, allowing us to grow closer, to know Him better, making life exciting, and an ongoing adventure.

God bless.

For more exciting stories and the free novella included in the deluxe print edition come to www.leewimmer.net/shop.

The special bonus beginning on the following page is one of six free short stories on my website. To read them you simply need to sign up for my newsletter. There, you will receive special savings, news about upcoming releases, giveaways, and more. You can unsubscribe at any time.

Charaka – The Last Snow Angel is a story similar in nature to *The Marks Boy's Rock.*

ABOUT THE AUTHOR

LEE WIMMER is an author living in Michigan with his wife, two stepchildren, and six grandchildren, where he often chases his golf shots deep into the woods. His writings often revolve around his favorite scripture, Romans 8:28 – "And we know that all things work together for good of those who love God, to those who are called according to his purpose."

Most of his novels include aspects of his own life that impacted him in deeply profound ways. As a late bloomer himself, Lee understands what Nick experienced.

Lee's life shows the "all things" can get messy and difficult before the breakthrough, but late blooming also created for him opportunities that wouldn't have existed if not for the trials of his teenage years. Through the trials he developed a creative side that may not exist if not for his teenage years. Now he is producing characters of depth to share the glory of God. You can connect with him online at leewimmer.net.

Visit Lee:
https://www.leewimmer.net

Find Lee's published books at:
https://www.amazon.com/author/leewimmer